HOW TO BREAK AN
UNDEAD HEART

HAILEY EDWARDS

Edited by Sasha Knight
Proofread by Lillie's Literary Services
Cover by Gene Mollica
Tree of Life medallion drawn by Leah Farrow

HOW TO BREAK AN UNDEAD HEART

The Beginner's Guide to Necromancy, Book 3

Grier finally has the one thing she's always wanted: Boaz Pritchard. Too bad her dream boyfriend is keeping her up nights, just not in a sweaty or fun way. Boaz has dialed down the Southern charm and stopped returning her calls. His job forces him to keep secrets, but his radio silence is cranking up her suspicions. He's a shameless flirt, but he's *her* shameless flirt...right?

Soon an attack on Woolworth House leaves her with bigger problems than *he loves me, he loves me not*. Vampires are on the prowl, and they aren't the only predators circling. A new threat has emerged, one with blood rights to Grier. With enemies closing in on all sides, she must choose her allies, and the decision could make or break her...and her heart.

Warning: This book contains a buttload of zombie parakeet poop. Like grab a poncho and thank me later. Watch out, y'all. It's about to hit the fan. Hearts will break, and heads will roll. Literally.

ONE

Thirteen nights into my new roommate situation had illuminated the myriad ways being an only child had not prepared me for having a live-in best friend. On Maud's orders, sleepovers had been restricted to one night per week when we were kids. Goddess, how I hated that rule. Each time I walked Amelie home, I vowed to Hecate that she and I would live together forever after we were grown.

No bedtimes. No rules. No parents.

Chocolate in all its various, glorious forms for breakfast, lunch, and dinner. Thirty-one flavors of ice cream for brunch. Pie for linner. Cake for dunch. Basically, I envisioned adulthood as one never-ending sugar high.

But what I hadn't pictured was my Type A bestie padding around Woolworth House in boy-short panties paired with mismatched tank tops stained by chocolate milk dribbles, her hair a bird's nest tangled at her nape, her teeth fuzzier than my socks. Or the all-cereal diet she had adopted, though I admired her dedication to marshmallowism. Or the bathing-optional clause she seemed to have penciled into her temporary lease. Or the stalking. The stalking was the worst.

Odette had a cat once, a familiar as old as the sand I tracked into her house, and it trailed her everywhere, including the bathroom. Once or twice while I was visiting, Jean-Claude would miss his cue and end up on the wrong side of the door. When that happened, he wedged his nose in the crack where the door met the frame and yowled to get in like his world was ending. But if anyone approached him to offer sympathy, he would whirl on them, hissing and spitting.

That was post-disownment Amelie in a nutshell.

Only, she was so much worse because thumbs.

When I was home, she walked a step behind me, her toes brushing my heels. When I left, she pressed her nose to the glass, her breath fogging the pane as she clocked my trips through the garden, across the lawn, or down the driveway.

Coming home was worse. Amelie waited for me in the foyer, foot tapping, arms crossed over her chest. She was ten times the nag Woolly had ever been, and even the old house was starting to fray under the constant strain of having Amelie pacing her floors night in, night out.

But what else could I do? I had ponied up the cash for the $3.5 million indenture she owed the Society for the crimes she committed during her voluntary possession by the dybbuk Ambrose, but the mandatory six-month sentence she was required to serve as a member of my household as a result of that transaction was immutable.

As far as the Society was concerned, I owned her and the rights to any services she provided during that period of time. As far as I was concerned, I had one hundred and seventy days and change to rehab Amelie before releasing her from her bond to carve out a life from the wreckage of her previous one.

A tentative knock drew me from my gloomy thoughts.

Shuffling out of the kitchen, I left Amelie shoveling in her first bowl of mini marshmallows and toasted oat cereal of the night. I hesitated in the foyer, hand on the knob, and glanced overhead at the elegant chandelier. "Well, girl? What do you think? Do I answer, or do I pretend I'm not home?"

"I can hear you," a woman replied primly, her voice muffled through the heavy wood.

The crystals tinkled with laughter at my expense.

Me and my big mouth.

The door swung open to reveal a young woman, maybe a year or two older than me, with wavy chestnut hair that brushed her narrow shoulders. Her wide, hazel eyes belonged on an anime character. High cheekbones gave her face a familiar shape, as did her thin lips and the severe point of her tiny chin.

Her smart black pantsuit smacked of taste and money, *old* money, and the frugal application of jewelry made a statement. Something along the lines of *I might only be wearing one ring, but I could sell it and pay off your mortgage.* The diamond perched on her left hand's ring finger might as well have been a grape. The glare nearly blinded me when she tucked her hair behind her ear. I had seen dimmer runway lights at airports. There was also the telltale hum of necromantic power haloing her. Now that I was paying attention, I sensed it through my bond with Woolly.

Crocodile tears sparkled in her eyes as she launched herself at me. "Oh, Grier."

Woolly, who was not a fan of strangers bum-rushing her threshold, flung up a transparent barrier that sealed the doorway. The woman bounced off the compressed air before her outstretched fingertips brushed my arm, and she hit the porch on her butt with an unladylike grunt.

With her hands cupping a button nose she may or may not have been born with, her voice came out stuffy. "W-w-what was that?"

"Who are you?" I really hoped Woolly hadn't broken her nose, plastic or not. At this rate, she was going to get a reputation. "Why did you try to attack me?"

"Attack you?" she echoed, lowering her hands to reveal her reddened schnoz. "I was going to hug you."

"Oh." Random tackle-hugs might even be more sinister coming from strangers than candy, if I'm being honest. "In that case—" I leaned against the doorframe. "Who are you?" The stubborn jut of her chin struck me as familiar. "Why did you try to hug me?"

"I'm Eloise Marchand." She rose with a wobble on her kitten heels then straightened her clothes. "I'm your cousin."

The lights overhead flickered in shocked bursts that matched the wild flutterings in my chest.

Dame Severine Marchand, the Marchand family matriarch, had disowned my mother, Evangeline, on the day I was born. Mom had refused to reveal my father's name when asked, and Dame Marchand had severed all ties with her youngest daughter rather than risk a potential scandal over my paternity.

Eloise's arrival might herald the extending of an olive branch, but I had been excised from their family tree before my first cry rang out through the world. Blood or no blood, I was a Woolworth, and this woman was no relation of mine.

"I heard voices." Amelie appeared at my shoulder, a spoon fisted in her hand like she knew how to use it. Which, considering the number of empty cereal boxes in the trash can, she did, but I doubted it would do her much good here unless she planned on scooping out Eloise's eyeballs. "Introduce us?"

"This is Eloise Marchand." I gestured toward the High Society poster girl. "My cousin."

"What are you doing here?" Amelie demanded, knuckles gone white. "What do you want with Grier?"

A delicate frown gathered between Eloise's brows. "I'm family—"

"No, you're really not." Abandonment issues, I had them. "Try again."

"I was three years old when Grandmother disowned Aunt Evangeline," she said, proving me right about our age gap. "You can't hold me responsible for the decisions she made for us all."

Amelie flinched in my periphery, her wounds in that area much rawer than mine.

"I thought you were dead," Eloise continued. "Our histories record you as stillborn."

Interesting that I rated a mention at all when disownment was meant to cleanse Mom from their annals.

Less interesting was learning the Marchands had decided I was literally dead to them.

"Why show up now?" That was the million-dollar question. "How did you find out I was alive?"

"Odette Lecomte," she whispered, reverence for the famed seer stealing her voice.

"Odette told you?" Skeptical as I was that she would pin my private business to the family bulletin board, I had begged a favor of her. While gaining entree to Dame Marchand, she might have made a few more discreet inquiries along the way. "What did she say?

"No, it was nothing like that." Eloise flapped her hands at the notion Odette might speak directly to her. I worried she might knock herself unconscious if that rock on her finger clipped her. "I'm a practitioner. I'm training under Grandmother at the family firm."

An unexpected pang hit me at the glimpse of yet another stolen future, one where I worked alongside a cousin, groomed by our maternal grandmother to take my place in the family business as a practitioner.

"She was supervising while I prepped the conference room for a new client meeting," Eloise explained. "When the receptionist patched a call through, we assumed it was the client. He was nervous about our suggestion he consider inducing death in order to jumpstart the resuscitation process. He was a high-profile client and required... special handling."

Inductions, ending human lives in their prime to raise vampires in peak condition, cost extra. "And?"

"I overheard Madame Lecomte mention Aunt Evangeline before Grandmother muted the call and sent me home for the day." Her cheeks reddened. "I was curious why Madame Lecomte would call and drop your mother's name." She ducked her head. "Our mothers were twins, you see, and that bond has always fascinated me. Our family has multiple instances of fraternals whose magic—"

"Twins?" A peculiar ringing started in my ears. "No one told me."

A heady truth swirled through me and left me weaving on my feet. *Can I see a picture?* That's all I had to ask. One question, and she could show me a glimpse of Mom. No, not Mom. One of her possible futures. The hair, the makeup, the clothes, the expression—no matter how similar—belonged to someone else.

On the spot, I decided I never wanted to meet my aunt. I don't think my heart could take seeing her.

"Mom sided with the family after the disownment," she said, picking her manicured fingernails. "To my knowledge, she never saw or spoke to her sister again but..."

"She regretted turning her back on family," I finished for her.

"Yes."

"And you hoped that fence might be mended through you and I?"

"Yes," she replied, slower this time. "After Madame Lecomte called, I scoured the family archives and discovered she lives in Savannah. A section of her file was dedicated to her friendship with your mother and Maud Woolworth." She gnawed her bottom lip. "When I noticed the former Dame Woolworth also lived in Savannah, I followed up on a hunch, and I found you."

Googling Maud would have turned up photos and mentions of me, mostly from fundraisers and galas, and those would name me as the Woolworth heir. But there was also Mom's obituary to consider, and my very public adoption. Connecting the dots wouldn't have been hard. Especially since a practitioner in Eloise's position would have access to the Society databases.

"Woolly, what do you think?" Armed with amped-up wards, she ought to be able to scan Eloise down to the marrow for a reading on her intent. "Is it safe to let her in?"

"Woolly?" Eloise glanced at Amelie. "Who is Woolly?"

Neither of us enlightened her.

The porch light beside Eloise hummed thoughtfully before flaring her consent.

"Come in." I made it an order. I wanted to get to the bottom of her interest in me. "Leave any weapons you're carrying at the door. She won't let you bring them in."

"Weapons?" Her wide eyes rounded. "I'm unarmed." Her hand lifted to her throat. "This is a social call."

Amelie choked on a snort, and I elbowed her in the gut. Once upon a time, we had been that naïve too. I wouldn't be the one to tear off Eloise's blinders. Truth be told, I relished the idea of at least one person thriving in our world who might never think to check for monsters under her bed.

"In or out." I rolled my hand in a hurry-up motion. "Class starts in fifteen minutes, and my teacher gets his suspenders twisted if I'm late."

Okay, so Linus had yet to wear suspenders, but I strongly suspected he owned a pair. How could he not? And if he didn't? I knew what I was getting him for his birthday.

"Maybe this wasn't such a good idea," Eloise murmured as she stepped over the threshold. Or made the attempt. Woolly suspended her midstride, and the wards slid over her skin, assessing every inch of her. Thirty seconds later, Woolly released her, and Eloise stumbled into the foyer beside us, flailing like a salmon swimming upstream. "What was that?"

"Magic." I took her by the elbow, guided her into the living room, and shoved her toward a couch. "Sit."

She perched on the edge of the cushion, her spine ruler-straight, her legs crossed at the ankles.

Still half-naked and rather feral, Amelie stood behind Eloise, clutching the spoon in her fist.

"Okay, Eloise, let's try this again." I hooked my hands on my hips. "You found out I'm alive and decided to visit. Why?"

There must be more to this visit than smearing salve over her mother's decades-old hurt.

"As I said, I hoped we could talk." Her manicured fingers twisted into knots on her lap. "That maybe one day we might be friends."

"Your family disowned her," Amelie snarled, jabbing the spoon at the back of Eloise's head like a deranged zombie fantasizing about using her skull as a bowl. "What right do you have to—?"

"Amelie," I warned, flexing my palm until she surrendered her weapon. "Let her talk."

"I understand your suspicion," Eloise began. "I read articles about your time in…"

"Atramentous," I finished for her.

Eloise swayed a bit, her hand again rising to her throat to clutch pearls she wasn't wearing.

"I was locked away for five years for the murder of Maud Woolworth." I cocked an eyebrow at her. "I'm sure you can imagine how imprisonment changed me."

The version of me who might have hugged her back and welcomed her into my home with happy tears had died locked in a cell buried so deep underground the tang of mold still coated the back of my throat on occasion.

"View this from my perspective." I swept my gaze up and down her, doubting her kittens-and-rainbows outlook would allow for such a thing. "Some long-lost relative popping up on my doorstep after my reinstatement as the Woolworth heir makes your timing suspect."

News of how the Grande Dame had pardoned her niece was circulating too. Eloise might be telling the truth. Maybe this was an innocent visit. Or she might be a ladder-climber who had spotted an opportunity to align herself with the Woolworth name under the guise of mending fences.

"This was a mistake." Eloise shot to her feet and backed toward the foyer. "I shouldn't have come." She wiped her palms on her pressed slacks. "I wish things could have been different between us, Grier, I do, but this is too much."

Woolly opened the door in an invitation to leave that Eloise was quick to accept.

I massaged the base of my neck after the locks snicked into place behind her. "That went well."

"She shows up out of the blue all these years later?" Amelie pulled aside the curtain on the nearest window, and we watched Eloise get in her hired car and leave. "I don't buy it."

"Odette did call Dame Marchand. That part is true. She was hoping to get a lead on my father."

"How do we know it wasn't Dame Marchand who sent her protégé to woo you back into the fold? High Society families are always shopping for an angle." The fabric crumpled in her fist. "Besides, you've already got one spy living on the property. You don't need a matched set."

"Better the devil you know." Defending Linus just put her teeth on edge. There was no point trying when her mind was made up about him. "What are your plans for the night?"

"I'll be diving into your finances here in a little bit." Her yawn illustrated how much the prospect excited her. "I'm almost to the good stuff," she assured me, retrieving her cell from parts unknown to check for messages. From Boaz. He was the only person calling her these days, and he checked in every forty-eight hours like clockwork. Yet he hadn't so much as texted me since leaving her in my care. "Before I get bogged down by all those decimal points, I'm putting dinner in the Crock-Pot."

Hope that this might signal a return to normal for her tightened my chest. "You're tired of cereal?"

"No, but cereal is tired of me." An unhappy gurgle welled in her stomach. "You off to meet Linus?"

"Yes." Cue my belly's anticipatory growl. "Lessons wait for no woman. Or parakeet."

"I'll be here when you get back," she joked, mostly, the words less bitter than in nights past.

When Amelie veered toward one of the downstairs bathrooms, she tapped each doorknob in the hall as she passed them, a new habit she'd developed that reminded me of a prisoner counting the bars on her cell. Tension ratcheted through my shoulders when her fingers brushed the glass knob leading down into the basement, but her stride didn't so much as hitch as she marched on.

Thank Hecate it was still magically sealed, and no one had figured out how to access it.

At least, not yet.

TWO

With Eileen, my eyeball-studded grimoire, tucked under one arm and what I considered Keet's traveling cage dangling from my fingers, I exited Woolly through the kitchen and entered the rear garden. Following the winding flagstone path to the carriage house, I put an extra bounce in my step that probably had more to do with the smell of cinnamon and butter wafting through the window over the sink than the lessons awaiting me.

The front door no longer stood open, and I missed that implied welcome more than I ever expected.

All thanks to Julius, who had arrived from the Lawson aviary last week to assist Linus in the next phase of my education: the familiar bond. Now that the great horned butthole was in residence, Linus's open-door policy had been nixed. Almost like he worried his owl might *accidentally* fly far, far away and never be seen or heard from again after I *accidentally* left the door open and *accidentally* chased him out with a broom.

Once certain I wasn't about to get dive-bombed, I darted inside and slammed the door behind me. I didn't have to search far to spot

Linus bent over the stove while he flipped French toast for our break-fast. Well, *my* breakfast. The man ate like more of a bird than his fowl-tempered familiar. *Ha.*

Tonight, he wore dove-gray slacks that molded to his backside. Having pants tailor-made did that. His white button-down shirt was likewise fitted to highlight his lean musculature, the cuffs rolled up over his forearms. His dark auburn hair brushed his shoulders, the ends curling slightly thanks to the humidity. "How is Amelie today?"

Each dusk, he greeted me with the same question. I might have drawn the containment ward meant to keep the dybbuk from repos-sessing her, but he had been the one to tattoo it on her ankle. His interest in her was the same as his interest in me—clinical. "Any new symptoms?"

"No, Dr. Lawson." A grin tugged at my lips. "The patient has not relapsed since dawn."

Linus glanced at me over his shoulder, his dark eyes dancing, bluer than black at the moment. "I don't have a medical doctorate." A smile blossomed. "Yet."

"Why does it not surprise me to learn you're chasing another suffix?" I slumped into my usual chair at the kitchen table, settled Eileen an arm's length away, then placed Keet's cage at my feet. "You're too ambitious for your own good. You make the rest of us look bad."

"You have plenty of time to catch up." He plated us each four toasty slices of heaven, cut them on the diagonal, and dusted them with confectioner's sugar. He carried them to the table before returning for the maple syrup and butter, and I noticed he only brought one fork. Not that I had expected him to indulge. I had yet to see him do more than nibble. As far as I could tell, he just liked keeping up appearances. "You're twenty-one." Back at the counter, he poured us each a glass of milk then claimed the seat across from me. "You've got centuries to accomplish anything you set your mind to, Grier."

"You're not eating," I mumbled around a mouthful of bliss. "Why bother cooking if you aren't hungry?"

"You're hungry." He cracked open the binder containing the syllabus for his beginner's guide to necromancy and flipped to where we left off last night. "That's reason enough."

"Do you ever eat?" Unrepentant, I stabbed the topmost piece of French toast on his plate and crammed it in my mouth before reaching for the milk. "Or drink?"

"Yes."

I waited for him to expound on his dietary requirements, but he appeared absorbed in his lesson plans. "When?"

"Does it matter?" He kept skimming, writing notes in the margin.

"Yes." I stole another wedge from him while he wasn't looking and decimated it in two bites. Maple syrup stuck one corner to my cheek, but I didn't let that slow the fork-to-mouth action. "Is this another side effect of bonding with a wraith?"

Call me paranoid, but I was starting to think that was his go-to excuse when he wanted a topic dropped.

"More or less." His gaze lifted to mine, and his eyes sparkled, a rich navy blue in this light. "Do you need a wet cloth?"

"No." Heat tingled in my cheeks, which were goopy with syrup. "I can get it." I poked the corner of toast glued to my face into my mouth with my pinky—like a lady—then turned up my glass of milk to wash it all down. "My compliments to the chef."

The chef in question stood, the blades of his sharp cheekbones ruddy beneath his freckles, and he padded to the sink where he wet a dish towel.

"Here." He returned to me, bending low to dab my cheek and jaw. "Let me get that."

"Have you ever considered teaching elementary school instead of college?"

"No." The rag, and his focus, slipped over my bottom lip. "Why do you ask?"

"You're a nurturer." I took the cloth from him, the fabric warmer than his chilly fingers. "You're good at taking care of people."

The praise stunned him into silence for a beat. "Caring for someone because you want to is a different beast than caring for someone because it's your job."

"Ah," I said eloquently while stinging heat crept across my chest like a spreading sunburn. The idea he might actually like having me around was...nice. "Can I ask you a question?"

A crinkle pleated his forehead into neat rows. "Yes."

I steeled myself for his response while scrubbing the sticky residue off my hands. "Have you met any Marchands?"

"No." He straightened at last and reclaimed his seat. "Mother and Evangeline weren't close. Mother was the stereotypical annoying little sister. She idolized Maud, but she wasn't allowed in her big sister's inner circle." He considered me. "She probably hadn't thought about your mother in years until Evangeline returned to Savannah. She can be..."

"Self-centered?"

"I was going to say *career-oriented*." He twisted his mouth like it might squeeze off the laugh twitching in his shoulders. "Why do you ask?"

"Eloise Marchand showed up on my doorstep tonight."

"That's...unexpected."

Black devoured his eyes from corner to corner while he conferred with Cletus. The wraith didn't update Linus in real time unless I was in danger. Clearly Linus wasn't willing to wait for the full report at dawn.

"Yes and...no." I fessed up before he put two and two together. "I *might* have asked Odette to call Dame Marchand."

"You're searching for your father." The statement came out with the slightest edge.

"Yeah." I ducked my head. "I thought it might help to know how he fits into all this."

This being the goddess-touched freak of nature that was his daughter.

"There was a reason your mother kept him out of your lives."

"What reason?" I braced my elbow on the table and rested my chin on my palm. "No one knows."

Eloise's arrival had sparked a new possibility, one I had never considered, and I couldn't ditch the idea.

Linus was shaking his head. "Your mother—"

"What if she never told him about me?" I tapped my bottom lip with my pinky. "What if he doesn't know he has a daughter?"

"What if she was afraid to tell him?" he countered. "What if their relationship wasn't...?"

The implication turned my stomach, but it made sense. "You think she might have been his mistress."

Divorce was taboo within the Society. Affairs were of no consequence...unless you got caught.

Having a love child smacked of incontrovertible proof to me. And yet, Mom had kept me.

"The theory fits with her leaving him after she learned of her condition. If the Marchands suspected, and after she refused to abort, it would explain why her family disowned her." He reached across the table, his cool pointer tapping my forearm. "The only truth to be found at this table, in this moment, is that we simply don't know."

"We moved around so much." I stared at the elegant bend of his fingers where they curled on the table, flexing as though comfort were a butterfly he feared crushing in his hand before gifting it to me. "Mom made no secret about our gifts. She never taught me, but she let me watch when she performed resuscitations."

Those had been off the books, a means of earning money to feed us, but I hadn't known that until I turned Woolly upside down in search of clues. Mom had kept a ledger with notations in the margin, in case she ever got caught, and it was packed away with her belongings in the attic. Sifting through those fragments of her life hurt too much. Tears in my eyes, I had folded the box shut and hadn't returned since.

"We changed cities so often, I couldn't get a familiar. She told me about them, and I wanted a kitten so badly, but there was no guarantee the next place we lived would allow pets." I blasted out a sigh. "I was so young when she died." Five years old and an orphan. "I don't remember much about her, just bits and pieces of our life together. I'm afraid..." I bit my lip, "...that what I do recall isn't real. Maud told me so many stories. I can't tell them from memory anymore."

The chair legs scraped as Linus stood. The cold of his touch bit through the thin fabric of my shirt when his palm came to rest on my shoulder, but I covered his hand with mine anyway.

"I have to know," I confessed. "Not only *what* I am, but *who* I am too."

"I understand better than you might think."

"There's no question of your paternity, buddy." I patted his hand. "You're one-part Woolworth to one-part Lawson. Mixed vigorously." I tasted bile in my mouth. "Scratch that last part. I really don't want to know if you were shaken or stirred into existence."

"No." His hand eased away. "I'm not."

"*What?*" I toppled my chair in a rush to stand and face him. "Are you...? Were you...?"

Adoption would explain how Linus could be both a decent guy *and* related to the Grande Dame. Admittedly, by eliminating the "related to the Grande Dame" part, but still.

"Don't get too excited," he teased. "Clarice Lawson is my biological mother."

Oh, well. No one was perfect. "And your biological father?"

"He was a donor, my father's cousin twice removed, to keep the bloodline pure. I was carried via surrogate because of Mother's advanced age, so no one was the wiser."

Surrogacy was common among necromancers due to a propensity for females to undergo menopause around three hundred years of age. Sperm donors weren't uncommon, either. Necromancers weren't the most fertile bunch. That's how we ended up with a Low Society in the first place. They were interbred with humans in a bid to increase fertility rates, and it worked, but they sacrificed magic in the bargain.

Actually, now that I thought about it, as a Woolworth seeking a financially and socially superior match rather than a genetic one, the Society would likely applaud the Grande Dame's choice to engineer her ideal heir.

"Advanced age," I echoed. "Maybe never retell this story within your mother's hearing if you want to hold on to your favored-son status."

Clarice Lawson was a lot of things, and vain was chief among them.

"This information is, as I'm sure you can imagine, sensitive." He studied the glossy tips of his dress shoes. "I would appreciate it if you kept this between us."

"You keep my secrets." Oscar, my ghostly ward, came to mind. "Keeping yours is the least I can do."

That earned me the tiniest smile, and my lips twitched to return his confidence.

"There's nothing more natural than to wonder, Grier."

"Speaking from experience?" A hungry mind like his wouldn't have let a mystery as compelling as his paternity go unraveled, confidentiality clause or not. "What do you know about the donor?"

"His name is Timothy Mercer." Linus tucked his hands into his pockets. "He lives in Montana with his wife and their daughters."

"You have half--sisters." A trill of curiosity shot through me. "Have you met him? Or them?"

"I met him once," he admitted. "He lived in Savannah at the time, so it was easy enough for me to take a bus to the Lyceum and confront him." He shrugged like it didn't matter when it must have for little Linus to brave public transportation alone. "Mr. Mercer was polite about the whole thing. He told me I was the spitting image of his grandfather." That memory earned a faint smile. "He called Mother, and she came to collect me. That was the last time I saw him. I went back once, years later, but he had already moved out west by then. Given their arrangement, it didn't feel right to pursue the connection further, even with sisters to consider."

Most likely, Mercer had been pink-slipped the night he met his son. "Thank you for telling me this."

All kids with question marks for parents longed for a link to their roots. A connection to their past. An understanding of who they came from that might shape who they became. I got lucky. I grew up hearing stories about Mom from Maud and Odette and flipping through the scrapbooks of their lives. My father might have been a blank page, but the others overflowed with proof I had been so very loved.

Mom had given up the right to call herself a Marchand, though she had anyway. She had forfeited her position within the family firm, forcing her to rely on her reputation to support us. She had cut ties with her relatives, forsaken her lineage. All for me.

So yeah. I had been lucky. The luckiest. Even if I had lost her all too soon.

Linus sharing his story with me might not count as a ringing endorsement for what I had done in recruiting Odette to make inroads with the Marchands, but it made me less ashamed for my curiosity.

The backs of my eyelids stung, but I blinked away the blurred vision to read him better. "What is it?"

"Let me help you find your father."

A tiny bubble of happiness rose in me. "Does this mean you approve?"

"Approval is not the issue here." Those six little words torpedoed that hope. "How you're gathering the information is what concerns me." He wiped a hand over his mouth. "Odette is family to you, and asking her for a favor might seem like a small thing, but she's a world-renowned seer. She's hardly inconspicuous. Having her contact

Dame Marchand was bound to raise eyebrows. There are members of the Marchand family, Evangeline's contemporaries, who will immediately make the connection between her and Odette and wonder what prompted the call given the disownment. Eloise might not be the only one who overheard their conversation. Even assuming her motives are pure, others' might not be."

The urge to smack myself in the forehead twitched in my palm. "When you put it like that..."

"The fewer people who know you're looking, the better chance you stand of finding your answers." His gaze cut to me. "I have contacts who can be trusted. Let me make a few calls, see what they can uncover."

"All right." Knowing a good deal when I heard one, I stuck out my hand to shake his. "I accept your offer under the condition that you let me foot the bill. Retainer, equipment, bribes, all of it. And—" I squeezed his icy fingers, "—you tell me everything. Every. Single. Thing. No matter how bad or how much you think it might rock my world, I want to know."

"I give you my word."

"Good." The bargain struck, I dropped back into my chair. "What's on the agenda for tonight?"

After clearing the dishes, he paid a visit to a nearby bookshelf and returned with a mottled tome he placed in front of me. "Open your text to page sixty-five."

The old leather creaked as I turned the pages. Several were stuck together with the cement that was parakeet poop. The chapter in question was titled *Trust Exercises: Testing the Bond Between Practitioner and Familiar*. The first subsection read *Play Dates: Working in Pairs*.

"Oh no." I grimaced. "Can we not and say we did?"

"Keet is your familiar," Linus scolded me. "You must stop viewing him as a pet."

"Your owl tried to *eat* him," I shrilled. "How can he do his job if he's terrified for his life?"

"He's already dead," Linus stated flatly.

"There's dead," I told him, "and then there's digested-in-stomach-acid dead."

Linus had, of course, chosen a great horned owl as his familiar. The symbol of Hecate herself. But Keet, a lowly parakeet, was terrified of him. He believed to the depths of his undead soul that the second Linus turned his head, yellow-eyed death would swoop down and gobble him up before I could intervene.

The poor little guy didn't sleep for a week after our first attempt at socializing our familiars.

The fact Keet was undead and didn't require sleep was totally beside the point.

"Familiars are like batteries for necromancers," he explained for the umpteenth time. "They boost our power, but they're drained in the exchange. They must be recharged, or they will die." He squinted at the cage. "Keet is a psychopomp. He's already dead. The only limit on his capacity to act as a conduit is the breadth of your power, when we haven't begun to understand your limits. That makes him uniquely suited to channeling your energy, but first you both must be trained on how to siphon."

"Fine." I strummed the bars of his cage like harp strings, finding the latch blindly and palming his quivering banana-yellow body. His round, red eyes pleaded for mercy. "But I make no promises."

A shrill whistle from Linus brought Julius sweeping into the room, and yep, Keet pooped his bird britches, which is to say my hand. Glaring at Julius, I wiped my palm clean on the towel Linus had wisely left on the table. That bird was all beak, talons, and bad attitude, in my humble opinion. The way he followed my every move through wide, unblinking eyes gave me the creeps. I really wished Linus would pack him up and courier him back to the Lawson family aviary.

In preparation for Julius's arrival, Linus had assigned a tome as thick as my wrist on cultivating a bond with your familiar. Parakeets rated one piddly footnote on page four hundred and twenty-three, but great horned owls? Four chapters. Four. Whole. Chapters. One even insinuated their golden eyes were windows into the goddess's soul.

I really hoped not. Mostly when I stared down Julius, I saw a predator in want of prey staring back.

THREE

Lessons ended that night with me speckled in fear poop, missing clumps of hair, and down one T-shirt. Julius had shredded the back of this one when I leapt between him and Keet during a trust exercise that required we leave the room for five minutes while they acclimated to one another. A bloodcurdling tweet sent me racing back in as Keet zoomed around in search of a hidey-hole while Julius did the owl equivalent of licking his chops then swooped down on him.

Linus had patched up the long furrows raked down my back and checked to ensure no damage had been done to my tattoo before I left. The shirt had too much blood on it to keep. It would have to burn.

As much as I loathed the idea, I might actually have to go clothes shopping soon.

I failed to suppress a shudder as it rolled through my shoulders, and that split second was the reason I noticed a shadow peeling from the rest and striding in my direction wearing butt-kicking boots, combat fatigues, and a matching black shirt. Taz wore her hair in a thick braid down her back, and the only part of her not dedicated to stealth was the bright red bindi dotted between her brows. Her brown eyes twinkled merrily—they did that when she was about to draw blood—and I swallowed. Hard.

Based on the broad grin stretching her cheeks, I was guessing she'd heard.

"Pause." I threw up a hand before her powerful legs got too close. "I need a second."

"Pause?" She threw back her head and laughed at the moon. "You can't mash a pause button when you're under attack."

A cage full of traumatized parakeet weighted my arm when I lifted it. "I need to put him somewhere safe."

"Oh, well, in that case... *Nope*." She cracked her knuckles. "You still have to go through me."

"Hang in there, fella." I scratched Keet's earholes through the bars of his cage. "This is going to be a bumpy ride."

"Get your butt in gear, Woolworth," Taz barked. "Moving targets are harder to hit."

Without me realizing it, she had managed to force me to circle around until she stood between me and Woolworth House. *How did she do that?* Now I really did have to go through her to reach the porch.

Fiddlesticks.

Faster than I could let out a squeak, Taz was on me, and I had no idea what to do except curl in a protective ball around Keet's cage. Sure, he was undead, but this was the only body he had, and I didn't want to have to pick the pieces of it from between her boot treads for a proper burial.

The first kick hit me in the ribs, and I swear I heard one crack. My breath left me in a rush, and black dots spotted my vision. I stumbled back, still keeping my body between her and my bird.

"I'm not here to teach you how to take a hit," she snarled her disappointment. "I'm here to teach you how to avoid getting struck in the first place."

"Sorry," I wheezed, forcing myself to straighten. "I'll do better."

"What you're failing to grasp is no conditions will ever be ideal when your life is endangered. In fact, I can guarantee that the circumstances will have been engineered to ensure the conditions are as far from ideal as you can get. They want you off your game. They want you running scared. Fear causes us to make mistakes." She cut her eyes toward the cage. "Love does too. You have to assess the risks."

"You're saying because I'm alive and my bird is technically not, I should prioritize myself above his welfare."

Stunned into a rare moment of stillness, she zeroed in on Keet. "Your bird is...what?"

Thanks to Maud, few people ever saw Keet, let alone knew what he was or how he had been made, but I had started thinking of Taz as a fixture in my life, and I had let my guard down around her. Big mistake.

"What I meant to say," I amended in a rush, "is I'm a person, and he's a bird, so my life is more valuable."

"Yeah." She frowned at the cage. "That's right."

Desperate to draw her attention back to me, I went on the offensive and swung my left leg out in a kick that hit her in the hip and sent her stumbling. I was about to sweep her legs from under her when she laughed—a gleeful sound that promised pain—and leapt back into the fray with a roundhouse kick that grazed my chin with a cool swipe of mud.

Momentarily stunned that I had dodged the first strike, I was too slow to miss the mule kick that struck me right in the gut.

Doubling over, I heaved and clutched the cage to my side. Bells rang in the distance, and my head swam. I had trouble hearing whatever insult she hurled at me over the thundering of my heart.

An inquisitive chirp cut through the wool binding my head, and for a fraction of a second, it was like standing in the eye of a tornado. Absolute peace, utter tranquility, and the firming of my resolve to stop being a victim.

Make no apologies for surviving.

"Remember what we practiced?" I panted at Keet. "You got this, buddy."

Against my better judgment, I popped the cage door open and released him. We had been working up to this for the last week. He had to learn to be part homing pigeon in case we ever got separated while he was assisting me. But I never imagined testing his radar under these conditions. Thank the goddess, Woolly was only a dozen feet away from us. Surely not even Keet could get lost between here and there.

Unable to track him unless I wanted to get a matching boot print on my cheek, I focused on Taz, who was incoming. She was always harping on me to make the best use of what I had, so I swung the cage at her. It clocked her across her right eye, and guilt swamped me.

"I am *so* sorry." Just not sorry enough to pass on the opening she had given me. I kicked out hard with my right foot and hit her square in the solar plexus. Oxygen exploded from her lungs, and she doubled over. More afraid of what she would do to me if I didn't finish her than if I did, I swept her legs from under her and watched her smack the grass on her back. From there, I hovered a safe distance away and squeezed the cage to my chest. "Are you okay?"

Wild laughter poured from her throat. "You don't apologize for kicking someone's ass."

Warmth swelled in me, but it was quickly extinguished. "I cheated."

"The cage?" She pushed into a seated position. "What have I been telling you all along?"

"To use the weapons at my disposal?" I rubbed my thumbs down the bars. "Somehow I doubt you meant a birdcage."

"You want to believe your enemies will show you mercy, that they adhere to the same moral code as yours, but they won't, Grier. They don't." She accepted the hand I extended to her, and I pulled her to her feet. "There's no such thing as a clean fight. Vampires will use their strength, their age, their skills against you. So will necro-mancers. So will humans. You must sacrifice your ego, accept there is always someone stronger, faster, or smarter than you, and do what it takes to survive." She gripped my shoulders until I winced. "Whatever it takes, understand? There is no shame in living to fight another day."

The sentiment drew me up short, almost an echo of the words I had melded into a personal mantra, and it occurred to me then while Maud might have been the first, she was far from the last to offer me that sage advice.

Tossing the cage aside, I sank into a ready stance. "Want to go again?"

Expecting the attack to come from below, as usual, I was stunned when her fist clipped my jaw.

Had my eyes not rolled back in my head, I would have cried foul.

"STOP BABYING HER," Taz grumbled. "She must have a glass jaw. I didn't hit her that hard."

"She bit through her tongue," Linus snapped. "Go wait in the garden before I return the favor."

"Kinky," I slurred, my words thick and wrong. "You canth...go 'round...bithing..."

"Shh." Linus cradled my cheek in his cool palm. His touch felt divine against the hot pain throbbing in my jaw, and I leaned into his touch. "Don't speak."

A jolt of alarm zipped through me, and I leveraged myself upright. "Keeth!"

"Keet is fine." Linus rested a hand on my shoulder. "Woolly noticed him on the porch and let him in the house." He lowered me back against the pillows. Pillows? Had they sprouted on the lawn like mushrooms? "Amelie caged him for you."

"Not Taz's faulth." It felt important that he remember that. "Asked for ith."

"I very much doubt you requested to have your tongue shortened."

A miserable noise rose up the back of my throat. "Thath...bad?"

"I've done what I can, but I require a second opinion."

"No." The last thing I wanted was a record of this incident in the Society databases.

"Yes." He smoothed sweaty hairs off my forehead. "He'll be here shortly."

Without making the conscious decision, I slipped through the door in my head and gave myself permission to rest there, away from the pain, until firm nudges forced me to return to my body.

"Hey, you." A young black man with a smile that promised trouble stared down at me through eyes the rich, deep color of my favorite triple dark chocolate brew from Mallow. "Remember me?"

A distant gurgle in my stomach, paired with the bitter taste in the back of my throat, told me I had hurled my breakfast while unconscious. No wonder I was framing the poor man's looks to align with my sweet tooth.

"Heinz," I murmured. "'member."

The shameless flirt was a medic attached to the sentinels. Maybe he was a sentinel himself. I hadn't thought to ask. All I knew for certain was Boaz had dialed him up after my dybbuk hunt on the *Cora Ann* went sideways.

A pen light swept back and forth across my vision. "What happened this time?"

"Taz."

Sympathy twisted his features. "Ouch."

"Yeah." I flinched when his fingers prodded my jaw. "Ouch."

"She called me up, but she didn't give any details." He answered the question I had just been pondering. "I'm a better medic than a sentinel, so I tend to ride around in the box, but I'm in Taz's unit."

"So you know." That she must be the love child of a centaur and a donkey the way she loved to kick.

"I do know." He pulled aside the collar of his shirt to expose a long scar across his collarbone. "She clipped me once during training, and I fell on a pile of volcanic rock. I hit a sharp edge and nearly got decapitated in the process. She thought it was hilarious. I thought I was dead meat."

"Thath sounds like her."

Linus peered over Heinz's shoulder. "Will she be all right?"

"Her jaw is bruised, but it's not fractured." He tapped my chin. "Say *ahhh*."

"*Ahhh*—crap. Thath hurths."

"I don't doubt it, but I need to see that tongue. Mr. Lawson tells me you bit the tip clean off, so I need to check and make sure it's been properly reattached. We don't want you to have mobility issues. Those might lead to problems with deglutition or articulation later."

This time my *ahhh* was more of an *AHHH*, but I let him examine me for as long as I could endure the pain.

"The seam is flawless." Heinz sought out Linus. "Are you sure you're not certified, Mr. Lawson?"

"No." His gaze touched on the books scattered across every available surface in what I was just realizing was his bedroom. That explained the pillows. "I read a lot."

"Huh." Heinz sounded unconvinced. "Maybe you should loan me a few of those books."

A ghost of a smile twitched his lips. "I'm happy to make a list if you'd like to borrow them from the Lyceum."

"I'll take you up on that." Heinz answered the challenge in Linus's tone then turned back to me. "You're going to be fine. You're also going to be on an all-liquid diet for the next five to seven days." He pinched the skin on the underside of my upper arm. "You're thin as it is. Don't skimp on the calories just because you have to suck them down. Drink those enriched shakes with lots of protein. Broth is also an option. Any soups that have small pieces that won't choke you, like tomato basil or wonton—minus the wonton—are good."

Visions of Mallow danced in my head. "Okay."

A snort to my left told me Linus had me pegged. "You can't live off hot chocolate and melted marshmallows for a week." He hesitated. "Well, *you* probably could, but you shouldn't." He fussed with the edge of my—his—sheets, as I was lying in his bed. "Pick your poisons, and I'll put soup on later. We can freeze it in batches. That way all you have to do is thaw them out when you get hungry."

I reached for his arm. "You donth have tho do thath."

He tensed under the weight of my hand. "I don't mind."

"Has anyone told Boaz yet?" Heinz inserted himself into our conversation. "He's going to flip his lid."

"I'm sure Taz called him the second my head hith the grass." I snorted, and goddess that hurt. "Oh, no. Whath abouth Amelie?"

"I called her," Linus assured me. "I'll update her once Mr. Heinz leaves."

"Thanks." I pushed out a tired breath and released him. "I donth want her to worry."

The expression he wore conveyed perfect neutrality, but I knew he wasn't thrilled that I had taken in Amelie. He worried about me being alone in the house with her, but I wasn't alone. I had Woolly, who never slept, and I had Oscar too. Although he tended to pop in and out on his own schedule.

"Okay, I'm all done here." Heinz passed over a prescription for painkillers I would ball up and toss after he left. "These will get you through the first two days. I'll leave my number with you. Call if the pain gets unmanageable, and I'll give you a lift to the hospital."

"Thanks." I took the paper he offered me. "I appreciathe you coming outh here."

"No thanks necessary. It's my job." He winked. "Plus, I get to call Boaz and tell him I conducted a *thorough* examination of your mouth while you were stretched out on Mr. Lawson's bed. You can't put a price tag on that."

Mortification singed me clear to my hairline. "Please donth."

"I like you, Grier, so I'll take it under advisement." He gathered his things and stood to leave, but he didn't make it far. Cletus barred the door. "What in the—?"

"This was a confidential visit," Linus answered, ice glazing his words. "You're free to tell Boaz what the instructor he chose for Grier has done to her, and you're welcome to update him on her condition, but you will not make any insinuations that might damage her reputation."

The wraith swelled until he filled the doorway with his tattered black cloak, his bone-white fingers curved into claws he clacked together at his sides.

"Confidential," Heinz agreed, his voice pitched higher. "My lips are sealed."

"Good." Linus dismissed him with a flick of his wrist reminiscent of his mother. "You may go."

"Imperious much?" I mocked his gesture. "You may go now, peasanth."

Linus didn't crack a smile as he sank into a chair angled toward the bed. He penned fresh healing sigils along my jaw where the ones he had inked on had begun to flake. Cooling magic enveloped my mouth, and my tongue tingled like I had eaten one too many jalapenos. The swelling reduced, and the pain eased to a dull throb. There were runes that would stop the ache entirely, but he knew I wouldn't go for those.

"You must end this madness with Taz." After dusting the reddish-brown crumbs into his palm to toss in the trash, he toyed with the ends of my hair where they fanned across his pillow. "She's too advanced for a beginner. She's a skilled fighter, but a poor teacher. She doesn't grasp that she can't beat the knowledge into your head."

This was a conversation I sensed had been a long time in coming. For weeks, Linus had allowed us to spar. No, that's not right. Unlike other men in my life, he didn't view my decisions as a thing he had the right to allow or disallow. More like he had kept his mouth shut, the way a friend might, while watching another friend embrace a bad decision with arms wide open because they craved recklessness or needed an outlet.

"I like her." From the hips up, at least. "She doesn't pull her punches, and she trusts me to take care of myself."

Catching himself, he withdrew his hand. "What would Boaz say if he saw you after one of your practices?"

I flinched, well aware I resembled hamburger meat most nights, and his eyes gleamed with triumph. "He would kill her."

"I've been tempted," Linus muttered.

"Linus." I must be hearing things. "You're supposed to be the rational one."

"Let me offer you an alternative." His muscles stiffened in expectation of a swift rejection. "I have a friend who teaches self-defense. Work with him a few months, learn the basics, and then you can graduate to Taz. Against all odds, I am aware of how much you like her. But she isn't for you. Not yet."

"I'll think about it." With my jaw pulsing in time with my heart, it was hard to argue the point with him. "I'll have to talk to her, and to Boaz, first. I don't want them to think I'm ungrateful or that I'm wimping out on them."

"May I?" Linus picked up my cell from where someone had placed it at the foot of the bed and held it out for me to unlock. Curious, I did as he requested then waited to see what he wanted to show me. "This was the first time."

He turned the screen toward me, and I got an eyeful of the picture I had taken to send Boaz as a sort of thank you before common sense prevailed, and I deleted the text. He would have blown a gasket if he had any idea how intense our sessions got or that Linus refereed with the caveat I allowed him to heal me afterward.

"Your lessons have escalated. You're showing marked improvement, but you're also sustaining worse damage." As my private nurse, he ought to know. "You owe neither of them gratitude for this."

"I'll handle it." With a grimace, I deleted the picture like I should have already done. "Promise."

Relenting at last, Linus blacked the screen then placed the phone out of my reach. "I'll bring your things in here, and you can get started on your homework."

"Are you serious?" I gestured to my face. "This doesn't earn me a free pass?"

"You're off tonight, you won't take the painkillers, and you won't let me paint on a sigil to dull the hurt." He moved in for the kill. "Woolly and Amelie and Oscar will hover over you if you go home, so you might as well stay here in the quiet and be productive."

"Teacher logic strikes again." As much as I hated admitting it, he was right. I didn't want to go home yet. I couldn't face an entire night of Amelie snapping covert pictures to text her brother along with updates when he seemed to have forgotten my number. One call, and he could get news right from the source, but my phone remained silent.

The uncharacteristic quiet on his end made me nervous. Usually bouts of introspection where relationships where concerned ended with him spouting *it's not you, it's me* or another canned response guaranteed to result in raccoon eyes for his current girlfriend.

Except, for the first time, that 'current girlfriend' was *me*.

"Fine." Despite the headache, and yeah, okay, heartache, I caved. "But I'm not reading another word on the greatness of horned owls."

FOUR

Night passed in blissful silence at the carriage house. Linus had his own work to keep him occupied, so he didn't hover while I studied. His mastery of the art of silence was so complete, I didn't notice him leaving to pick up soup for our dinner. The logo on the cup he pressed into my hand matched an upscale bistro in town I avoided like the plague due to its High Society vibes. They might not hand out fourteen-karat spoons, but their clothlike to-go napkins were stuffed with gold-tone utensils.

I forgave them their ridiculousness when I took my first mouthful of French onion soup heavy on the Gruyere and decided maybe I could revisit my avoidance policy.

Lounging in bed with a full stomach made me drowsy, and I blamed that for musing on how nice it must be to live in a house unable to form its own opinions on your life choices. Instantly, I regretted thinking I could get along without Woolly when I was all she had left. If that meant she clung a little tighter than necessary, then so be it. Though, truth be told, the break from Amelie was welcome, and I didn't experience even a twinge of remorse for acknowledging that.

Maybe Maud had been onto something by only allowing us to sleep over once a week.

"Are you ready to go home?" Linus appeared in the doorway, black-framed glasses sliding down his nose and eyebrows raised. "I can walk you over, but I'll have to call Amelie to help you upstairs."

"Sorry about that." I sat up and swung my legs over the edge of the mattress. "Woolly cultivates her grudges the way Maud used to nurture her plants."

"I broke her trust." He rushed over and tossed his glasses on the bed before helping me stand. "It will take time for her to forgive me. I understand that." He hooked his right arm around my waist to hold me steady then draped my left one across his shoulders. "Though, at times, I'll admit it is inconvenient."

"She'll forgive you eventually," I assured him. "She loves Oscar, and she knows you're the reason he's here with us. That alone earned you tons of bonus points."

Though I didn't have the heart to tell Linus that Oscar was still shy of him, which meant grateful or not, Woolly wasn't going to let him in anytime soon.

We shuffled our way across the yard, and she allowed him on the porch without so much as a reprimanding flicker. Amelie flung open the door and her arms at the same time, and I felt like a dirt sandwich accepting her hug when I had been avoiding her for hours.

"I'm going to murder Taz," she growled, and I stiffened in her hold. "Geez, Grier, I don't mean it in the literal sense." She drew back and examined me. "Though my brother might once he gets a load of this."

I thought back to my phone, which hadn't rung a single time tonight. "Have you talked to him?"

"Yes." She released me to rub her ears. "I'm shocked you didn't hear his bellows from across the yard."

"I haven't heard much of anything from Boaz." The words slipped out before I could call them back.

Ugh.

I didn't want this to be me, the jealous-girlfriend type who craved each meager scrap of attention. But I also had no idea how the whole relationship thing worked. Did I have the right to demand more? Or was I supposed to let him dole out what he thought was enough? And was the reverse true? Not that I'd had much chance to ice him out thanks to smacking up against the brick wall of his inattention.

Amelie mashed her lips into a hard line, her gaze skittering like a spider up the far wall behind me.

That...was not reassuring.

"I'll come for you at dusk," Linus said from the porch. "Call if you need anything."

"Go home. Rest." I took his hand and squeezed it. "You've done enough for me for one day."

Pink saturated his cheeks as he tightened his long fingers around mine. "It's my pleasure."

At least Amelie had the good manners to wait until the door shut behind Linus to mock him. *"It's my pleasure."* Her arm slid around my waist. "Who talks like that?"

"He does." A prickle of irritation made me wish I could manage the steps up to my room alone. "What's your problem?"

"Why didn't he bring you straight back here?" she demanded. "Woolly and I were worried sick."

The old house groaned, a sure sign she didn't want to be used as leverage in our latest spat.

"He can't enter Woolly, remember? The carriage house was closer, so he took me there."

"Convenient," she grumbled.

"Heinz popped in for a house call—" I kept going, talking over her mini rant, "—and he told me to take it easy. Since I was off tonight, Linus propped me up and put me to work on a lesson." I slid her a stern look. "It was nothing nefarious."

"I don't trust him."

"You don't have to, Ame." I patted her back. "He's not your problem."

Amelie tensed at my tone but kept going. "Boaz is pissed."

"When is Boaz ever not pissed when it comes to Linus?" All that navel-gazing earlier had given me fresh perspective. "He's not my boyfriend. We went on *one* date. That means he doesn't have the right to an opinion. Especially one he can't be bothered to call and voice himself."

Jealousy might be a new concept for him, but his past antics had turned me green often enough to know it did nothing for my complexion. And, okay, yes, I was still in a snit over the fact he had made no effort to communicate with me since the night he dropped his sister off at my house. Yet another keepsake of his for me to store until he wanted it back.

The Elite deploy where they're sent, I got that, but wherever he was stationed had plenty of cell service as far as I could tell. How else could he touch base with his sister every other day? And I know it was him, their banter so familiar I would recognize the back-and-forth anywhere.

Now, I'm not saying I was eavesdropping on her phone calls. I'm just saying her voice carries, especially when I press my ear against her bedroom door.

"He may not be your boyfriend, but he's your *something*. I think that earns him the right to be concerned when you get hurt or when you spend the night in another man's bed."

My head snapped toward her. "How do you know I was in his room and not the guestroom?"

"I saw you through the window."

"No, you didn't." I had plenty of time to soak up my surroundings while pretending to be studious. "The curtains were shut. Heinz closed them before he left so the rear porch light didn't bother me."

The angle was all wrong too. From the porch, maybe. But she wasn't supposed to be out there.

"Okay, you got me." We reached the landing, and she shepherded me toward my room. "I called Taz and asked for details."

Groaning, I toddled into my room and eased down onto the mattress. "I don't remember seeing her."

"Who do you think carried you?" She snorted. "Linus?"

"Yes." Actually, that's exactly what I'd thought. Taz, having been the one to KO me, must have beat him to the punch. "You're saying she put me in his bed then lit up the phone tree to broadcast the details."

"We have the right—"

"I get it." I sagged back against my pillows. "You're my best friend, and Boaz is my *something*, but that doesn't entitle either of you to every detail of my life."

She flung her arms out to the sides. "You know every detail of my life."

"Uh, no. I don't. Or I didn't. Not until it was too late." I bit the inside of my cheek, but the buildup of annoyance had bubbled over my lips. "Ame, I'm sorry. I didn't mean that the way it sounded."

"I'm grateful for what you did for me," she said, voice flat. "But no one asked you to save me."

"You're right." The snide comment erased all that came before it, and that was my breaking point. "In fact, your mother ordered me *not* to."

Tears glistened in her eyes as she spun on her heel and hit the stairs.

I was too exhausted to go after her and too afraid of what I might say when I caught her.

Instead I curled up against my pillows and closed my eyes.

A SCREAM TORE from my throat, raw and aching, and fresh pain lanced along my jaw before I clamped my mouth shut. As awareness settled over me, I grasped that I wasn't huddled on the hard floor in a corner as I expected, but balanced across warm thighs and cradled against a wide chest.

"Hush, Squirt." Boaz caressed the length of my spine. "It was just a dream."

"Just *the* dream." I ran my newly healed tongue along the edge of my teeth before asking, "How are you here?"

"Magic."

"Mmm-hmm." All the anger I had been carting around for the past two weeks smashed to pieces at his feet. He was here. That was all that mattered. "You can't drop your life and come running every time I stub a toe."

"Watch me." His lips brushed my forehead. "For as long as I can, I will."

Fear of how long that might be had me snuggling closer. "You're sweet."

"I can be." His chuckle deepened. "With proper motivation."

"What were you doing before Amelie and Taz blew up your phone?"

"It's classified." His gaze dipped before meeting mine again. "It's also boring as hell."

"Poor baby." I reached up and patted his prickly cheek. "How long can you stay?"

"Twenty-four hours." He turned his face and pressed a kiss into my palm. "That's the best I could do."

A tiny corner of my heart deflated at the brevity of the visit, and I fisted his shirt like that might hold him here with me. "We need to talk."

"Am I in trouble?" He ruffled the longer hair on top of his head into a tousled mess. "I should have called before inviting myself over, but I didn't think. I heard you got hurt and I—"

"I'm glad you're here." I blasted out a sigh. "The problem is how you knew to come in the first place."

"Taz called me right after it happened. Amelie reached out thirty minutes later with an update." A frown knit his brow. "Did you not want me to know?"

"It's not that." I traced the logo on his T-shirt with my fingertip.

"Of course I want them to call you when it's important, but it feels like every time I get a paper cut, one of them is texting you."

"I didn't ask them to if that's where you're headed with this." He tangled his fingers in my hair. "I haven't discouraged them, though. I'll give you that."

"I would appreciate a touch more privacy, that's all I'm saying."

"Ah." The weight of his hand pulled on my scalp in a pleasant way. "You're waiting for me to lose my cool over you convalescing in Linus's bed."

Aware he was cataloging the damage and not going in for a kiss, I still allowed him to tip my head back. "I will admit I expected fireworks."

"Grier." The rare use of my name released butterflies into my stomach, and he smiled down on me until the bruising drew his eye. "Are you attracted to Linus?"

Thinking I misheard him, I straightened on his lap. *"What?"*

Our gazes clashed, and he repeated the question. "Are you romantically interested in Linus Andreas Lawson III?"

Had the pain not stopped me from dropping my jaw, it would have scraped the floor. *"What?"*

"Your shock is priceless." Amusement lightened his eyes. "You've really never thought about it?"

"He's got pretty hair but..." I tried and failed to frame a response. He was smart and kind and funny and so many other unexpected things. "He's Linus."

A smirk tugged up one corner of his lips. "And I'm Boaz."

I frowned. "Exactly."

"See, I don't care how you ended up in his bed. I don't care that you stayed there all night. I don't even need to know what happened while you were there, alone with him."

"You don't." I heard the doubt thick in my voice.

"I trust you." His eyes searched mine. "You would tell me if you wanted out."

I huffed a frustrated sigh. "You're barely in."

Boaz trapped his bottom lip with his upper teeth right over the scar I remembered so well, but it didn't stop his shoulders from bouncing with laughter. "You have no idea how much restraint I'm showing by keeping this conversation PG."

"Perv."

"I'm your perv."

Unable to resist being amused, I rolled my eyes. "That shouldn't sound as sweet as it does."

"I told you," he said with a wink, "it's all about proper motivation."

"Stop distracting me." I pinched his nipple and relished his yelp. "We need to talk about Taz."

"No, we don't." A grimness settled over his expression. "I cut her loose."

"You don't get to make that call." Contrary, yeah, but I hated that he had pulled the trigger without asking me first. "I can continue working with her if I choose."

"Tell me the truth." His fingertip skated through the air over my jaw. "Was this the first time she's hurt you? I don't mean scratches or bruises from training, I mean damaged you enough to require medical intervention."

My silence answered for me.

"Taz believes in tough love, and I know you appreciate that, but this is taking things too far."

"I like her." That she didn't pull her punches after hearing my name was a bonus. "She's taught me a lot." But facts were facts. "You guys might be right, though. She may be too advanced for me right now."

"Linus knew?" His derisive snort required no response. "He should have stepped in sooner."

"I asked him not to interfere." And guilt had eaten him up on the sidelines. I never should have put him in that situation. "He's taken care of me...after...but he wasn't happy about the choices I've made."

"Have you ever stopped to wonder if there's a reason you let it go so far?" His voice dipped into a lower register. "You should have set her straight after the first time it happened, but you didn't. Why is that?"

I got a bad feeling about where this was headed. "I thought I could handle it. I *was* handling it."

"Are you sure you weren't taking the punishment because you felt like you deserved it?" Boaz gentled his hold on me. "You internalized so much of what happened to you, it's become your default to bury what you're thinking and feeling. I never know what's going on in that head of yours." He scanned my face. "Can you look me in the eye and tell me you weren't using Taz as an outlet?"

A quiver tightened my stomach. "I am *not* a masochist."

"Atramentous—"

"No." I shoved at him. "I don't want to talk about it."

"That's the problem." He captured my wrists. "Are you still confiding in Odette?"

"I've been busy." Guilt if I kept Amelie waiting was driving me home earlier and earlier these days. "I don't have to schedule weekly therapy sessions."

"Don't take this the wrong way, Squirt, but maybe you do." His hands drifted higher until he held me by the shoulders. "Have you seen your face?"

Maybe Taz had once accused me of walking into punches I could have blocked, but I had been sick with the knowledge I was leading Linus into a trap set for the dybbuk at the time. Truthfully? I may have been jonesing for punishment then, but it's not like I go around rubbing my hands with glee when I imagine all the pain I'll be in during or after sparring with her.

And fine, yes, so I have a backlog of pent-up rage searching for a target. I could admit that much. There was something cathartic about striking another person as hard as you could when you knew they would deflect the blows to minimize the damage.

Life had been using me as a punching bag for so long, it felt good hitting back.

"I will consider scheduling regular head-shrinking sessions with Odette *if* you agree not to interfere with my self-defense classes." I braced for a mantrum of epic proportions when I added, "Linus offered to set me up with an instructor he knows who can teach me the fundamentals before I pick back up with Taz."

A muscle jumped in his jaw, but Boaz nodded. "I had my shot. Why not give him his?"

"It's not like that." I braced my forehead against his chest. "It's not a competition between you two."

"Feels that way sometimes," he muttered under his breath.

"Mmm." I linked my arms around his neck. "Whatever happened to trust?"

"This has nothing to do with trust." His eyes met mine. "Or you, really."

"Ah." I nodded sagely. "This is one of those manly contests that involves the whipping out of—"

"Please finish that sentence." He settled his arms around my waist. "I've never heard you say a dirty word in your life."

"Hmph." I jutted out my chin, wincing at the bite of discomfort. "I can be dirty."

"I look forward to a demonstration—after you're healed." Pushing me back against the pillows, he shifted until his weight dented the mattress beside me. "You're not going to tempt me into misbehaving when I came all the way here to make sure you were okay."

I fluttered my eyelashes at him. "Came all the way from...?"

"Nice try." He nudged me onto my side facing the wall then spooned behind me. "You sure talk a lot for someone with a missing tongue and a broken jaw."

A snort escaped me. "It wasn't *that* bad."

"Do you know how lucky you are that you didn't swallow it? That Linus found and reattached it?"

"Gack." I tasted acid in the back of my throat. "Let's not talk about self-cannibalism."

"We don't have to talk at all," he murmured, lips pressing against my neck. "I'll settle for cuddling."

"I missed you," I whispered into the darkened room. "You've been hiding from me."

Using the same taunt he'd fired at me on his first night back in Savannah caused all that heat behind me to freeze. "I haven't been hiding. I've been working."

"You make time for Amelie." Goddess, I hated sounding like a butthurt girlfriend.

Warm breath skated across my throat. "You're jealous."

A laugh escaped me. "No, I'm not."

"Yes, you are." His teeth closed over the tip of my ear. "It's cute."

"Given everything that's happened, I get why you want to keep in closer touch with her."

"The only person I wish was closer, so I could touch her, is you." He rubbed his stubbly cheek over mine, and a delicious thrill coursed through me. "We're all she's got, Squirt. For now, it's just you and me, and she knows she's driving you crazy. You've shown the patience of a saint in dealing with this situation." His lips plucked my earlobe. "Amelie needs me more than you do right now. That's all. It won't always be this way, but I have to prioritize her."

Amelie did need him more than me, but it stung hearing him sweep my needs under the rug to address later. It's not like he couldn't alternate calls between us, giving us equal attention, or spot me one of her days every week. No, this felt like a shutout. But pointing that out would set him on edge, and I didn't want to waste the hours left to us.

The thing was, I couldn't tell how much of my annoyance stemmed from how he was treating me versus how she had treated me. Amelie and I still had wrinkles to iron out if our friendship was to survive. The lengths she had gone to in the name of acquiring magic left a bad taste in my mouth.

Though she claimed the deal she had struck with the dybbuk was to protect me, Ambrose must not have gotten the memo. He almost killed me to get at Oscar, and he had killed nine vampires. True, six of them had trespassed on my property with the intent to recapture me, but three of them had been innocents.

"Have you visited her yet?" I wriggled underneath the crisp sheet. "She must have heard us talking."

"I said *hi* on my way in." He made an appreciative noise in the back of his throat while I snuggled closer. "I'll make time for her tomorrow. We can watch one of those cheesy movies while you're in class."

Amelie did enjoy a good B movie. Her running commentary was often better than watching *MST 3K*.

"You can't stay in here," I said drowsily. "The dream..."

"Hush." Warm lips blazed a trail down the column of my throat. "You just close your eyes and rest."

Sleep never came on command for me, but I still lowered my eyes. "I've never slept with a man."

"Are you trying to kill me here, Squirt?" Boaz adjusted his hips, but all he managed to do was emphasize the point where our bodies touched. "I'm trying to be good here."

Bundled up in a Boaz blanket, I settled down to snatch a few winks from the jaws of the dream before it snapped closed over me.

FIVE

oaz was gone, his side of the bed cold, by the time I woke with my heart lodged in my throat. A small mercy. I preferred keeping the nightmare to myself. As I made my way downstairs, I hunted for signs of the Siblings Pritchard. Though I suppose they technically weren't that anymore. Their muted voices lured me downstairs, and I padded toward them, freezing on the staircase when I realized I was the topic of conversation.

"I was asleep down the hall," Amelie was saying. "That's way too close for *that* to be happening."

"*That* didn't happen," Boaz countered. "I might be a dog, but I can resist leg humping an injured woman."

Amelie burst out laughing. "Since when?"

"Since Grier," he said with an edge that killed the conversation dead on the spot.

"I'm kidding. Sheesh." A spoon clanged against the side of a bowl. "I tease Grier all the time. I used to anyway. Mostly we just tiptoe around each other and avoid topics more controversial than the weather."

"You guys will be okay."

"I almost killed her," she rasped. "How can she forgive that?"

"She loves you. That's how." Chair legs raked across the tile, and she grunted. No doubt she was the unwitting recipient of one of his bear hugs. "I love you too. You know that, right?"

"Yeah." Her voice came out muffled, and I had no problem imagining her face turned into his shoulder. "I wish you loved me less."

"Nothing doing," he murmured. "You're my sister."

With a great sigh, she resumed clicking her spoon. "Some choices can't be forgiven."

"I don't expect absolution," he said grimly. "I don't want it, and I don't deserve it."

"I'm sorry," she whispered.

"So am I," he breathed. "So am I."

A cold stone dropped into the pit of my stomach, but I had no way to ask what he meant without revealing I had been eavesdropping on them.

Amelie cleared her throat. "How is Macon?"

"He's heartbroken. He doesn't understand why you don't live at home, why he can't talk to you. Goddess only knows what *those two* told him." Not Mom and Dad, but *those two*. "He called me after his first day back to school. The kids are..." A growl revved up his throat. "You know how cruel kids can be."

"I didn't mean to hurt him." A hiccupping sob broke through her chest. "I didn't mean to hurt anyone."

"But you did." Gravel churned in his voice. "Now we have to live with the consequences."

Feeling like a creeper, I backed off up the stairs then made a clomping entrance. Amelie didn't glance up, she was too busy blotting her cheeks dry, but Boaz swept his gaze down my body and left me tingling down to my toes.

"Hello, gorgeous." He puckered up and tapped his lips. "You gotta pay the toll."

"This is my house." I moseyed over, helpless to resist that teasing glint in his eyes. "Shouldn't you be the one paying me?"

"Hmm." He appeared to consider this. "Good point."

Faster than I could squeak, he was out of his chair and gunning for me. I made it three steps into the living room before his arms banded around my waist, and he lifted me off my feet. He peppered the side of my neck with kisses while he swung me in a dizzying circle. Right when I was starting to be thankful for my empty stomach, he laid me on the couch then climbed over me, pinning my hands to either side of my head.

A furious blush rose up my throat. "Amelie is in the kitchen."

"Amelie is a grown woman." He lowered his voice while pressing his lips against my ear. "I'm pretty sure she knows how this works."

"There better not be anything *working* out there," she called from the bar. "I have a full stomach, and I'd like to keep it that way."

Cackling at his indignant expression, I wriggled my hips. "You are kind of smooshing me."

"Sorry, Squirt." He leveraged himself off me. "I didn't hurt you, did I?"

"Nah." I sat up along with him, straddled his thighs, and plastered myself against his chest. "I liked it."

His brows quirked. "Then why...?"

A loud rumble in my stomach told him I had breakfast on my mind.

"Want me to whip up some grub for you?" He brushed his fingers along the uninjured side of my jaw. "There are plenty of waffles and syrup to go around."

"As tempting as that sounds, Heinz told me I'm on a liquid diet for the next few days." I touched my cheek. "It doesn't hurt as much today, but I'm not putting pressure on it, either." I swiped my tongue along the backside of my teeth. "Oddly enough, my tongue feels as good as new."

That probably had something to do with the amount of magic Linus had channeled into healing me.

"I'm glad to hear it." Concern tightened his expression. "Still, you should eat something before you go."

Hating to ruin the moment, I saw no way around telling him the truth. Especially since I was certain that Amelie had already spilled those beans. "I usually eat with Linus."

"Ah." He gripped my hips and set me on the floor in front of him. "Well, that's okay, I guess." He rubbed his hands over his scalp. "I can see how it might have been lonely over here until Amelie moved in."

The faintest suggestion I ought to bail on Linus threaded his words, but he didn't press me on the issue, and I was grateful not to have to shoot him down. Breakfast at the carriage house was part of my nightly routine. Depending on the menu, I often left convinced it was the best part. I wouldn't miss that date for anything less than...

Fiddlesticks.

Date was not the right word. Even in my head, it sounded too dangerous.

"I should get going." I hooked my thumbs in my belt loops. "Are you guys still watching a movie?"

"That's the plan." He did the same, not pushing for more, just holding on like he wanted to keep me here with him. "How long do these lessons of yours last?"

"Two hours on a good night. Four on bad ones. Six if I'm a total dunce." My hand cramped just thinking about the last eight-hour stint I earned for utterly failing one of Linus's infamous pop quizzes. "I'm still working aboard the *Cora Ann* part-time, so I have a freer schedule these days."

Boaz gave a sharp tug. "Has Cricket mentioned Amelie?"

"Neely says Cricket was ready to kick puppies when Amelie called in and quit. She's been a fixture at Haint Misbehavin' for years. She was one of their most dependable ghost tour guides." I gave a helpless shrug. "I report to Cricket once a week on the *Cora Ann*'s progress, but I'm not around to hear more gossip about Amelie if there is any."

That wasn't what he was really asking, though.

"Amelie had a solid alibi," I reassured him. "Everyone knows she's been working toward her degree. Her cover story about spending six months as an intern at a firm in Atlanta isn't that big of a stretch." I glanced toward the kitchen, but Amelie was nowhere in sight. "She ought to be able to pick up her job and her schooling right where she left off."

"Let's hope." He squeezed my fingers. "I want her reentry to be as normal as possible."

For a Low Society necromancer, life wouldn't be that altered. In the big-picture sense, at least. Most of them worked human jobs, attended human schools, and led human lives. Some even married humans, though the difference in lifespans made such unions bittersweet.

Amelie could resume her job as a Haint, and she could return to college, but she would never step foot in the Lyceum again. Her days of attending lavish moonlit balls and studying under her mother as the spare heir were over. Her ties to the Pritchard family had been cut, and most Low Society families would be hesitant to risk ostracism for welcoming her into their midst.

"Me too." I kissed his cheek then twisted out of reach before he distracted me again. "Do *not* leave without telling me goodbye."

His answering grin was wicked. "Yes, ma'am."

After gathering Keet and my grimoire, I passed through the kitchen on my way to eat with Linus.

Amelie must have slipped out while Boaz had me otherwise occupied. Unsurprising since her threshold for PDA was nonexistent where he was concerned. I couldn't blame her. I wouldn't want to watch my brother tickling my best friend's tonsils with his tongue either.

A pang struck each time it hit me she had traded on her family name for power that had almost killed me.

Miserable all over again, I plodded the rest of the way to the carriage house where the closed-door policy irked me for no reason. I knocked, but Linus never appeared. Leaning in, I pressed my ear to the door and heard a loud whirring-grinding noise. Curious, I decided that since he must be expecting me, I could let myself in.

Linus was, as usual, in the kitchen. But this time, he manned a fancy blender I knew hadn't been in the cupboards when he moved in. Its throaty growl would have given Jolene a run for her money. No wonder he hadn't heard me.

Jars of supplements littered the counter along with fresh fruit sliced into cubes, two percent milk—bleck—and a tub of protein powder. The mixture swirling in the glass basin was pink enough to remind me of strawberries, but I had my doubts about its tastiness based on the rest of his arsenal.

Honestly, who put grass in their shakes? Wheat or otherwise?

I meandered up to him and tapped him on the shoulder.

Turns out Linus was not a fan of surprises.

A wraithlike cloak flickered in my vision, overlaying his usual slacks-and-dress-shirt combo, to ripple in a wave of black mist that lapped at my ankles, a frigid pond I had waded into without taking the first step.

Though he had been busily blending since I arrived, his back to me, he was now in my personal space. His nose was an inch from mine. Less. And his icy fingers trapped the wrist of the hand that had touched him.

Ink spilled across his eyes until I was staring into a fathomless pool of still waters that lapped against the shores of my mind, eroding the memories I kept caged until I gasped and stumbled back.

"Linus?" I massaged my wrist, not because he had been rough, but because his glacial touch stung.

Midnight eyes dropped to my hand, and his lips tipped downward. "I hurt you."

"No," I rushed out, breathless. "I'm just cold."

"I'm sorry." He turned from me and braced his hands on the sink. "You startled me."

"I let myself in. It was totally my fault." This time I didn't take liberties without first alerting him. "Linus?" I rested my hand on his shoulder, and the fabric crunched like frostbitten blades of grass. I forced myself to leave my fingers where they settled instead of jerking back on instinct. That seemed important somehow. "Next time I'll wait until you answer the door."

A shudder moved through him, and he covered my hand with his. Gooseflesh coasted down my arms, but I didn't budge as he turned his head, his fogged breath skating over my skin. "That might be for the best, though you're always welcome here." He huffed out a laugh. "It is your house, after all."

Manners ingrained in me and every other High Society girl since birth breached the surface.

"You're living here. That makes it your home too." *Home* wasn't the word I'd meant to use, but the quick jerk of his head toward me and the surprise glinting in his eyes—a crisp blue that reminded me of the ocean during storms—made me glad I had misspoken. "You get to make the house rules."

Linus might have started out as an uninvited guest, but the truth was I liked having him around. Early on, I made no secret of how unhappy I was about the arrangement. The Grande Dame offering hospitality as if Woolly were her home tweaked my tail, but it had been rude of me to take it out on him.

The guy had saved my life when the dybbuk attacked.

As far as I was concerned, I owed him mints on his pillow each dawn.

A sliver of warmth brightened his expression. "I appreciate that."

"So..." I cleared my throat and took a seat. "What's on the agenda for the night?"

"Breakfast first." He returned to the blender, flipped it off, then poured me a tall glass of his concoction and a smaller one for himself. "You still like strawberries?"

"I do." Chocolate-covered strawberries were one of my favorite treats. "That explains the pink."

"I researched protein shake recipes. I hoped mixing in the fresh fruit would help with the taste."

"You stayed up working on this?" He must have made a grocery run while I was sleeping. "I can buy protein shakes at the store, and cans of soup. You don't have to put yourself out."

"I don't mind." He stabbed bendy straws into our glasses, having realized from our last meal that silverware was part of the illusion, and joined me at the table. "You don't have to worry about my feelings." He handed me my breakfast. "Tell me if you don't like it, and I'll make something else."

"Here we go." I took a hesitant sip and let the smoothie melt on my tongue. "*Goddess.*"

Linus swirled his straw through his pink drink. "Is invocation this time of night a good thing or a bad thing?"

"How do you know how to do all this?" I took another pull. "You're like a kitchen ninja."

A pleased smile broke across his face. "I enjoy cooking."

"You know that saying?" I said around a third slurp. "Jack of all trades, master of none?"

His pleasure dimmed a few watts. "Yes."

"They never met you." The cold numbed the inside of my mouth, and the dull ache in my jaw faded to nothing. "It's ridiculous that you excel at everything."

"Not everything," he murmured, his gaze colliding with the table. "Only what I can learn from books."

"There are books on every topic imaginable." I pinched my eyes closed after giving myself brain freeze. "You realize that, right?"

"True," he allowed. "How about this? I'm better with books than people. Books I understand. People..."

Seeing where this was headed, I squinted up at him while my brain thawed.

"You have to talk to people, hang out with them, observe them, to get them," I explained gently. His mouth opened, and somehow I knew what was about to pop out. "Teaching doesn't count. Your students don't act like themselves around you. They want to impress you. You're going to see the best versions of them. Same for faculty. They're going to posture with you because of who you are." I glanced around the carriage house. "Are you going out at all?"

"Yes."

"Society business doesn't count. Neither do covert ops." Chatting up Volkov and doing goddess knows what else he did in the name of science was *not* social interaction. "Have you visited any of your friends since you arrived? Or family?"

The hand stirring his drink stilled. "No."

"Why not?" I kicked him under the table. "You've got time to get out and have a life while you're here."

"I don't consider anyone I left behind in Savannah to be a friend, and family is...complicated."

"Oh." Considering my inner circle included a pair of siblings, a house, and a parakeet, I wasn't one to talk. Neely and Marit were friends too, but they were also human, and yes, complicated. "What about your friends in Atlanta?"

"We've chatted." Genuine fondness softened his expression. "Mary Alice is threatening to drive down for a weekend. So is Oslo. He wants to pick up some sketches I've been working on. I offered to scan them, but he wants the originals and doesn't trust the postal system. He's a bit of a conspiracy theorist."

"Are Mary Alice and Oslo an item?" I flexed my straw back and forth. "Or...?"

Laughter exploded from him, lighting up his entire face until even his eyes shone bright. For a minute, I worried he might rupture something the way he was carrying on. I had never seen him do more than an under-his-breath huff of amusement. I hadn't thought him capable of full-on belly laughs.

"No." He cleared his throat a few times. "Mary Alice is like a den mother to everyone who works at the Mad Tatter—the tattoo shop where I apprenticed. She appears to be a well-preserved sixty-seven, though I suspect her true age is closer to four hundred and sixty-seven. Oslo is seventeen. He's an intern."

I hadn't noticed the slight pressure building in my chest until it eased after hearing Mary Alice wasn't...

No. Absolutely not. No with a side order of no way, no how. Nah-uh.

Who Linus dated was none of my business. I didn't like him in that way. I didn't think of him in that way. He was family. Sort of. We grew up together.

You grew up with Boaz too, a helpful inner voice reminded me. But Linus was the Grande Dame's son. I couldn't trust him. Sure, he had saved my life, but—but—

Goddessdamn Boaz for putting the idea of Linus as, well, a *man,* in my head in the first place.

Groaning, I wedged my elbows against the table and covered my face with my hands.

I was going to kill Boaz. Except I could never admit to him why he needed to die, or he'd murder Linus.

Cool fingers brushed my knuckles. "Are you all right?"

"Brain freeze." I lowered my hands and smiled weakly. "Hate when that happens."

Except my glass was empty. Noticing this, Linus passed his over in case I wanted more. I stared at the straw, hoping he thought I was wondering if it had cooties instead of being curious if his mouth had—

Fiddlesticks.

Fire consumed my cheeks in a raging inferno that made my jaw heat like infection had set in. Too bad that didn't excuse the sting racing across the rest of my face.

"You're flush." Linus still held my hand. "Do you have a fever?"

"Maybe?" Anything was better than admitting what was on my mind. Namely *him.* "I don't feel so good."

For as long as I could remember, I had wanted one thing, and that one thing was Boaz Pritchard.

Now I had him, some days more than others, and I was blushing over drinking after Linus.

Ridiculous. Absurd. Impossible. Ludicrous.

I didn't like Linus. I didn't want Linus. I didn't find Linus attractive.

He has pretty hair.

"No," I grumbled. "He doesn't."

I clamped my jaw shut, winced, but it was too late. The words had already tumbled out for him to hear.

"I'm calling Heinz." Linus punched in the number he must have gotten from Taz. "He's not my first choice, but you seem to have a history." His mouth pinched. "This is Linus Lawson. I'm calling on behalf of Grier Woolworth."

Shaking my head frantically, I tugged on the cuff of his shirt. "I don't need to go to the hospital."

"Her face is scalding," he told Heinz. "She was talking to herself. I worry she might be delusional." His shoulders stiffened. "I didn't realize. I'll call over there." He ended the conversation, and his expression shuttered. "Boaz is here."

"He got in early this morning."

"I don't have a thermometer, and my hands..." He lifted them, palms up. "I can't determine others' body temperatures well thanks to mine running lower than most." He scowled at his fingers like they had individually banded together to betray him. "Call him."

Linus drifted to the sink and started washing the blender, the measuring cups, and the spoons he'd used, a sure sign he was agitated. Yeah, he liked to clean when he needed to think, but what was he thinking? Better yet, what was *I* thinking?

"I'll just go home." I pushed away from the table and stood. "I'll feel better after a nap."

A hundred years of sleep might clip the thorns off the prickly idea Boaz had planted.

"I'll go with you to the doctor if Boaz needs to leave." He kept his back to me. "I won't make you do it alone."

"That's not..." I crossed my arms over my stomach. "You don't have to do that."

"All right." Tension curved his shoulders as he dried a bowl and set it aside. "Suit yourself."

"I need to learn to be okay alone." I crossed to him and kept my gaze on the bubbles in the sink. "I can't expect you or Boaz or Amelie to drop everything and run to my rescue all the time." To prove my point, I washed out my glass. "I can do this on my own."

"I understand." He swung his head toward me, his eyes searching mine. "You need to feel like your actions don't set a domino effect into motion with everyone around you."

"Yes," I breathed. "That's exactly it."

"Amelie was wrong to blame you for what she did to herself." He pulled the plug in the sink. "There's nothing wrong with having friends who love you enough to drop everything and come when you call. The problem is those friends blaming you when the things they drop shatter." The swirl of gurgling water held his attention. "Our actions have consequences, Grier. We are all responsible for what we do—or don't do—and that's it."

"Thanks for the pep talk." I curled my fingers into my palm to avoid touching his hand before I left, a recent habit I ought to work on breaking. "Do you want to assign me homework before I go?"

"No." His forearms flexed when he gripped the sink, the strain a fine tremor in his muscles. "You should rest. I'll bring over dinner later." His head lifted, brow pinched. "Unless you're going out with Boaz?"

"No." I rested my hand on his shoulder before my brain threw on the brakes, but I couldn't ignore the way his muscles relaxed under that small contact, like my touch soothed him. "Dinner sounds great."

I lingered a moment longer, watching him for signs the black cloak might emerge as it had earlier, but he kept control of whatever I had unleashed, and it got awkward with me standing there, staring at him. There was no point in peppering him with questions. No matter what I asked, he would say it was a side effect of bonding with his wraith.

He told me once that he had never lied to me.

I didn't want him to start now.

SIX

Needless to say, I did *not* go to the hospital. Or to see a doctor. There was nothing wrong with me that a pint of ice cream wouldn't fix, but I couldn't very well explain to Boaz that I was bingeing because he had opened my eyes to an unsettling realization that had been creeping up on me for weeks.

I liked Linus. Maybe not epic love story *like*, the way I used to feel about Boaz, the way I maybe still did?

As much as I wanted to hit my favorite ice cream parlor to hide my sudden need for a double chocolate chunk fudge cone, I had obligations. Boaz had cleared his schedule to visit me, and I couldn't duck out on him. And, yeah, maybe I was counting on the way his larger-than-life personality blocked out everything else to shore up my resolve that I didn't *like-like* Linus.

I took the stairs two at a time, the birdcage swinging from my fingers, and the porch creaked in question. I was back early, and the old house knew something was up. Linus was no slouch, and he never cut classes short. She was right to be suspicious. But there was no good way to tell her I was having impure thoughts about the guy who had violated her trust instead of the one she adored. Though impure might be too strong a word. It's not like I was picturing him naked, I was just...picturing him. And that was bad enough, all things considered.

"I'm not feeling so hot," I told her, and it was the truth. "Linus let me go early."

Concern warped the boards under my feet until I had to choose between stopping or face-planting.

"It's not my jaw." I brushed my fingers across Linus's handiwork. "I'm just out of sorts." The door swung open to reveal Boaz standing in the kitchen shoveling in cereal. "Have you eaten all your waffles?"

"You say *all* like there were dozens of them when in fact..." his lips moved in silent calculation, "...there were only sixteen fatalities."

Suspicion confirmed, I made a mental note to buy more the next time I went shopping.

Casually munching, he gestured toward me with his spoon. "I wasn't expecting you back so soon."

That made two of us. Three if you counted Keet, who was thrilled to skip our lessons. The little dork was actually tweeting his heart out while hanging upside down from his perch. "Linus gave me the night off."

"Really?" His eyebrows climbed. "Did Mumsy need her toenails painted?"

I cracked a forced smile. "You're bad."

"I never claimed to be otherwise." He turned up the bowl and drank down his milk. "I've got a while before I have to go." Whatever he saw on my face had him ducking down to kiss me with sugary lips. "I'll be back soon. I get four days off in two more weeks."

"I'll add it to my calendar," I grumped.

"Are you pouting?" He tapped my chin with his hooked finger. "You can't miss me that much." A purely masculine gleam brightened his eyes. "Do you?"

"Stop fishing." I stuck out my patchwork tongue. "You just got here, and you're already leaving."

"Work sucks." His gaze fixated on my mouth. "I would quit all this if I could."

"Do you mean that?" Joining the sentinels hadn't exactly been his idea.

"I enjoy the job. I like my unit. Becky is a hoot. She's a good partner to have at your back." His knuckles grazed my cheek. "What I don't enjoy is the leaving." His voice softened. "I want to be home more often."

"So you can spy on Amelie?" Goddess only knew who he had watching her since I wasn't a snitch.

"I need to keep an eye on her." His rough thumb glided over my bottom lip. "I need to keep an eye on you too." He exhaled. "It kills me not being where I'm needed."

"Will things always be like this?" I had no idea what the career of an Elite sentinel entailed, not really.

"I can't say for certain." His expression shifted into thoughtful lines. "Things are intense right now."

"The Undead Coalition?" The governing body for vampires balanced on the knife's edge of an all-out civil war. Longtime members, wealthy and powerful clans, were withdrawing from the organization, forsaking the protection of the Society, and joining a movement spearheaded by the master vampire responsible for kidnapping me. The clans left behind were getting antsy. A war with this splinter cell meant pitting them against their brethren or suffering the wrath of the Society. Rock, meet hard place. "Are things still destabilizing?"

"Yes." He dropped his hand. "Half of the master vampires in the Coalition are in favor of maintaining the old laws. The other half are fighting over every damn thing and bogging down the system. Of those masters, half have established ties to vampires we found at the estate where you were held or to the vampires the dybbuk killed. Odds are good they're plants meant to gum up the works, and they're doing a damn fine job of helping chaos reign."

"Any fresh leads on the Master?"

"I would have updated you if there had been." He hooked an arm around my shoulders and led me into the kitchen. "Classified intel or not, your safety is my first priority." He put his bowl and spoon in the dishwasher then turned back to me. "Has Linus mentioned what his mother learned from the masters involved in the attack?"

"Four out of the six committed suicide by ingesting UV capsules prior to interrogation." Perhaps scenting the trap, they came prepared with a pill stuffed between their cheek and gums. All they had to do was bite down and incinerate. "The others carried their secrets to the grave."

Boom.

A percussive blast struck the wards surrounding Woolworth House, and the resulting tremors rattled the foundation beneath my feet.

Panic seized my lungs in a vise as I ran into the living room. "Woolly?"

"Grier," Boaz snapped. "Get back here."

With the wards operating at full power, I had nothing to fear as long as I was in contact with the house. Before he could catch me, I bolted out onto the front porch and kicked off my shoes. I stood barefoot on the peeling boards, flexing my toes, reading the magic.

Mentally, I reached for the wards, drawing their weft and warp into sharp focus. Ear-splitting dissonance near the front steps clued me in to where Woolly had been struck. I examined the area, turning over the weave in my head, but found nothing. Confident she remained secure, I scanned the yard, my gaze landing on the carriage house.

Linus.

Fingers trembling, I palmed my phone and jogged down the side of the wraparound porch. I thumbed the keys and pressed the phone to my ear, relaxing when it connected with a static burst of background noise that hinted at a location downtown. "Where are you?"

"I'm at the Lyceum." A dark undercurrent sharpened his tone. "What's wrong?"

"Woolly was attacked." The planks under me shivered, and I amended, "She's under attack, right now."

A furious growl rose behind me, and I didn't have to turn to know it was Boaz and that he was pissed.

"Get your ass back in the house." He wasn't looking at me, he was scanning the garden for signs of intruders. "I mean it, Squirt. There's nothing you can do out here except make yourself a target."

"For once, we agree," Linus murmured. "I'll be there as soon as I can."

Hating that they had ganged up on me, and that they were right, I stomped back into the foyer and stared up at the chandelier. "What can you tell me, girl? You've got to give me something here."

Woolly projected images in my head, the chaotic jumble difficult to understand since houses and people didn't process information the same way. One picture I had no trouble recognizing. The front porch stood out in stark relief. That was the unharmonious area I had already identified. There were other flashes too: a radiant starburst, a fallen tree limb, and two English peas. None of them made sense.

I patted the wall to let Woolly know I was proud she had done her best. "Where's Amelie?"

Boaz, right behind me, no doubt to make certain I followed orders, blanched. "She didn't do this."

"What?" I fully disconnected from Woolly and shook my head clear. "I didn't say she did, but we both felt the tremors. Where is she? Why didn't she come running too?"

The rest of the blood drained from his face. "I don't know."

"Let's split up." She had to be here somewhere. Linus hadn't bound her to the house as he promised his mother, but surely Amelie wasn't so foolish as to have used the distraction to escape. "We'll cover more ground that way. Start in the attic? I'll take the second floor."

We raced upstairs together, peeling apart on the landing. I shoved into her bedroom. *Empty.* I moved on to mine. *Empty.* Other rooms lined the hall. I ducked my head into each of them. *Empty, empty, empty.*

Amelie wasn't here.

A flash of blue light snared my attention as a small boy popped into existence beside me. He wore a dark blue sailor suit with sagging ankle socks and dirtied canvas shoes. A matching cap, wrinkled within an inch of its life, sat at a jaunty angle on his mass of blond curls. "What's wrong? I heard yellin'."

Apparently good diction was a respect paid only to strangers or parents, and I was neither. The more comfortable Oscar got with me, the more he relaxed, and the more suffixes he axed off words.

I affixed a smile on my mouth for his sake. "We can't find Amelie, that's all."

"Is she playing hide-and-seek?" The black voids of his eyes sparkled like polished coals. "Can I play?"

"Sure thing, kid." I could use all the help I could get. "First one to find her wins."

"Deal!"

Magic swelled in the room, easy to sense through my connection to Woolly, and he vanished.

I met up with Boaz out in the hall as he was climbing down from the attic. "Well?"

"No luck." He folded the access ladder up then secured the hatch behind him. "She wouldn't leave."

Blue light blasted my corneas as a boyish face appeared at the end of my nose.

"I found her," Oscar crowed. "I win! I win!"

Smiling to acknowledge his victory, I cut my eyes toward Boaz, but Oscar wasn't great with hints.

In all the excitement, the little ghost had forgotten we couldn't talk openly in front of Boaz for his safety.

"Since she's not inside," I reasoned with Boaz, "she must be outside." I made a subtle gesture at hip level for Oscar to lead the charge. "The wraparound porch covers a lot of real estate. We need to search all four sides."

Indecision warred with Boaz's driving need to secure his sister. "I'm going with you."

On the porch, I nudged him in one direction while Oscar and I went another.

"This way." Oscar gripped my hand and tugged me along after him. "She must have felled asleep."

"Fallen," I corrected absently, and then winced at the habit I had picked up from Linus.

We raced around to the left side, which pulled the carriage house into view, but there was no Amelie. The back porch was the same. Not expecting much from the right side, I almost tripped over her crumpled form before Oscar slammed on the brakes.

Hitting my knees on the wood, I checked her pulse. Steady. That was all I knew to do.

"Good job, kid." I ruffled his hair. "We'll talk prizes later, okay?" I held a finger to my lips in a reminder that his living with me was a secret between Linus and me for now. Not even Amelie could know since telling her was the same as whispering in Boaz's ear. "Can you go play with Woolly?"

"Sure." He bobbed on the breeze. "She lets me play in the secret room when I behave."

Gut sinking into my toes, I grasped for him. "I don't think that's such a good—" my fingers sliced through air, "—idea." The urge to smack my forehead itched my palm, but at this rate I would give myself brain damage. "Woolly, tell me you're not letting him play in the basement."

A breeze whistled innocently through the eaves.

Fiddle-de-dee-sticks.

We three had to have a chat about boundaries before he went poltergeist and got us all in trouble fooling around unsupervised down there.

"I found her," I called out as Boaz rounded the corner. "She's breathing, but she's out cold."

On a hunch, I pulled up the leg of her pants, exposing her sock and the tattoo Linus had given her to contain the dybbuk's energies. The reddish-black ink glittered and swirled, almost alive under her skin. I touched it, and the magic burned hot. I yelped and stuck my fingertip in my mouth.

"What is it?" Boaz crowded her other side, phone pressed to his ear, but his attention shifted to his call before I could tell him. "Heinz, hey, my sister's unresponsive. I need you here yesterday." He paused. "Thanks, man. I owe you."

"Her tattoo is hot." I turned down the top of her sock and checked for scorch marks, but the fabric appeared to be fine. For the sake of thoroughness, I also checked the cuff of her jeans, but it wasn't blackened either. "Can you feel it?"

He pressed a single finger to the intricate design that reminded me of a Celtic knot. Showing no visible reaction, he cupped her whole ankle in his wide palm. "Her skin feels normal to me. The ink does too."

"I don't get it unless—" I chewed my bottom lip. "You can't feel it because you're..."

"I've been Low Society all my life." An amused smile tugged up one side of his mouth. "You can say it. I'm not ashamed."

"It's not that," I hurried to assure him. "It's about magic."

"Ah." He took my hand and examined the pinkened skin on my finger. "That makes sense." He kissed the stinging tip. "You designed the tattoo. Does that link you to its magic?"

"I redesigned the sigil, but Linus tattooed her." I was having trouble looking away from his mouth. "If anything, it should respond to him, not me."

Embedding ink *in* skin wasn't the same as using ink with a brush or in one of his modified fountain pens *on* skin. But he must have proven the method safe or else the Society wouldn't have granted his patent. The one thing I still believed in was their dedication to customer satisfaction as it applied to their profits.

A faulty product created no revenue stream and kicked the door open for lawsuits that cost money, two fates worse than death according to the High Society. Therefore, tattooing sigils must be a valid magical application with no lasting side effects that might prompt a disgruntled customer to demand restitution.

All my anger toward Amelie stalled out as I held her hand, linking our fingers, waiting on help to arrive.

The distant clang of the garden gate as it closed had me straining to hear footfalls cushioned by grass.

"Grier," Linus expelled my name on a relieved breath when our eyes met.

"Oh, look. The cavalry has arrived," Boaz grumbled. "Will Woolly even let him on the porch?"

I don't think I imagined the smug twist to his lips at the knowledge she approved of him, not Linus.

"Some days more than others." She was grateful to him, but she was also still hurting from his betrayal. Forgiving him for breaching her wards, kidnapping Keet, it would require time. "I better go make sure." I rushed around to the back porch and found Linus standing in the grass, fists clenched, with Cletus wavering behind him. "Woolly, let him in."

The porch light brightened in acknowledgment of my request. For once, she wasn't fighting me.

"It's safe now." Under different circumstances, I would have laughed at his hesitance, but nothing about this struck me as funny. Woolly and I were under attack. Again. I stood on the bottommost step and held out my hand. He took it, wrapping his cold fingers around mine, and I hauled him through the barrier encompassing Woolworth House. "Come on. Amelie's this way."

"Amelie?" He matched his stride to mine. "Was this her doing?"

As much as I wanted to defend her with a vehement *no*, I had to admit, "I don't know." We rounded the corner. "We found her out here like this."

Boaz swung his head our way, and his gaze dragged down my arm to the hand still holding Linus's.

"Any idea what happened?" Boaz demanded, his tone sharp. Under his stare, I broke away from Linus so fast he flinched. "Grier is picking up on an anomaly within Amelie's tattoo. Care to give your two cents?"

Having his arm almost yanked out of its socket mustn't have fazed Linus as much as I thought. He knelt beside Amelie and examined her tattoo, jerking his hand back the instant his fingers brushed the ink.

"That was unexpected." He didn't meet my eyes, just angled his chin in my general direction. "You sensed the heat too?"

"It burned me." I rolled my thumb over the sore spot. "I have a blister."

The thoughtful way he inspected his pointer made me think he had suffered the same negative reaction. I half expected him to offer to soothe my hurt, and when he didn't, it almost stung. "Does Woolly have any ideas about who or what attacked her?"

"No." I patted the nearest railing. "The images she sent me don't make much sense. She's aware of where she was struck—on the front steps—but not how or who initiated the strike."

"What do you think it means?" Boaz asked Linus. He wasn't looking at me either. Great.

"There's no residue on the lawn that I noticed or shrapnel on the stairs. The blow must have been magical in nature." He confirmed what I had been thinking. "That might explain why a siege against Woolly resonated through the tattoo on Amelie. Grier designed them both, and Amelie was within Woolly's protective bubble at the time."

A chill scrabbled down my spine. "You're saying Amelie is linked to Woolly?"

"No." Linus tugged her sock over the design. "I'm saying she's connected to you."

Somehow that made it worse. I was used to being responsible for Woolly, but Amelie? Forever?

"Whose blood did you use?" I rubbed my forehead. "Yours or...?"

"Maud was the donor." He angled his head in my direction without meeting my gaze. "I involved myself as little as possible to make Amelie and Boaz more comfortable."

That brought Boaz's head up, and a frown pinched his forehead, but he didn't share his thoughts with us.

"The wards were inked using Maud's blood too," I reminded him. "Her blood could be the connection."

"There's power in her blood, potent magic, but it's..." he searched for the word, "...inert."

Meaning the energy had survived, but its origin no longer existed. The remaining power took on the tenor—for lack of a better word—of the practitioner. And since I had applied Woolly's wards, and he had applied Amelie's tattoo, there was no harmony between them. Each carried its own tune.

"That only leaves the design," I said, praying he contradicted my logic but not holding my breath.

"Practitioners are inventing original designs and mass distributing them all the time. There's a thriving patent business. I'm proof of that. There are hundreds of textbooks put into the hands of thousands of children that never elicit this response." He rose with a frown fixed in place. "No designs are specific to the person who created them. Any residual link, if there was one, should dissolve the first time the sigil is used by another necromancer."

Thanks to my rare designation, sharing my work with others was unlikely, but it worried me that I might not be able to use it either without running the risk of connecting my client to me. "I'm a freak of nature."

"No, you're not." Halfway to brushing his fingers against the back of my hand, Linus dropped his arm to his side. "I'm going to conduct a search. I can start with Woolly and work my way toward the property line." Head down, he lingered a moment longer. "How certain are you that Eloise left Savannah?"

"We saw her get into a car. She left the grounds, but we can't be certain where she went from there." He nodded and took a step back, but I pinched the fabric of his shirt where it rolled over his elbow to hold him in place. "Do you think she did this?"

"We'll know more soon," he promised, easing back until I lost my grip on him. "I won't be long."

Flashing lights strobed over us, washing his pale face in reds and blues, as an ambulance screamed into the driveway. Two doors slammed, and two sets of footsteps pounded up the flagstone path. However, in a surprising move, neither of them braved the steps. One must have possessed enough magic to sense the wards. Or they came armed with equipment that helped them perceive any hidden dangers they might encounter on calls.

"Medic," Heinz called. "Get your hot, fresh medic."

"We're back here." As Linus left, I stood to go fetch him. "I'll come get you."

Woolly, for her part, was as polite as could be to the men, allowing them on the porch with nary a flicker of her opinionated porch light. Both men were Low Society and gaped as her curtains flittered, and she preened beneath their regard. Nudging them out of their stupor after she batted her blinds at them, I guided them to Amelie. Luckily, a downed patient was enough to snap them out of their trance.

Chewing my thumbnail, I hovered behind the guys while they examined Amelie.

"Let me try something," Heinz said at last. "Does she have any allergies?"

"No." Boaz beat me to the punch. "What do you have in mind?"

"I've seen kids with these symptoms. Only High Society, though." He snapped on a pair of gloves. "A magical interaction in the blood causes the problem. The condition is linked to new bonds formed with familiars. For a while, it's push and pull while the two acclimate to one another. Most animals have a stronger survival drive than people. They pull too much energy from the kid, and the drain knocks them out cold." He held out his hand, and his partner slapped a plastic kit across his palm. Inside, vials filled with what resembled diluted ink sloshed. "This mixture won't break the bond, but it confuses the magic long enough for both parties to normalize."

There was no hesitation in Boaz. "Do it."

Amelie gasped awake ten seconds after Heinz depressed the plunger.

"W-w-what...?" She sucked down huge lungfuls of air. "Boaz?"

"Everything's okay, sis." He pinned down her shoulder. "You winked out on us there for a minute."

"Miss Amelie, you're coming with us." Heinz conducted a quick examination then nodded his satisfaction. "I've never seen a Low Society necromancer exhibit these symptoms. We need to run a full screen on you."

"That's out of the question." Boaz rubbed a hand over his face. "Know any phlebotomists who make house calls?"

"Sorry, man." Heinz cringed while yanking off his gloves. "I wasn't thinking."

High Society necromancers learned early how to tap their own veins, but Boaz's training wouldn't have been the same. Given the circumstances, I wasn't about to suggest he allow Linus to do the honors, and I was too out of practice to offer to do it myself.

"Amelie is under my protection," I informed Heinz. For the next six months, I was her sole means of support. "Contact whoever can do whatever she needs and send them out here. I'll cover the bill."

The look Heinz turned on me conveyed many things, but chief among them was gratitude for taking care of his friend by providing for his sister. "I'll do that."

Once the paramedics left, Boaz carried Amelie inside then made her comfortable on the couch. Wanting to give them a moment of privacy, I waited for Linus on the porch. I was a tad concerned Woolly might bar his entrance now that Amelie was out of danger. I needn't have worried. Linus appeared not five minutes later, exchanged words with the house, then joined me near the door.

"We can't send those samples to a Society-owned lab."

"You're worried someone will trace her condition back to me."

Hearing our voices, Boaz snapped his head toward us, his gaze bouncing between us. After kissing Amelie on the forehead, he ambled over to add his two cents.

"What do you propose we do then?" An ugly, bitter noise rose in his throat. "You must have all the answers, right, Professor?" Muscles fluttered in his jaw. "You're the one who oversaw Grier when she designed the new wards on Woolly, and you're the one who tattooed my sister. Seems to me if you don't know what you're talking about, then you ought to get a damn clue before you go around handing out advice."

Linus stared him down. "We both know there are extenuating circumstances."

Vertebrae popped when Boaz jerked his head from left to right. "What do you propose we do?"

"Discuss this in private, for one." Linus still wasn't looking at me when he said, "Put her to bed then meet me at the carriage house."

"*We'll* be there," Boaz assured him before turning to me. "Help me get her upstairs."

Imperiousness must be bred into Society males of all castes.

"Yes, sir." Snorting, I saluted him then headed inside after shooting Linus an apologetic look that glanced off his cheek. He went his way, and we went ours. At the couch, I wedged my shoulder under Amelie's armpit to give me leverage to heave her onto her noodly legs. "Whatever you say, sir."

"One day that smart mouth of yours is going to get you in trouble," he threatened, eyes glinting.

"Gonna be...sick," Amelie moaned. "Stop flirting. It's disgusting."

"I won't take that personally," Boaz said magnanimously, "since you've suffered a fainting spell and possible head injury, which would explain your lack of respect for my prowess."

I turned my head against my shoulder to stifle a laugh, but they both heard, and Amelie grinned.

"I don't need a head injury to know you and your moves are gross."

"She is your sister," I reminded him. "I'd be more worried if she did admire your, uh, *prowess*."

A full-body shudder rolled through him. "Good point."

Once we situated Amelie on the bed in her room, Boaz and I approached the carriage house.

The door was shut, of course, and required knocking, which made my jaw clench. He was expecting us. Surely, he would have confined Julius by now. Why not leave the door open? Or at least greet us when we arrived?

Linus appeared six knocks in and gestured toward the kitchen, indicating we should sit at the table. He opted to stand in his usual spot near the sink, like he had set himself apart on purpose, and that self-imposed isolation got on my last nerve.

Maybe I was just having a bad day.

"I have a friend in Atlanta who can conduct the tests we need done." Linus got straight down to business. "I can drive the sample there for testing. Reardon will handle the case personally, I can assure you, and I will remain with him at all times to ensure the sample is destroyed along with all testing supplies. No one else will have access to Amelie's blood."

"Who's this Reardon?" Boaz demanded. "How do we know we can trust him?"

"Reardon McAllister is a made vampire with no affiliations to any clans. He's technically a rogue, but he considers himself neutral."

"What about the clan that made him?" They didn't vouch for humans they didn't mean to hold on to.

"He has no clan." Linus leaned a hip against the counter. "His wife was a necromancer, but she didn't tell him. He died in a carriage accident early in their marriage, and she turned him against his will."

"That's horrible." I linked my fingers in my lap. "Even so, the Undead Coalition just let him go?"

"Oh, they want him returned to the fold," Linus said, a cold smile in place, "but he was a human victimized by the Society, and that puts him under the Grande Dame's purview. He's a brilliant chemist. His mind is what attracted his wife to him despite his humanity. He teaches at Strophalos, has for decades. That's how we met. He's one of the few teachers with dispensation to live on grounds year-round, safe behind the wards."

"You're going to Strophalos?" I strained forward like that might get me closer to the acclaimed college for the necromantic sciences. "How long will you stay?"

"Three days at most." Slowly, his gaze met mine. "You're welcome to come."

On my periphery, Boaz tensed, a stone-cold statue hewn from granite.

"I..." the moisture dried in my mouth, "...can't."

A flicker of something—disappointment?—shadowed Linus's face, but he nodded as if I had done what he expected.

"I have to consider Woolly. I can't leave her alone." Unable to let it go, I rambled. "And Amelie. I can't leave her unsupervised. Keet would be fine, but then there's—" I clamped my mouth shut before I outed Oscar in front of Boaz, "—work."

"I understand." Linus kept his tone all business. "You don't have to explain yourself to me."

The towering stack of valid reasons I had for not going tottered under that direct hit.

I wanted him to look at me like this was any other night, like there was a breakfast spread between us. I wanted him to listen to me the way he did when we discussed our lessons, not tune me out when he got his answer and it wasn't what he wanted to hear.

I hated when he reverted to this aloof version of himself who couldn't be bothered with anyone who failed to meet his exacting standards. Tip his nose up any higher, and he'd drown if it rained.

"Would it help?" Boaz asked, voice strained. "Having Grier there?"

"If there are any markers in Amelie's blood that are magical in nature, it might help to crosscheck them against Grier to see if we can isolate the cause and create a cure. Otherwise..." grim lines bracketed his mouth, "...she can't practice if there are known side effects to her magic."

Which put me right back to square one. Don't get me wrong. I don't want to be a Society lackey who asks how high when the Grande Dame tells me to jump, but practicing necromancy was a dream out of my reach for so long. Having it offered up to me only for it to be snatched away again was a cruel joke.

"That's not all, though, is it?" Boaz studied him. "You're dropping everything to hand deliver this to a reclusive colleague in Atlanta. What aren't you telling us?"

"Mother's interest in Grier is contingent upon her ability to practice." He stuffed his hands into his pockets, but I saw them ball into fists through the fabric. "She views her as an investment."

Boaz asked what I was afraid to wonder. "What happens if there's no payoff?"

"Atramentous," I whispered, folding in on myself, sick with possibilities.

"Double jeopardy," Boaz soothed. "You can't be tried again for the same crime after an acquittal."

Unwilling to be coddled, I bit out, "Forgive me if I have my doubts about the legal system."

"Mother can't return you to the prison without weakening her reform agenda." Linus mashed his lips into a bloodless line. "Calling your innocence into question allows for too much speculation on her role in your release."

"You're saying the danger isn't in a direct strike," Boaz reasoned. "You think, if it comes down to it, she'll withdraw all support from Grier and let the problem handle itself."

"Mother would never allow a weapon as powerful as a goddess-touched necromancer, whose fledgling magic might prove capable of binding her progeny to her, to fall into the Master's hands." Muscle fluttered along his jaw. "She would execute Grier before allowing vampires control of her."

An odd lightness spread through my limbs and left me tingling. The wrongness of preferring death to life in a cage pinched my conscience, but only for a second. "Okay."

"No," Linus contradicted me, a frown tipping his lips. "Nothing about either scenario is *okay*." Boaz grunted reluctant agreement with Linus, who wasn't done yet. "That's why I will do everything in my power to understand the connection between you and Amelie, if one exists, and nullify it before anyone suspects such a bond might be possible."

"Thank you," I murmured, wishing I had better words for what he was risking for me.

Linus, uncomfortable with my gratitude, inclined his head in acceptance of my appreciation.

Boaz scratched his jaw, his brow furrowed at Linus like he was working through a complex puzzle.

"Reardon's only interests are in the pursuit of science," Linus continued, "but there will be dangerous questions asked. Even if we present our case as wanting to examine an accidental bond between a Low Society necromancer and a familiar, he might uncover more of Grier's secrets on a cellular level."

A shiver twitched between my shoulder blades. "You're worried about handing him a new specimen."

"Yes." His gaze cut to me then dropped to the floor. "There's also the dybbuk contamination to consider."

With Ambrose's magic swirling through Amelie's blood, there was no telling what the tests would reveal. It might act as camouflage for whatever havoc my sigils had wreaked on her, which might be a good thing as far as Reardon was concerned, but that also meant yet another layer for Linus to peel back to find our truths.

I was gambling with my future by allowing him to seek out Reardon, but I had no real choice.

"He doesn't have to know why you're there. I could tell him you're one of my students, that I'm tutoring you. He knows I'm on sabbatical, but it's not unheard of to tutor for extra cash," Linus said, and I snorted so hard I almost choked on my own spit. Oh yeah. That was totally believable. The Grande Dame's son needed pocket change. "Or favors if the student's family has political sway."

"That might work," I allowed. "I have zero clout, but I can still trade on Maud's name if I have to."

Make no apologies for surviving.

As much as I hated using her name for leverage among the curious, I would do it to protect myself. She would understand. How could she not when she had given so much to keep me safe? Even from myself.

The thrill at his first mention of the campus shriveled. "I still can't go."

"Yes, you can." Boaz reached across the table and took my hand in his, linking our fingers in clear view of Linus, staking his claim. "We can ask Odette to stay with Amelie for three days. Woolly's a big girl. She can take care of herself for seventy-two hours." He rolled his thumb over my knuckles. "A short break might do you good."

"The new wards are holding..." I allowed, willing to be tempted. "But Woolly was just attacked. We don't know who or what was responsible. I can't leave her alone. What if they come back?"

"Have you considered hiring full-time security? You've just ascended as Dame Woolworth. Everyone will expect you to start building your staff. Why not start there? The rumor mill won't think twice about why you're fortifying Woolly if you act now. It's expected for new heads of family to secure their residences if such measures aren't already in place." There was no point in him reminding me how long she had sat unoccupied, how many years she had been vulnerable, so I was glad he didn't poke that particular wound. "It's better to have the extra bodies and never use them than to need them and not have them. Say the word, and I'll handpick a team for you and have them in position by the end of the week."

More eyes meant more opportunities for Boaz to snoop into my life. I would have to hire a team without ties to the sentinels or to his family, if such a thing existed, to preserve my privacy. Low Society sentinels had cornered the security market. Meaning I would have to look outside the Society for guards loyal to me, a daunting prospect when you removed vampires from the candidate pool. "I'll consider it."

"You do that." His mood buoyed, as if I had already agreed. "In the meantime, I can ask Taz to patrol the grounds while you're away. Woolly is used to her presence. She might be miffed about her hurting you, but as long as Taz doesn't touch the house, she ought to be safe. How does that sound?"

"Like you're trying to get rid of me." I was only half kidding. Shoving me together with Linus was not his style.

A more normal response from Boaz would have been to toss me over his shoulder and stomp from the carriage house while shouting "Go to hell" at Linus. A reasonable Boaz was a dangerous Boaz.

"Your eyes lit up like stars when he mentioned the campus. I might have been the lame older brother, but I know what you girls had planned. I know what college meant to you, and taking lessons, alone, in your own backyard is a poor substitution." He glanced at Linus. "No offense."

"None taken," he said drily.

"It's not like I can absorb the whole college experience in three days anyway." I hated admitting, "Seeing what I can't have might make it worse, actually."

Until Maud...and Atramentous...I had dreamed big dreams as a kid. Getting a degree alongside Amelie. Planning how we would live together and how I would marry Boaz to make us real sisters. But those were old wishes for an old life. I wasn't that person now, and neither was Amelie. Neither was Boaz. None of us were the same. Time and distance and life experiences did that to people.

But I couldn't ignore the uptick of my pulse when I imagined walking those hallowed grounds.

If Maud had proclaimed me a practitioner instead of an assistant, I would have attended Strophalos the same as any Woolworth.

All this time I had been jealous of Amelie going to college here in Savannah when I was starting to think it was Linus and Strophalos I truly envied. Maybe Amelie had been right all along. Maybe I had been settling. But it had never felt that way, not to me.

These days I had no choice but to embrace my High Society birthright, and I'd had no clue how hard I had been tamping down my resentment until the limitations placed on me were wiped away thanks to a few drops of blood.

"Sleep on it," Boaz urged. "You don't have to go if you don't want to, but it might be a good thing for you to get out and see more than Savannah. You haven't left town since you were released."

For the longest time, I hadn't had funds or a reason to go anywhere. My whole life was in Savannah.

I still had no reason to leave, but maybe...I wanted to go?

"I have calls to make," Linus said in dismissal. "You've got time to think it over and make your arrangements."

"Okay." I blew out a breath and stood. "I'll let you know at dusk."

Boaz and I headed for the door but not fast enough.

Linus angled his head toward me. "What did the doctor say?"

"Doctor?" Boaz wheeled toward me. "What doctor?"

"There was no doctor." I pointed through the wall toward Woolly. "There was no time."

Wise man that he was, Linus said no more, but he let the disappointment shine through his eyes.

Much less circumspect, Boaz growled, "What doctor?"

It was like he hoped the third time would be the charm.

"Come on." I hooked my arm through his. "I'll explain on the way home."

SEVEN

melie recovered from her fainting spell with no clue what had happened or why. Since we didn't know either, conclusively, I elected to keep her in the dark. Truthfully, she might have to learn to like it there. Any explanation I gave about a possible connection to Woolly through wards I designed meant explaining this newly discovered quirk in my magic. That was impossible without also explaining I was goddess-touched.

That's where things got tricky. Ambrose had known what I was from the moment we met. I wasn't sure if that meant shades, the souls of deceased necromancers, had special insight from the other side or if his experience was more personal. As much as I would love to sit him down and play twenty questions, he *had* tried to kill me. Any information he shared would be suspect. Assuming we could communicate with him. Things would be so much easier if Amelie had retained his memories.

Wincing, I renounced that thought with my whole heart.

Things would have been easier, all right. For *me*, not for her. Recalling the vile things he'd forced her to do had given her nightmares. Meaning Woolly was treated to a nightly symphony of screams ringing out from both ends of the hall. So far, she hadn't volunteered any information she might have gleaned from Ambrose, and neither Boaz nor I had pressed for details.

The problem with the kid-glove approach was it meant we were operating under the assumption she had no idea I was goddess-touched when she might know more about me than everyone else squished together.

"Boaz said you might be heading to Atlanta."

Torn from my thoughts, I spotted Amelie lingering in my doorway, waiting for permission she never used to have to ask. But the last time we had been alone in this room, things had gotten heated.

"I'm considering it." I patted the mattress beside me. "What do you think?"

"A tour of the campus might be fun," she allowed. "Maybe, one day, you could go there. If you wanted."

Atlanta was three and a half hours away. I could drive that in a day. Not close enough to commute, though I could come home on weekends and holidays. But that meant leaving Woolly alone for whole weeks at a time, and I couldn't bear abandoning her again so soon. With the wards renewed, the bond between us was stronger than ever, and each pang that wracked her when I left arrowed through me.

"It's not like that." I scooted over to give her room. "It's more that I want to lay an old dream to rest."

"Do you have to bury it?" She plopped down beside me. "College was always goal number one for you." An exhale puffed out her cheeks. "Okay, so it was number two behind becoming Mrs. Boaz Pritchard, but it was still up there."

"So much has changed, though." I plucked at the comforter. "The big appeal back then was what we have now—girl nights every night, no parents to boss us around, no rules except the ones we make." I thought about Boaz, about the phone that never flashed with his number. "I'm not sure I know what I want anymore."

"Life is funny that way." She flopped onto her back, staring up at the ceiling. "Boaz partied all night, slept through most of his classes, and still managed to get an associate degree in criminal justice." She kicked her heel against the mattress. "I never partied, studied all night—heck, my last professor asked me to donate my binder full of class notes and diagrams to her—and I still managed to ruin my life."

"Ame..."

"This is not a pity party." She shoved my shoulder. "This is not about me. This is about *you*."

Lately it felt like everything was about me, and I hated being the center of so much attention.

"What do you want to do?" She turned on her side facing me and braced her cheek on her fist. "Can you deal with Linus for three days?" A chuckle moved through her. "Just make sure you don't drive. He might start lecturing and put you to sleep at the wheel."

I smiled. It was what she expected. But it bothered me how quick she was to cut him down when he had done so much to help her. Even Boaz was acting nicer to him these days. Then again, maybe that was part of the problem. What I saw as an act worthy of thanks, she might view as him kicking off a chain reaction that landed her nameless, jobless, and hopeless.

"He's not so bad." I palmed her forehead and shoved her down on the mattress. "You played peeping Tom through his bedroom window. What happened to that?"

"He's easy on the eyes. I'll give him that. He grew up *hot*." Gaze distant, she linked her hands across her navel. "I don't..." She wet her lips and tried again. "I don't remember everything that happened. With Ambrose." The cracked plaster ceiling held her rapt. "But in my dreams I'm him again. We're being chased. Standard nightmare fare, really."

Barely daring to breathe, I nodded my encouragement before the words dried on her tongue.

"The thing tracking us is like a wraith but not. Black mist come to life, and I do mean *life*. It's not insubstantial. It's real. Alive." A tear streaked down her temple. "When it catches me, and it always does, it whirls me around, and its hand is like ice. The creature carries a scythe, and it..." Her hand lifted to her vulnerable throat. "He takes my head, Grier. Every time. And the last thing I see is always the same. Linus's face beneath the hood."

A quick flash of Linus standing at the sink, black mist pouring off his skin to pool on the floor where it lapped hungrily at my ankles, burst into the forefront of my mind. "Linus isn't the grim reaper." But he was bonded to a wraith, and he was the keeper of Society law in Atlanta. "You're atoning, Amelie. Bit by bit, day by day. He won't harm you."

Unless she went off the rails, but Amelie didn't need me to spell that out for her.

A hoarse laugh left her throat. "I had no idea my imagination was so vivid."

Repressed memories weren't the same as imagination, but I would be inviting her to dig around in my head if I did the same to hers. "It will get better."

She wedged her elbows under her. "Has it gotten better for you?"

"Not yet." I stood and finished dressing. "But I have to believe that it will."

She shoved up the rest of the way. "When do you give Linus your answer?"

"In about fifteen minutes." I fiddled with the hem of my shirt. "I have to talk to Odette first."

"I'll give you some privacy." She pulled out the collar of her tank top and took a sniff. "I need to shower. It's been a few days."

I wrinkled my nose. "I wasn't going to say anything but..."

The pillow smacked me square in the face before I could finish.

The next ten minutes were a blur of feathers, linen, and squeals.

Just for a second, it almost felt like the good old days.

THE SENSITIVE NATURE of my conversation meant I could no

longer use speakerphone outside of Woolly. I was forced to hold my phone against my cheek, which limited me to using one hand to dead-head the wilting flowers. Amelie teased me about investing in a Bluetooth earbud, but I wasn't a fan. I tried hers once, and it kept popping out of my ear. The cheap ones were crap, and I was too thrifty to invest in a piece of tech I didn't want. Ugh.

"Ma coccinelle," Odette cooed. "How is your jaw?"

There was no point in asking how she knew. While Odette couldn't see into *my* future, she had become a pro at glimpsing it from reading others who knew me or whose lives intersected with mine.

"It's not too bad." I touched my cheek in reflex. "Little sore, but it hasn't slowed me down." I gave an odd laugh. "The weird thing is my tongue was actually separated from my body, and it's fine. I can barely see the scar when I stick my tongue out at the mirror, and it doesn't hurt at all. But my jaw? Which is still firmly attached to my face? Now that sucked."

"When we cut away that which hurts us most, that which remains compensates for the loss."

Unsure what to say to that, I kept swiping my tongue along my teeth, going for a thoughtful silence.

"Linus is every bit as skilled as Maud was at his age." Amusement suffused her voice. "How is Boaz? And our Amelie?"

"She's adjusting, bored out of her mind, but she's making peace." I got all gooey inside when I told her, "Boaz came for a visit when he heard I was hurt. I wish he could have stayed longer. I miss having him around."

The sound she made in the back of her throat could have meant anything from *ain't true love grand* to *it's easier to miss what's not in front of you.* Sometimes it was hard to tell with Odette.

Without question, her attachment was to Linus. She was fond of Boaz, in the way Maud had been, content with our friendship as long as it led to nothing more. But I lived in fear of her picking a side, not that there were sides to be chosen, but I wanted a surprise. I wanted to make my own choices, my own mistakes, even if that meant getting my heart broken.

"You're excited," she decided. "I can tell. What's making you happy, so I can join in the celebration?"

"Linus invited me to join him in Atlanta for a short trip. He's meeting a colleague at Strophalos to work on a project, and he thought I might enjoy a tour of the campus."

"Ah. Already he has learned the way to your heart." She cackled. "What do you need from me?"

"I don't always call begging favors." Thinking back on the reasons for my last several calls, I deflated. "Maybe I do only call when I want something, but I don't mean to. I don't want you to feel like I'm using you."

"You're family," she chided. "You can ask me for anything, *bébé*, and I will give it to you if it is within my power." Laughter threaded her voice. "You want me to spend a few days with Woolly, yes? To keep an eye on Amelie while you're in Atlanta?"

"I thought you couldn't read me?"

"You have an unorthodox houseguest. You have an unorthodox house. You want to go on a short trip, and you would never leave either unprotected. You don't have to be a seer to understand that, Grier." The ocean roared to life across the line. She must have stepped out onto the beach that was her backyard. "I will pack my things. Let me know when you need me."

"I'll do that." I paused. "Odette?"

"Yes?"

"Thank you."

"You're more than welcome." Seagulls cried in the distance. "I'll talk to you soon."

Pivoting on my heel, I tapped the phone against my chin and watched Woolly for a moment.

I might have won this battle, but the war was far from over.

EIGHT

"Seventy-two hours," I stressed to Woolly. "Three days, a long weekend."

Woolly killed the lights throughout the house, leaving me standing in the dark.

"Amelie will be here," I reminded her. "You won't be alone."

A death rattle of laughter shook the blacked-out chandelier.

"Okay, bad example." Woolly's grudge was airtight on that front. "How about Oscar?"

Light flickered in a single bulb. She was listening.

"I can't bring him with me. It's too dangerous. You're the only one I trust to protect him." I played my trump card. "*And* I asked Odette to stay. What do you say to that?"

Two more bulbs sparked to life, and a third blinked with indecision.

"She doesn't know about Oscar moving in yet," I tempted her mischievous side. "Think how much fun you two can have with her until she figures it out."

Brightness exploded in the room, and my eyes ached like they had been stabbed, but she was onboard.

"Boaz might have been half the reason I was always in trouble as a kid," I told her, "but you're the other half."

Warmth spooled up my leg from the floor register, and I leaned into her hug. Right in time for her to blast arctic air up the leg of my pajama shorts.

"Dang it." I hopped out of range. "That was evil."

Lights winked to life throughout the rest of the house as her laughter trailed her.

With two out of three parties in agreement, I sought out the third. I found Amelie in the parlor Maud had decorated as an office. She never worked in there. It was all for show. But Amelie was putting it through its paces. With her damp hair swept up in a bun on top of her head, and her matching pajama set—a marked improvement over the tank top and boy shorts combo—she looked like a young professional at work. If you overlooked the Smurfs frolicking across her thighs.

"So," I started. "Atlanta."

"You cleared it with TPTB?" She kept writing until she finished her thought. "The trip is a go?"

"The Powers That Be have agreed to let Odette hang out while I'm gone."

"Woolly is still mad at me."

"Yeah, she is." She took things like attempted murder seriously. Given Maud had bled out on these planks while Wooly bore witness, unable to save her, I couldn't blame the old girl for clinging to her remaining family.

"That's fair." She tossed her pen on the desk. "I hope you have a good time."

"Me too." I sank in the chair opposite her. "I'm nervous."

"This is your first trip after..." Her lips twisted against speaking the word. "You'll be fine. Linus will protect you." A shrug rolled through her shoulders. "He proved that at the Lyceum."

Amelie's recollection of those events was hazy at best thanks to the whammy from the wards Linus and I had used to contain her aboard the *Cora Ann*. All she recalled for sure was what happened after, during her trial, when Linus uncovered a plot to send half a dozen vampires to attack Woolworth House.

The Grande Dame had played to her audience and made them all believe the vampires had wanted to do me harm, but we both knew the truth. They wanted to capture me and drag me back to the Master.

At least Volkov was no longer booking our honeymoon trip. Though his absence might make things worse. There was no guarantee just because he was out of the picture that the Master hadn't lined up another goon to tie the knot with me in the misplaced hope it would bind me to his clan by vampire law.

"I'm tired of being protected," I sighed, "but you're right. I'll be safe with Linus." And Cletus.

Amelie twisted her fingers on the desktop. "Grier..."

"Hmm?"

"I support what you're doing. You're making yourself stronger and smarter, better able to take care of yourself." Her hesitation told me I wasn't going to like what came next. "But you have to keep in mind there's a reason *why* you're being protected."

Ice glazed my spine as I stood there, frozen, waiting on her to out me as goddess-touched, and it was almost a relief to have it in the open.

"First Atramentous, then Volkov, then *me*." Her chin dipped. "It's like you've got a bull's-eye painted on your back. I don't know why that is, but maybe we should find out?"

Torn between relief and disappointment, I nodded. "I've been thinking along the same lines."

"That's why you contacted the Marchands," she realized. "You're already digging."

"Yeah, I am." How deep, I couldn't tell her. Not yet. Maybe not ever. "I want to know what happened to Maud." While the truth, it wasn't the whole truth. "There might be answers there."

After all, Maud had known what I was, and had been terrified enough to lock her library and throw away the key to keep others from reviving her knowledge.

"Have you tried asking Woolly?" Amelie glanced around the room. "Your connection is back online, right?"

"Yeah." I swallowed hard. "And no. I haven't asked her."

I had no excuse for not posing the question now that our bond had been revamped. Except fear. More like pants-wetting terror.

Whatever she had witnessed would get shot straight into my head, and I...wasn't sure I could handle it.

What if she flipped through the scrapbook of her memory, reliving each snapshot of Maud's death? What if I had to watch her die in slow increments that I could do nothing to stop? I would be trapped, as helpless as Woolly had been, caged in her memory and unable to act as my whole world shattered. Again. What if...? Gah. I hated this game. I had played it on too many nights in my cell.

"It's okay to wait." Amelie glanced up at me. "It's all right if you're not ready yet."

Nodding was the best I could manage, and it still felt like my head was so wobbly it might pop off and roll across the floor to stop at her feet.

"You're late for class," she informed me with an arched brow.

"How can you tell?" Her phone was tucked behind her laptop, and there was no clock in the room.

"Oh, I have my ways." Her eyes darted toward the window. "Let's just say I've got this feeling."

I rose from my chair and drifted toward the window to find Linus standing near the back steps, waiting.

Usually, the promise of good food kept me punctual. No wonder he was worried about me.

"Time to face the firing squad," I said wryly. "He does not appreciate tardiness."

"Want me to write you an excuse?" She scooped up her pen. "Grier was late to class because she was planning a trip with a pretty boy nerd who—"

Face going up in flames, I turned on my heel to go. "I'll bring him an apple and take my chances."

Evil laughter trailed me into the kitchen. Turns out I had no apples, so I lifted a pack of strawberry oatmeal and carried that and my grimoire out with me. Our eyes clashed the second my foot hit the porch, and Linus exhaled, long and deep, like he couldn't breathe until he laid eyes on me.

"Heads-up," I called and tossed him the packet, which he caught with ease. "I brought you an apple."

"Oatmeal?" He rubbed his thumbs along the crinkled edges. "This says it's strawberry flavored."

"Check the ingredients." I met him in the garden and winked. "Skip the big words you don't know."

His eyes glittered with humor when he looked at me and then the packet. "Ah. Dehydrated apples."

"Yep." I moved to reclaim the packet, figuring he would just throw it in the trash. He wasn't much for convenience foods, or food at all, really. "They chop them up, dye them pink, add flavoring, and call them strawberries."

Linus held it out of my reach. "You gave it to me."

"You can't want that." I crossed my arms over my chest in challenge. "You won't eat it."

"You gave it to me." He cupped his hands around it like he was scared my next grab might be successful. "I'm keeping it."

"You can't be so hard up that you're going to hold on to an oatmeal packet. It's not even brand name."

Pink brushed his cheekbones, highlighting his freckles and the adorable cluster that resembled a daisy beneath his left eye, and he gestured for me to follow him into the carriage house, where he placed the oatmeal packet in the china cabinet.

I meant to trail after him, but my feet got stuck in front of that china cabinet. A packet of oatmeal, not even an actual apple, and he had given it a place of honor in his home.

Thinking back on all the little things he had done for me, all the not-so-little gifts he had bought me, all the meals he had cooked for me, I cringed from the comparison. The grimoire alone was worth a small fortune while I had gotten the entire box of oatmeal for less than two dollars.

Sensing his eyes on me, I rushed to catch up and dropped into my usual chair. "About this trip to Atlanta."

The tension in his shoulders ratcheted higher. "Have you made up your mind?"

"I want to go." I set Eileen on the table then petted the grimoire, its multiple eyelids fluttering in ecstasy. "If you still want me? To go, I mean."

"I want you," he said, tendrils of black chasing across his irises, "to go."

The temperature in the carriage house shot up about a thousand degrees, and I started to sweat.

Thanks to Boaz, my brain had twisted Linus's innocent comment until his pause made it sound flirty.

Resisting the urge to fan my face, I smiled weakly. "Well, that's settled then."

"You'll enjoy Strophalos." He sank into the chair across from me and flipped through his syllabus, which did nothing to hide his smile. "Every necromancer should see it at least once."

My excitement dimmed a fraction when I recalled the actual reason for the trip. Linus wasn't escorting a potential student. He was seeking more answers about my condition, ones that could reshape my future yet again or even cost me my life. "It's worth playing lab rat to get a guided tour."

"I planned on taking you there in three months, during the faculty tourney." He glanced up at me then. "I'm required to partici- pate each year." Annoyance flattened his lips. "The university parades us around to entice new students and encourage benefactors to dig deep. The whole event is nothing more than peacocks strut- ting." He shrugged. "You're welcome to wait until then if you'd prefer, assuming you want to attend. You're under no obligation to go now if you're uncomfortable."

No amount of flapping my lips produced more than a wheezing gasp. *The faculty tourney?*

When I was a kid, Maud had regaled me with stories about the complex and unique magics performed during the tourney. According to her, it was one of the few events where the Society played nice alongside vampires, wargs, and all manner of supernatural competitors who had only their tenure in common.

In a world where the Society kept us segregated from other supernaturals as often as possible, to an almost xenophobic degree, the event was legendary for its diversity.

For some, attendance was a truly once-in-a-lifetime opportunity.

Exerting great effort, I muffled my inner fangirl for moment. *"How?"*

Campus security was rumored to be airtight to protect all those Society darlings. Students and staff were issued ID cards that allowed them passage through its outmost ring of wards, but that was just the start.

"We each get a plus-one." His lips quirked in a knowing smile. "It's a shame to let the ticket go to waste."

"This is amazing." I sprang from my chair and dashed behind him, bending down to wrap him up in a backward hug. "Thank you." The chill of his skin seeped through his clothes into me, but I was getting used to the cold. "In case you can't tell, that's Grier for *count me in.*"

"We really have to work on your early-warning system," he chided, but he didn't shrug me off him. "There are requirements for attendance, but we can discuss those later. You're moving along quickly in your studies. I doubt it will be an issue."

I planted a smacking kiss on his cheek then returned to my seat. "What's on the agenda for tonight?"

No response.

"I'm not opposed to working with Keet again, but I think it's time we accepted that Julius is never going to play nice with him. Keet is too small. He sets off Julius's predatory instincts."

I cracked open my grimoire and thumbed to my notes on our last lesson. The pages were smeared with dried poop. I could read my notes through the flaking mess, but ugh. I didn't want to touch it. Surely there had to be a sigil for cleaning paper we could use without erasing all my work.

The utter silence finally registered, and I peeled myself away from the grimoire to check on Linus.

Frozen in his chair, fingers pressed to his cheek, he stared at me like he had never seen me before.

"Too much? Sorry about that. I get excited." Sinking low in my seat, I attempted to vanish in the face of his apparent mortification. "I'll keep my lips to myself next time."

"No," he rasped, lowering his hand and shaking his head like he was waking from a dream. "Don't."

The shiver racing through me this time couldn't be blamed on the temperature of his skin, and I wasn't sure how I felt about that. "So...familiars?"

"Ah. Yes." He corrected his posture. "Familiars." He flipped a few pages through his syllabus. "Julius is exceptionally well-behaved, but you're right. He can't fight his instincts with Keet. After thinking on it, I don't believe the issue is the typical predator-prey response. I'm starting to wonder if it's not because Keet is undead. Julius might view him as a potential threat to me, which would explain why he keeps attacking him despite my orders."

"Hmm." For someone whose brain was working triple time, you'd think I could come up with something deeper than what sounded like me clearing my throat, but I was still hung up on the rasp of that single syllable: *Don't*. "You might be right. I hadn't considered that." There. Much more focused and studious. "Too bad we can't test the theory, but there's not another familiar like Keet."

The glint in Linus's eyes betrayed his curiosity. "Have you tried making another?"

I almost choked on my snort. "No."

The quirk of his brows invited an explanation I might as well give him.

"Maud was never the same with me after that. Our lessons shifted overnight. She confiscated my copies of *On Human Souls* and *Progeny: What to Expect When You're Resuscitating* to *Build a Better Ward* and *Our Homes, Our Castles*. The last thing I ever would have done was create another." I winced under the burden of memory. "He's the reason she declared me assistant material."

Linus smoothed his hand across the page while looking at me, like he might absorb the information through his fingertips.

"All my life, I thought it was because I wasn't good enough. Now I get it. Or I think I do. He was a symbol of what I was capable of, and she must have been thinking ahead to how that magic would translate to humans when I performed my first resuscitation." A hint of bitterness soured my mood. "That's why she made sure that would never happen."

Except it had, in Atramentous. Somewhere out there, I had progeny I didn't remember making.

"Maud loved you very much."

"She did." That truth was the bedrock my life had been built upon. "I just wish she had trusted me."

"We can't know what long-term plans she had for you, but I doubt she would have kept you in the dark forever. She must have known that, even as an assistant, you were bound to draw attention to yourself. She'd seen your drawings. She knew your brain is hardwired differently than ours."

"So what you're saying is...I really am a freak of nature."

"No." He reached across the table and covered my hand with his. "I'm saying you're a miracle."

"That's not how it feels." I held very still beneath his touch. "I wish she were here, that I could talk to her." I huffed out a laugh. "Or Mom. Mom would be nice. She must have had all the answers."

No one ran that hard for that long unless they had a good idea of how afraid they ought to be.

"Maud was a packrat. She kept everything. There are boxes full of letters in the basement." He stifled a laugh. "I spent an entire summer down there sorting through correspondence between her and Dame Hildebrand Gershwin after Maud received a wedding invitation."

"Husband number eight?" That seemed about right. Dame Gershwin was a man-eater.

Divorce might be frowned upon by the Society, but there were no laws against marrying humans, fragile by comparison, who lived much shorter lives. Still, eight husbands in four-hundred-odd years must have set a record.

"Nine," he decided after a moment's pause. "Dame Gershwin wrote an inflammatory note about Maud's taste in men back in the twenties, after Maud stole her boyfriend. Almost eight decades later, Maud wanted to throw the words back in Dame Gershwin's face when she married the man, who Maud dumped after a weekend fling, but she couldn't remember the exact phrasing." His tone sobered. "Some of those letters might be from Evangeline."

A hard clench in my gut had me sliding my hand back to my lap. "I can't access the basement."

"I'm thinking on some exercises that might help with that." He picked up a pen and smoothed the page in front of him flat. "It requires some advanced techniques we haven't covered yet. We can try in a few months, if you're comfortable with that."

A few months would give me a firmer grasp on his character, and it would give me time to decide if I wanted to unleash the secrets she felt safer locked away. "Okay."

Pleased, he returned to where he'd left off earlier. "Let's get started. Turn to page..."

It was going to be a long night.

THE WALK back to Woolworth House left my nape prickling with the certainty I was being watched. Most likely it was Amelie, but I had grown so used to Taz leaping from the foliage, legs scissoring, that it took a conscious effort to keep from scanning the bushes for her.

"I'm off to work," I told Woolly as I hit the stairs and ducked in my bedroom. I placed Eileen on a stand I had rescued from the attic that allowed her to see out the window. Once I got her settled, I dug around in the top drawer of my desk. When my fingers brushed metal, I pulled a necklace strung with a dented brass button over my head. "See you in four."

Mr. Voorhees, the owner of River Street Steam, had yet to let me work more than half a shift for him. He blamed me for the brutal attack on his daughter, Marit. Though, to be honest, I wasn't sure if his grudge came from him believing I was directly responsible or if he was grumpy I hadn't sacrificed myself to save her fast enough.

My first encounter with Oscar had ended with him hurling a handful of steak knives at Marit. Not fun. But he had been a terrified little boy defending himself the best way he knew how, and I couldn't fault him for that. Sadly, as the only witness to the stabbing besides the victim, my boss wanted nothing to do with me. Marit's conviction I had saved her life was the only reason I still had a job.

Had I been dependent upon my income from working in the demo crew aboard the *Cora Ann* to keep the lights on and food in my belly, I would have turned in my notice by now. As it was, I could afford to work part-time, and it suited my schedule.

Linus got two hours, most nights, Taz got two, or she used to, and work got four. Homework cost me another two, but that still left me six hours to stream TV or hang out with Amelie before battling the last eight out in bed. At least tonight I was shaking things up by spending those hours packing.

With a bounce in my step, I hit the pavers and opened the garage. Jolene and her big sister, Willie, stood together near the front, both gleaming in the moonlight. I took my new jacket off the hook and snuggled into it, taking a moment to enjoy that new-leather smell, then I straddled Jolene and walked her out of the garage.

While the segmented door rolled closed behind me, I tugged on my gloves and helmet. She greeted me with a rumbling purr after I twisted the key in her ignition, and I did a double take at the gas meter. *Full.* Boaz must have topped her off before he left. This type of small kindness had his name written all over it.

"Ready?" I called out to Cletus, who materialized over my head, cloak billowing. "I'll take that as a *yes.*"

The ride to the *Cora Ann* left me cackling as the wraith wove in front of me, racing me. I got the feeling Linus had no idea how sentient Cletus had become or else he might worry about sending us out together. I wasn't in any hurry to lose my shadow now that I had gotten used to having him around, so I kept my mouth shut. Linus was a smart guy. He would figure it out eventually. In the meantime, I didn't see the harm in letting Cletus live a little.

Headlights caught my mirror as I turned on Bay Street. The curve slowed me down enough to confirm my suspicions. Yep. A nondescript sedan was tailing me, and if I squinted, I could almost make out the grimace twisting Detective Caitlin Russo's face as she hunted her quarry.

Russo had been escorting me to work for about a week, but she hadn't attempted to talk to me since Neely livestreamed her threatening me on the world's most popular social media platform, so I ignored her and let Cletus watch my back.

I parked on River Street, snagging a prime spot near where the *Cora Ann* was docked, and the sedan rolled past, casual as you please.

The walk down to the river was peaceful this time of night, but the boat herself thrummed with activity. As I crossed the gangway, I pulled the necklace from my shirt and rubbed my thumb over the button like Oscar was a genie to be summoned from his lamp. "Have at it, kid. Keep the action PG, though."

"You're funny." The small boy zoomed around me in dizzying circles. "I won't hurt nobody. Promise."

And then he was gone, off to harmlessly prank the crew for a few hours.

While I might not win any Mother of the Year awards for encouraging his shenanigans, I had a thriving, well-adjusted ghost boy, and that's all that mattered to me. He deserved happiness after so many years of loneliness, and if he enjoyed blowing in people's ears to watch them jump and slamming doors to hear them scream, who was I to tell him no?

Plus, I figured faking a haunting was the least I could do for Cricket after all the second chances she had given me. And, I'll admit, I was hoping the incontrovertible proof of a ghost onboard would clear my name with Mr. Voorhees and the crew in time for me to snag one of the coveted hostess spots for the launch party. After shedding my blood, sweat, and tears for this boat, I had more than earned the chance to revive Blue Belle.

No one called out a welcome as I crossed the gangway, but I had given up on the crew accepting me. All but a handful believed I was responsible for Marit's near-fatal injury, and there was nothing I could do to convince them otherwise when they wouldn't stand still long enough for me to defend myself.

"Hey, Trouble." Marit waved down at me from her throne, a cracked plastic lawn chair her father had placed near the second deck railing where she could help oversee demo. She had twisted her brown hair into a tight bun, and her bangs swept across her forehead. She tapped a clipboard against the vibrant red birthmark covering her chin and lower jaw, concealing where it spilled down the front of her throat. "Come on up."

These days my calves barely burned at the climb. I had jogged the stairs too many times. When I approached the queen of the night shift, I gave her a subtle once-over. "How are you feeling, my liege?"

"Will you stop that?" Marit flushed until her cheeks matched the wine-colored birthmark. "You know this was all Papa's idea. He won't let me go to the bathroom without an escort these days."

I dropped my jacket and gear at her feet to collect after my shift ended.

"You shouldn't be at work period." I tsked at her. "Your thigh is still wrapped up like a mummy."

"I pulled a few stitches," she admitted, her blush deepening. "Papa forgot to leave me with the remote on his way to work yesterday, and one of those Humane Society ads came on. I ran to the TV to change the channel before the waterworks started, but I tore something in the process. Papa was not amused to come home and find me sitting in yet another puddle of blood."

"Those ads are intense," I allowed, "but maybe put a pillow over your face or plug your ears instead?"

"Hindsight." She dismissed me with a wave of her hand. "I wrote them a big, fat check. Maybe next time the guilt won't force me to sprint into action to alleviate the sad."

As usual, it was just the two of us on the upper deck. No one else wanted to risk bumping into Oscar. I swept my gaze over the hot mess of dining room that was starting to take shape then back at Marit. "What's on the agenda tonight, boss?"

"Finish the wallpaper near the restrooms, sweep up, and then you can start priming the floor." She pointed a finger at me. "Watch out for nails, bolts, and other pokeys. You've had your tetanus shot?"

"I have, and I will." I located the toolbox I had taken to leaving onboard and popped the lock to give me access to my battered work gloves and tools. "Watch my gear, your highness."

Showing her *highness*, she used her middle finger to wipe imaginary dust from her eye.

Without Taz wearing me down prior to my shift, I had ridiculous amounts of energy as I ripped, scraped, swept, and painted. Falling into the soothing routine, I turned off my brain and let the work carry me away from my troubles. All too soon it was time to pack it up and go home, which meant facing Marit.

"You're smiling mighty big." Marit squinted at me. "Spill. You got plans with that hot blond tonight?"

"Nah. Boaz is out of town." I could still smell his cologne on the pillow he'd slept on, and I missed him already. "But I need to ask a favor." I gripped the railing, surprised by how much her answer meant to me, how much I wanted this. "I need the next three days off."

"Hmm." She leaned back, elbows on armrests, and steepled her fingers. "Going somewhere?"

"Atlanta."

"That's all I get?" She tapped her fingertips against her lips. "How can I make such an important decision with so little information?"

"You are a tyrant." I picked at the chipped paint under my palm. "I'm going to tour a university campus."

Her jaw hung open. "You're moving?"

"No." Sweat beaded along my spine just thinking about trading in Woolly for a sterile dorm room. "I have a friend who teaches there. He's going to show me around."

A wicked smile curved her lips. "A friend who isn't Boaz?"

"Linus is a friend of the family." No, that wasn't exactly right. "We grew up together." I winced when a dried shard slipped under my nailbed. "We're practically cousins."

"Kissing cousins?"

"We're not blood related." I cast her a withering glare. "He's my adoptive mother's sister's son."

"Interesting." The cadence of her tapping increased. "So is that a yes to the kissing?"

A burst of heat spiked my nape when I realized my mistake. "There has been no kissing."

Except my lips on his cheek, and even that had short-circuited his brain long enough that I worried about oxygen deprivation killing off hundreds of thousands of his billion brain cells.

"It's short notice, no notice, really, but I can spare you for three days." She nudged my calf with the tip of her boot. "But I want pics of this 'cousin' and updates so I can live vicariously."

"Deal." We shook on it. "I would have asked sooner, but he didn't invite me until yesterday."

"In that case, tell him he sucks." A flick of her wrist dismissed me. "Go on. You don't have much time to pack."

"I'll text you your first payment before we leave." Not that I was looking for excuses to sneak pictures of Linus, but the opportunity had presented itself. I scooped up my gear and tucked it under my arm. "Take it easy."

"Like I've got a choice," she grumbled. "Party in my name, okay? Drink until your eyes cross."

The only spirits we would encounter were of the undead variety, but I shot her a thumbs-up all the same. "Will do."

NINE

I made a pit stop at Mallow on my way home, figuring it was the least I could do since Amelie couldn't buy for herself, but Cletus stopped me in the parking lot with a gnarled hand on my shoulder. I was about to ask what his deal was when I spotted the issue sitting at my usual table with ruler-straight posture, wearing a pensive expression and a cream pantsuit with black beading in geometric patterns.

A prickle of unease raised the hairs down my arms, but it's not like Eloise could have followed me from work since she beat me here. Maybe sweet teeth ran in the family. This could still be a coincidence.

"She's not going to assault me in public," I assured the wraith. "She probably wants to talk."

Cletus moaned a rattling warning, but he released me.

"I'm not going to approach her. I'm going to the counter, placing my order, and then I'm going home."

Unhappy with my plan, if his snapping cloak was any indication, he drifted behind me to the door.

I pushed inside and hit the counter, ordered our usual, then took a seat in a chair beneath the picture window so Cletus could keep an eye on me. While I waited for my name to be called, I texted Neely, who I only saw when reporting to Cricket on the *Cora Ann's* progress.

Going to Atlanta for a few days.

>>Boaz taking you out on the town?

Nope. Family stuff.

>>*Yawn* Will you have any downtime?

Maybe. Not sure yet.

>>Call if you want company. I could drive up and surprise Cruz with dinner.

He's gone this week?

>>Always.

I hear you. Boaz is never home either.

>>All the more reason for us to get together.

Let you know tomorrow?

>>Works for me. Drive safe!

The worst part of being kicked out of the Haint's main operation wasn't the hard labor required aboard the *Cora Ann*. That I actually enjoyed. It was the severe shortage of Neely. We hadn't made much of an effort to get together since the whole livestream incident. He thought I was still mad, though I wasn't, and I had my hands full with the million things happening in my personal life.

I missed him. There was a gaping best-friend-shaped hole in my heart in need of filling. Not that I expected him to take Amelie's place, but an uncomplicated friend with mundane drama would be nice right about now. I bet a visit would cheer up Amelie too. We would just have to work on our cover story, so he wouldn't be suspicious of finding her crashing with me.

"Grier?" a hesitant voice ventured. "I thought that was you."

Busted.

I set my phone aside and braced myself to play nice with my cousin. *Cousin.* How weird was that? Linus was the closest thing I'd had to one growing up, but I never viewed him as family. For most of my childhood, I had simply considered him the nerdy son of Maud's snooty big sister.

"Hey." Glancing up, I gave her a finger wave. "I see you found my favorite café."

"Is it?" Her left hand tightened around her cup, and I noticed her grape was missing. The evenness of her skin tone made me think the engagement must be recent since there was no pale band to indicate otherwise. Maybe she needed a break from hauling around that rock. I could picture her spraining her wrist lifting her hand with each sip. "I don't drink coffee, but I wanted a place to sit and think. This fit the bill."

Smiling politely through my disbelief, I attempted to make amends since this might be the last time I saw her. "About the other day..." I cleared my throat. "I'm sorry I was rude."

"No, I get it." She sank onto the empty chair beside me. "I should have called or emailed before inviting myself to your house."

"A heads-up would have been nice." Maud had never stood on ceremony among friends, and neither did I. But there was a difference in having Amelie or Boaz let themselves in my home versus an unknown quantity inviting herself for a visit. "Things are crazy lately, and I get nervous when strangers appear on my doorstep."

The word *stranger* made her flinch, but I wasn't sure what else she wanted me to call her. We didn't know each other. The rift in our family hadn't affected her. No, it had been my mother who paid the price for Dame Marchand's decision, and she was past worrying if I ever kissed and made up with her family.

"I'm heading home tomorrow." She picked at the lid on her to-go cup. "I couldn't decide if I ought to say goodbye or just leave, so I'm glad you're here."

Ah. Her vigil at Mallow began to make more sense. Though the only way she could have known where I hang out was by following me. That wasn't creepy at all.

"Look, Eloise, I'm not saying we can't be friends. We can start small, with emails or texts. You can call me when you want to chat. We can fill each other in on our lives and go from there."

"That sounds fair." She opened her arms and went in for a hug but froze halfway to embracing me like some elegant bird of prey swooping down on a grungy field mouse. "Are you a hugger? I don't want to intrude on your personal space."

"I'm down with hugs." I embraced her quickly, and we stood. "It was nice meeting you, Eloise Marchand."

Eyes bright with what I hesitated to label as hope, she backed out the door. "Back at you, Grier Woolworth."

While I had it on my mind, I texted Boaz and Linus each an update. *Eloise Marchand is on her way home tomorrow. That means Amelie and Woolly ought to be safe enough while we're gone if she was involved.*

There was always a chance she had been feeling out the wards to see what made them tick. Professional curiosity. Though Eloise hadn't struck me as the ambitious type, the hungriest ones learned to hide their appetites early.

She came back? Boaz demanded.

Cletus mentioned you bumped into her at Mallow, Linus replied.

To the first, I clarified, *Not at Woolly. At Mallow.* To the second, I teased, *That Cletus. He's such a gossip.*

The barista called my name, and I paid for my order while signing off with the guys. Packing my goodies on Jolene required ingenuity, but I was an old pro at food wrangling. By the time I got home, Linus was standing in the front yard, and my phone was ringing. Boaz, if I had to guess.

"Overprotective much?" I gathered my treats and met him on the lawn. "She didn't follow me home."

As if the smarty-pants comment had jogged his brain, he scanned the road. "Russo?"

"Her sedan was sucking on Jolene's tailpipe the whole way to work, but I haven't spotted her since."

"That's good news at least."

"At least?" My pulse kicked up a few notches. "Does that mean there's bad news?"

"There's been another attack." The grim cut of his mouth should have warned me. "I was checking the perimeter when I heard Jolene and came to meet you."

"Is Woolly okay?" I took a step toward her before remembering we could commune without contact these days. *"Woolly?"* Curtains flipped in the window, a hearty wave to show that all was well. "What about Amelie?"

"Woolly is fine," he answered, unaware of her presence in my head. "Amelie is woozy and nauseated. She crawled out onto the back porch after the attack, the same as last time, but whatever Heinz gave her must still be in her system. She didn't black out, and she's able to talk."

Not even the scents of hot chocolate and marshmallow perked me up. "This proves there's some type of connection."

"Yes," he allowed, voice gentle. "We'll figure out how to protect her." His fingertips skimmed my forearm. "And you."

Swallowing past the lump in my throat, I nodded. "Did you hear another *boom?*"

"No." He lifted the cellphone dangling from his hand. "Woolly called me, and I came."

His cell, not the carriage house landline. "How did she get your number?"

How will Boaz feel once he realizes you've got another boy's digits? I projected at her.

The front door opened, and the hallway runner flapped like someone had taken one end and shook it.

I think my house had just stuck out her tongue at me.

"I gave it to her," he said as though it ought to be obvious.

Okay, so it should have been. It's not like I was jealous my house had his number. He could toss it out like beads at a Mardi Gras parade, and I wouldn't care. The implications are what worried me—that the two of them talked when I wasn't around to police their conversations. Woolly was smart enough to recognize the value in having his private line, but it still left me torn between happiness that they were mending bridges and concern over what an all-access Linus might be like if she greenlighted him to enter the house again.

As usual, he read me too easily. "Should I not have done that?"

"It's fine," I decided. "I'm sure it comforts her knowing she's got a better way to get in touch with you."

His expression told me he wasn't buying the level of okayness I was projecting, but I wouldn't relax until I put eyes on Amelie and hands on Woolly.

"I almost forgot." I selected a to-go cup and held it out to him. "I brought you something."

Linus accepted the cup, and a laugh escaped him before he cracked the lid and checked the contents. "It's empty."

"You don't eat or drink. I figured chocolate-scented air was as close to a treat as I could bring you."

"I do eat and drink." He cradled the cup between his hands as if the nonexistent contents warmed him, but it must have been the thought that counted. "Just not much or often." He brought the cup to his nose and inhaled, smiling. "Thank you for thinking of me."

"You're welcome." I poked him in the side. "How come you can skip meals and stay fit while I work five nights a week on the *Cora Ann* but I'm a scarecrow?"

"You've been through a lot, Grier. Recovery takes time." His shoulders hitched, and I could tell he was suppressing laughter. "Besides, you love food. Would you really give up churros?"

"No." I recoiled from the very idea. "Churros are my favorite food group. I couldn't live without them."

There had been too many years spent living on drips of water and scraps left over from the guards' lunches. Treats, sweets, churros—those were things about as likely to appear on your food tray in prison as the goddess herself.

"Then leave it be." He put it gently, but I sensed the firmness behind the command. Lifting his cup, he turned toward the carriage house. "Make sure you're packed and ready to go. Our ride arrives at dusk."

A sour tang splashed the back of my throat. Our ride. I hadn't put any thought into how we would get to Atlanta. The urge to volunteer Jolene almost overwhelmed me, but we had luggage to consider. There was nothing for it. I had agreed to go, I had made the preparations, it was time to suck it up and endure.

I took the stairs and kicked off my shoes, wiggling my toes against the flaking planks. The symphony that was Woolly's wards rose around me, blanketing me in her love, and I exhaled with relief that she was unharmed.

"That's odd." I twisted around until I faced the steps. "Another hit in the same spot?"

Last time, when vampires had been at fault, they had tested her wards methodically. This was a battering ram approach, blunt and obvious. No real harm was being done, so what was the purpose? Testing the strength of the new wards? How had they known about them to check them? Unless they assumed, rightfully so, that after Volkov, measures would be taken to protect me and my property.

The timing of the second attack cleared Eloise's name. She had been across town at Mallow with me when it happened. Sigils could be activated after a countdown, but that felt like reaching. Time-delayed magic was complex, and therefore, rarely used. More than likely, this was the fumbling work of vampire goons the Master had set on my trail.

"Did you see anyone this time?"

A sigh moved through the decking as she flashed the same set of images at me: a fallen limb, a radiant starburst, two English peas.

"Thanks, girl." I patted the nearest wall. "You did good. Those new wards have you snug as a bug in a rug."

A swell of light was her answer, pride in her ability to defend us both.

Following the wraparound porch to the side, I found Amelie

sitting with her back against the house, legs extended in front of her while she stared at the yard.

"How are you doing?" I mimicked her position. "Linus said you didn't black out this time."

"I wish I had some of those soft peppermints to crunch." Her hands went to her middle. "I haven't been this queasy in..." She inhaled then whipped her head toward me. "Mallow?"

"I thought you might—" I released her drink and bag before she ripped them from my hand, "—be hungry."

"Thank you, thank you, thank you." She gulped several times before smacking her lips. "That's the good stuff."

"What about your stomach?" I inched away to escape the splatter zone. "Can you hold it down?"

"I don't care how sick I am." She tipped her drink toward me. "I'm not wasting this."

Laughing, I got to my feet. "I have to start packing. Want to keep me company?"

"Nah." Her gaze slid past me to the yard that might as well have been on another planet for how far away it was for her. "I want to sit out here a while longer if it's okay. Come get me before bed?"

"Sure." I left her to enjoy the fresh night air and entered the living room. Dipping my fingers into my shirt, I fished out my necklace and rubbed my thumb across the raised emblem. "We're home, kid." I pulled the cord over my head and placed it on the mantle next to the silver box holding Maud's heart. "Scat."

Oscar materialized inches from my nose and yelled, *"Boo."*

Clutching at my chest, I staggered backward until my knees hit the couch and pretended to faint dead away from sheer terror.

"Grier?" His small voice squeaked. "Grier?"

A prickle of energy along my arms told me he was within reach. I couldn't stop my smile as I popped my eyes open, shot up, and grabbed an armful of wriggling, giggling ghost boy. "You scared me half to death." I tickled him until he was gasping. "Is that any way to behave?"

"I'm a ghost," he squealed. "I'm supposed to scare people."

"Oh, sure." I hugged him close then released him to float in the air. "That's what they all say."

The register beside us ticked as Woolly scolded us both, but her lights brightened, making it impossible to hide her pleasure. She was thrilled having guests in the house and on the grounds. Those early days hadn't been full of fear only on my behalf. Without me, Woolworth House had no heir. I was the last. The best she could hope for was Linus moving in, but he was a Lawson. Maud's blood or not, it wasn't the same to her. Her whole existence was wrapped up in the family legacy, and that meant *me*.

"Float with me." I gestured that he should follow me up to my room. "I'm going on a trip tomorrow. I'll be in Atlanta for three days. Amelie will be here, and so will my friend, Odette. You're welcome to stay here with Woolly, or you can come with me. Your choice."

"I don't sleep good in new places." He trailed me so close I shivered. "I want to stay with Woolly." He bumped into me when I stopped at the landing to open my door. "You promise to come back?"

Heart in my throat, I glanced over my shoulder at the desolate certainty he was being abandoned again.

"This is my home, and you're part of the family." I tweaked his nose. "You've got nothing to be scared of. I promise." Still skeptical, Oscar hovered over the threshold. "All right, all right. I wasn't going to do this, you're too young to have a cellphone, but let me show you how mine works."

Though his appearance had frozen as the six-year-old boy he had been when he died, that sad day had occurred more than a century ago.

And yes, I was rationalizing.

Ten minutes later, Oscar was wide-eyed and mesmerized by the phone. All those years of haunting the dining room on the *Cora Ann* had given him only a partial education. Most folks tried to behave during meals and kept their phones muted or in their pockets or purses. Thanks to the hardcore addicts, he had seen enough of them to know what they did, but he had never gotten to play with one.

I might have created a monster.

But at least he knew how to call me if he was ever in danger.

Thank Hecate, it required so much energy for him to go corporeal, he exhausted himself quickly.

Once Oscar scampered off to tell Woolly all about his adventures, I flopped on the bed and made a packing list. Thirty minutes later, I stood over my choices where they covered the bed in mismatched outfits. I wasn't impressed with the selection.

Society training was kicking in, the urge to look my best, to look my part, when in the presence of peers.

Ugh.

Jeans and T-shirts were fine when I was at home, so they would have to be fine where I was going.

Money might not be an object these days, but I wasn't going to buy a new wardrobe just to walk the grounds at Strophalos. Who would do that? That would be insane.

I WAS INSANE.

In a moment of total weakness, I texted Neely and invited him to join us. As my unofficial fashion consultant, I wasn't comfortable shopping without him. He would stay with his husband, which spared us the awkwardness of explaining why he couldn't bunk in Linus's building. It was a Society holding, and humans weren't allowed.

The discrimination might have bugged me another time, but it was for their own good. Non-predatory species had no place in a building that housed necromancers, vampires, and various other supernaturals. Animal instincts were at their highest in their dens.

"You ready to go?" Amelie asked from the doorway of my room. "Linus is waiting in the driveway."

"Ready as I'll ever be." I turned another circle, ticking off my mental checklist. "I always feel like I'm forgetting something."

"Whatever it is, you can buy another one when you get to Atlanta." She hefted my suitcase in one hand and linked her other arm through mine. "Try to have fun, okay? Don't let Linus keep your nose stuck in a book the whole time."

Fiddlesticks.

Linus hadn't mentioned if we would continue our lessons on the trip or not. I was hoping for field exercises instead of classroom busywork. But I had packed Eileen, ink, brushes, my modified pen, and a few other things that ought to get me over the hump if he assigned homework.

"It's only three days," I reminded her, and myself. The more often I said it, the less anxious I felt leaving her and Woolly. "That's not much time to go sightseeing."

"Forget sightseeing." She dragged me down the stairs. "Hit the clubs. Drink in the bars. *Live.*"

"I'll think about it." I hadn't been to a bar (except to pick up take-out) or a club since I turned legal. I wasn't keen on doing it the first time alone, and I would be alone. Linus was not the kind of guy who club hopped or bar crawled. Neely might go out on the town with me, but if he was missing his husband, he would drag Cruz along, and Cruz was not a big fan of mine. "You can text me a list of your favorite spots. Maybe I'll hit one."

"That's what I like to hear." She deposited my luggage at the front door then cupped my shoulders. "Everything is going to be fine. The house, me, Odette. Everyone and everything. Fine."

I wavered in my belief. "What if there's another—?"

"Neither attack has done any damage. I doubt the third time will be the charm." She held up her phone. "I've got Heinz on speed dial in case I kiss the floor again, and Boaz will be checking in with me at regular intervals."

Trying not to think about how I hadn't heard a peep from him since bumping into Eloise at Mallow, I smiled rather than show my hurt.

A knock on the door brought our heads up as Odette strolled in with a small bag over her shoulder. "Thank you for your hospitality, Woolly."

"Odette." I launched myself at her, wrapping her in my arms. "Thank you for doing this."

"It's no hardship, *bébé*. I will keep myself busy in the garden." After a moment, she pushed me back to see my face. "That is, as long as it's all right with you. I don't want to overstep."

"I would appreciate any help I can get out there." I had trouble meeting her eyes. "I keep meaning to clean up, and I do tiny chores, but it's like…"

"Everything is as she left it." Odette nodded in understanding. "Only nature has changed things since she passed."

"Yeah," I agreed, voice hoarse. "That."

"I will honor her memory." She kissed both my cheeks. "I promise."

I savored her mothering while I had the chance. "Are you sure you don't need anything before I go?"

"Amelie and I can entertain ourselves." She reached for Amelie and took her hand. "Can't we?"

A peculiar expression flickered across Amelie's face, a close relative to panic, but she schooled her features before I could be positive. "Sure. Yeah."

I collected my bag from Amelie, stepping on the porch as Odette led her into the house. I watched them walk arm in arm toward the kitchen, wondering what Odette had up her sleeve and wishing I could linger and be part of whatever treat she planned on concocting. I was trying to banish the annoying sensation I was forgetting something important when an impact to my spine slammed me against the rail.

"You didn't say goodbye." Oscar cinched his arms around my

neck until I couldn't breathe. "I was hiding, but you didn't come find me."

Ah, that would be the thing I was forgetting.

"Sorry." I pried him away from my throat and sucked in oxygen. "I searched for you through Woolly earlier, but I couldn't sense you. I thought you must not be home."

One day I ought to ask if he made a conscious decision to go wherever ghost boys went or if he simply dissipated when his reserves petered out, but I wasn't sure he knew, and I didn't want to upset the kid.

"I was in the basement," he announced proudly. "It's the best place to hide *ever*."

Safe behind Maud's wards, wards he shouldn't be able to cross to a basement he shouldn't be in.

"I bet." I glared up at the porch light, but Woolly pretended not to notice. "We're having a chat when I get back."

Woolly flickered the bulb in a *so what* gesture that had me second-guessing—or was that tenth- or eleventh-guessing?—the wiseness of this trip. I couldn't afford for my house to start sassing me now.

"The Odette lady has a bright glow," he told me. "Is she nice?"

"She's the best." I collected my suitcase, ready to try again. "Remind her you're a secret, okay?"

Odette was known for talking to herself, or at least to things outside our perception, so Amelie wouldn't think too much of it if she got caught chatting with Oscar, but there was no sense in taking unnecessary risks. With Boaz only a phone call away, I wanted all mentions of the little terror far from her thoughts when her brother called.

There was no reason to believe the Elite, let alone Boaz, would have a problem with me keeping the kid, but they had wanted to use him as dybbuk bait, so I wasn't keen on that crowd learning of his continued existence.

Better to ask forgiveness than permission, or something along those lines.

"I'm tired of being a secret," he pouted. "You said I'm family."

"Yes, you are." I patted his cheek. "But you're also family that not everyone can see or understand. It won't always be like this. Amelie will move out in a few months, and you'll have run of the house. After that, I can bring over friends who can see you for you to play with. How does that sound?"

He sank like a lead weight had been attached to his ankle. "Like Mr. Linus?"

"Yes, Linus is one of them. He's a good man, Oscar. I promise he won't hurt you. He's the reason why you got to leave the *Cora Ann*. He wouldn't have—" found his remains then returned them to his family, "—relocated you if he didn't want you to have a better life. Afterlife. Whatever. That doesn't make sense, does it?"

"I guess not." He sighed in the way only small children can, as if all the oxygen in their bodies has been expelled, leaving only a boneless sack of meat behind. "I'll be nicer since you like him."

"I do like him." I collected my bag. "You will too once you get to know him."

Movement drew my gaze to the front yard and the man standing there, who had probably overheard our whole conversation.

"It's time for me to go." I waggled a finger at him until he laughed. "Be good for Woolly. She'll tell me if you misbehave."

"I'll be good." He squeezed me so hard I decided he must have been a boa constrictor in his previous life. "Promise."

After disentangling from Oscar, I leaned against the wall and rested my forehead on the siding. "I'll be home soon. Call me if you get lonely or scared, and I'll come straight back. Okay?"

The porch light flared with sudden warmth as good as a hug, and when I straightened, I noticed the curtains in all the windows shooing me toward Linus.

I took the hint and met him in the grass, cringing at his sleek Tumi carry-on in black. Mine was also Tumi, an older model, but still serviceable, despite its custom purple shell being spackled over with

Lisa Frank stickers that shouted tween me's eye-gouging taste for all to see.

"Now I know how Maud felt when she left me behind with a sitter." I toyed with the telescoping handle. "I never thought of myself as particularly maternal but..."

"They'll be fine," a voice promised from the darkness.

"Taz?" I jogged toward her as she stepped from the shadows, only the twinge in my jaw reminding me why it was never smart to rush Taslima. "Hey." I stopped six feet away. "It's good to see you."

"I owe you an apology." Head bowed, she planted her feet at parade rest and pinned her arms behind her back. "I assured Boaz I could handle this assignment, but I failed you." Unable to glimpse the fire in her eyes, I didn't recognize her. "I have trouble separating the past from the present sometimes. It's why I had to leave the army and go sentinel. Only my own kind understands the switch that gets flipped in my head."

Slowly, I approached her. "Did I do something wrong?"

"No." She shook her head once. "It's not you, it's me."

"You hang out with Boaz too much if you're spouting his favorite lines."

The laugh I expected never came, and she raised her chin to look at me. Measure me, more like it.

"My baby brother was all mouth and not willing to bow to his betters." Lingering fondness curved her lips in a bitter smile. "He sassed the wrong boy and was killed by a High Society punk when he was eleven. That boy used magic to trap him one day on his way home from school so he couldn't run away, and then the punk beat Rajib to death. I almost returned the favor. I would have if my father hadn't peeled me off him."

A sour taste clogged my throat. "I had no idea."

"It was a long time ago." She peered up at me. "I like you, Grier. You're different. You're like us, not like them." She cut her eyes to Linus. "But I can't spar in your gardens, in front of your talking house, with the Grande Dame's son playing referee, and pretend you're one of us when you're not." A thread of anger wove through her voice. "You're the farthest thing from it."

"Why would Boaz do this?" Pairing us up to fail. "He had to know how hard this would be for you."

"See?" She laughed, a crazed sound. "You don't think the way they do. You care about others." She tugged on her earlobe. "Boaz thought that goodness might fix me, that you might—I don't know —heal me."

Never in a million years had I expected her to say that. As often as I had to peel him off the ceiling when I did something he disagreed with, I had no idea he thought I was capable of more than getting in trouble.

"I'm going to take some basic self-defense classes for a while," I found myself telling her, "but I'd like to train with you again when I'm ready. You're amazing, and I want to learn to move the way you do." To flow like water and kick like a freaking mule. "We can rent space in a dojo if meeting here is too hard."

"I'll think on it." Her posture relaxed, and she squinted up at me. "What about Boaz?"

I packed as much defiance into my smile as it would hold. "What about him?"

Cackling, she bared her teeth in a sharp smile. "You'll do, Grier. You'll do." She saluted me as she faded back into the shadows. "Call me when you're ready. We'll see what you've learned."

Feeling smug over my minor rebellion, I strolled to Linus, who shook his head at me. "What?"

"I still don't understand." He jerked his chin toward Taz and started walking down the driveway.

"She doesn't go easy on me because of who I am." There was more, but it was hard to put into words. "She's angry." Until tonight, I hadn't understood that anger was the well she was drawing her water from, but looking back, I should have guessed. "So am I." Lost family, lost time, lost hope. "We might be good for each other."

"Perhaps," he allowed without pushing. "Would you like to meet your new instructor while we're in Atlanta?"

Dread started creeping up on me in anticipation of the crimson Lincoln that ferried Linus around town, the model identical to the one Volkov had favored. "He's not local?"

"Most of my contacts are in my city."

Until that moment, I couldn't have told you if Linus had ever referred to Atlanta as *his*, but I heard the possessive edge, the anticipation, like being parted from it was a physical ache. Proving once again I was a crap friend, I had never asked if he was magically bound to his city. Was his anticipation homesickness or a magically fueled compulsion?

He wasn't meant to stay in Savannah forever. Only long enough to help me get my feet under me.

The sudden *tick-tock* of a countdown rang in my ears, and I shook my head to clear the noise.

"You'll like Mathew." After frowning at his watch, he scanned the road. "He offers basic self-defense classes at Strophalos twice a year, that's how we met, but he travels all over the state."

The suspicious part of me perked its ears at a resume befitting a spy for the potentate. But, to be fair, that's exactly what Taz had been. The only difference being she reported to Boaz. Using that logic, I couldn't strike Mathew from the list of potential replacements without meeting him first.

"You took classes from him?" Lessons would be a perfect cover to disguise any covert meetings.

"No." He fiddled with the zipper on his bag. "But we spar on occasion."

Linus sparring.

Linus.

Sparring.

While I understood he had hunted the dybbuk, which meant he must work in the field in Atlanta, I had trouble picturing him in the role. Even with Cletus for backup, I had difficulty wrapping my mind around him being the defender of a city. Atlanta's own Bruce

Wayne/Batman. Unreal. Picturing him in a mayoral role came easy, but down in the streets? Fighting? His elegant hands used as weapons?

No, that I couldn't imagine.

"How are you going to entice him down to Savannah?" That must be his plan. "How long will he stay?"

"His home base is in Atlanta, but he doesn't live there. He couch-surfs or stays in hotels. He hoards his money like a dragon." He reached for his suitcase. "Now that I think about it, I don't think I've ever seen him pay for anything."

I wanted one thing clear upfront. "He's not a dragon, though, right?"

"No." Linus shook his head, amused. "He's not a dragon. Those all live on the West Coast."

The taste of dirt filled my mouth, which probably had something to do with my chin scraping the grass. "Dragons are real?"

"Most everything is real if you know where to look." He grasped my wrist, turned it over, then traced the crease bisecting my palm. "We hold the balance of life and death in our hands. We can make, unmake, and remake humanity, and you can do so much more." His thumb pressed over my pulse point. "Your blood is proof that all things are possible."

The cold of his touch spiked chills up my arm. "I spent too much time with one foot in the human world. There's so much I don't know, so much Maud kept from me."

Muted pop music blared at the same time an engine revved, the noise unheard of in this neighborhood of the quietly wealthy. A horn honked at the gate leading onto my property, and I gawked at the nerve. But Linus was on the move, so I followed him.

This couldn't be our ride. The driver must be lost, and Linus wanted to hurry him on his way.

Beyond the glare of the headlights, I spotted a familiar white van coated in dust with profanity written across the hood and windows.

A young man with greasy hair popped his head out the driver's side window and waved to us with a folded slice of pizza. "You guys call for a lift?"

I choked on a laugh. "Are you serious?"

"Do you approve?" Linus glanced over his shoulder, making certain I understood he was serious. "I thought you might—"

Catching up to him, I looped an arm through his. "This is perfect." I chuckled again. "I can't believe you're going to let people in Atlanta see you arrive in this. What will your friends think?"

"They won't be paying attention to him." The stiffness that always seized him when experiencing unexpected physical contact began to melt, and he softened against me. "They'll be looking at you."

Shoulders hiking up to my ears, I wished he had kept that to himself. "I hope not."

"You'll be arriving with me," he said, an odd smile flirting with his lips. "People will be curious."

"Well, in that case, I'm happy to play the role of Nameless Arm Candy."

The slight curving of his mouth blossomed, and I grinned at having made him smile.

"I invited Neely to meet us there," I confessed while he was in a good mood. "I hope that's okay."

Quiet for a few steps, he lowered his voice. "Are you uncomfortable being alone with me?"

"No, nothing like that." I tugged on his arm until he turned his head toward me. "He was looking for an excuse to visit Cruz in the city, so I gave him one." Unsure why it embarrassed me to admit it, I glanced down at my least holey T-shirt and the jeans with ripped knees. "We're also going shopping." A flush warmed my nape. "I want to look not like a street person at Strophalos."

The frown Linus bestowed on me while sweeping me from head to toe with his dark-water gaze made me want to plant another kiss on his cheek. His honest confusion that I needed help in the wardrobe department buoyed my spirits. Boaz didn't care what I wore, minus his conviction that less was more. Volkov had been all about playing dress-up with me, which put me off the role of Society darling like nothing else. But Linus didn't seem to mind the style I had adapted, a mix of thrift store finds and pieces from my teenage years scrounged from my closet, and that won major points with me.

Sadly, Linus was not a High Society dame or even a Low Society matron, and anyone we met in *his* town would hold me to the standards of my station.

Savannah might be used to me schlepping it, but Atlanta was all glass, steel, and glitter.

"We meet Reardon tomorrow at dusk." Linus opened the gate and held it for me. "You'll have to shop tonight if new clothes are on your agenda." Brackets framed his mouth as he made his own addition to our schedule. "I have a meeting. One I can't postpone."

Our driver watched us over the end of his pizza slice as we loaded our luggage. I shot him a look he answered by taking a healthy swig from a twenty-ounce bottle of soda.

Linus had spoiled him. He wasn't budging without the promise of another fifty-dollar bill.

The cargo area was crammed with speakers, which meant our bags got stacked on the front passenger seat, leaving us to share the middle bench.

"It's no problem." As much as I hated shopping, I would never subject another person to it unless I already knew their preference. After snapping my seat belt in place, I woke my phone. "I'll shoot Neely a text and see if tonight works for him." While I was at it, I took a covert shot of Linus and sent it to Marit as promised. "I'll need to snag him before he meets up with Cruz. Their reunions last for *hours*."

And Neely was useless afterward, all soft-eyed and boneless, smiling goofily and texting his husband when he thought I wouldn't notice. Goddess only knew how I would end up dressed if I left it up to him in that condition. Probably lingerie. With accessories that required batteries to operate.

TEN

I jolted awake, chased from a blessedly dreamless sleep by the hand shaking me.

"We're here." Linus's cool breath hit my cheek. "We're also in a no-parking zone in front of my building."

The numbness pervading the left side of my body clued me in to the fact I had fallen asleep on his shoulder.

"Parking here is a nightmare." Our driver grinned at Linus in the rearview mirror. "Besides, you can afford the ticket."

"You've created a monster," I whispered, yawning as I sat upright and took in our surroundings.

"I think you're right." Linus passed him a fifty-dollar bill and a printout with a hotel logo in the top left corner. "Your reservation has been made, and your room paid for. You're responsible for any room service you order, movies you rent, or other fees you incur during your stay."

"Yeah, yeah. I got you, man."

"Keep your phone on you at all times. You are only to accept fares from myself or Grier. Do you understand? No freelance work while you're in the city."

"I told you I got you. Sheesh." His scowl tightened. "You need to take a chill pill, man."

"Come on, man." I shoved Linus out of the van, and we collected our luggage. "He's got this, man."

Linus sighed as he took my elbow and led me to the entrance. "I can't tell if you're mocking him or me."

"Both?" I hopped onto the sidewalk, purple suitcase trailing at the maximum distance the handle allowed, like maybe I wouldn't have to acknowledge it if it arrived after me. "Two-for-one special?"

"His name is Tony," Linus informed me, flashing digits on his screen at me. "Put his number in your phone."

Happy to oblige, I added Tony to my contacts list then included a pizza emoticon lest I forget him.

Air shimmered as Cletus materialized, brushed his bony knuckles over my jaw, then swirled into nothing.

Pressing fingers to my cheek, I turned to Linus. "What was that about?"

"I'm not sure." The expression on his face was difficult to parse. "Wraiths aren't allowed in the Faraday." Amusement peeked through his eyes. "Odd, wasn't it? Almost like he was saying goodbye."

Nodding thoughtfully, I zipped my lips before I gave my part in Cletus's newfound awareness away.

Though I doubted my doe-eyed innocence act had fooled Linus for a minute.

Fiddlesticks.

A giant of a man watched our approach through hooded eyes the tawny brown of crushed pecan shells. His sandy-blond hair hung in dreads down the small of his back, twisted into a loose tail. The crimson and black uniform did nothing to hide his muscular build or the menace in his bearing. How humans saw him and accepted him as one of them blew my mind.

"Mr. Lawson," he boomed down at us, gripping the curved handle on the ornate glass door leading into a gilded lobby. "I wasn't aware you were back in the city."

"I'm only here for the weekend, Hood." Between the curb and the door, Linus had donned one of the masks from his extensive collection. This was Scion Lawson, with a stick so far up his butt he probably coughed up bark, and a faint sneer tinged with just enough boredom to make you feel like simply addressing him was wasting his time. "This is Grier Woolworth. She'll be staying with me. She has full access to the building and my loft, understand?"

Hood blinked once, but that was the extent of his reaction. "Yes, sir. I'll make sure the rest of the staff knows to treat your guest with the utmost respect." He turned his warm eyes on me. "Ms. Woolworth, it's a pleasure to welcome you to the Faraday."

"It's a pleasure to meet you, Hood." I wondered what on Earth he was but knew asking was gauche.

Hood pressed a button, and the door slid open, allowing us to step into the foyer.

The layout reminded me of every five-star hotel Maud and I had ever visited, including the check-in desk. There was an air of permanence about the place that suggested this was more than a temporary dwelling for those who entered, but the gleam of metal and sparkle of glass made it hard to imagine there were people who called such lush environments home.

A spindly man with a hawkish face popped up at the sight of Linus and rushed around his desk.

"Scion Lawson, what an unexpected blessing. So good to have you home, sir. The Faraday hasn't been the same without you. The city herself has mourned your absence." He bowed almost in half. "How is your exquisite mother? Lovely as ever, I'm certain."

"Mother is well, thank you." Linus dared me to laugh with a scowl, his mask slipping a fraction, before addressing him. "Hubert, this is Grier Woolworth. She is my guest. Treat her as you would treat me."

"Yes, sir." Hubert unfolded and eyed me as if I were the morning sun rising. "Madam, you are glorious. I see why Scion Lawson favors you so. Your hair—like the darkest chocolates. Your eyes—like spun gold. Your—"

"If you'll excuse us," Linus cut in before Hubert broke out the full-on sonnets, "we have plans this evening and would like to freshen up before we head out."

"Of course, sir, of course. Let me take your bags." He reached for our luggage. "It's my pleasure, truly."

"We're good," I found myself saying, unnerved by the adoration shining in his eyes. "Thanks, though."

"As you say, madam." Crestfallen, Hubert slumped his shoulders. "I am yours to command, should you need anything, anything at all. Your slightest whim is my greatest desire."

Pretty sure I've never powerwalked to an elevator so fast in my life.

Once the doors slid closed behind us, I lost my grip on my laughter and brayed to do Maud proud.

That was all it took, like I had taken my fingers and pried off the mask to find Linus underneath.

Lips twitching, he was fighting a losing battle with a smile that had me grinning back at him. His starched posture had wrinkled into comfortable lines, and I saw so clearly the moment he sank into his skin and became simply himself that my heart pinched that this Linus was the one hidden away. Except from me.

"Wow. You've really been slumming it with me. I had no idea." Straightening my spine, I pushed my shoulders back until the blades rubbed. "Sir, it's such a pleasure to have you home, sir. Do you have any boots in need of licking, sir?"

Linus wiped a hand down his face. "Living at the Faraday was part of the deal I made with Mother."

"Ah." I counted the floors as we rose higher and higher. "That explains Hubert." I pulled out my phone and shot off a quick text to Amelie and Odette to let them know we had arrived safely. "I'm sure he called your mother the second our backs turned."

"You're probably right." He sounded tired. "He's not usually so obnoxious."

"Hood seems cool." Again, the temptation to ask what he was had me tasting curiosity. "Hubert is probably not going to be my favorite person, though. I dealt with enough sycophants on Maud's behalf to last me a lifetime, and he had a smudge on his face from all the brownnosing he's been doing."

"I've never brought anyone home with me." He allowed himself a tiny smile. "Outing one of my lovers to Mother would be the highlight of his career."

"Surprise." *Jazz hands.* "Mother already knows all about me."

And *one* of his lovers? Just how many did he keep? Or did he mean that in a general sense?

"Not *all* about you," he corrected me, snapping me back to attention. "But she knows you're here with me. There was no point in not telling her what her spies will make sure she finds out eventually."

Keeping secrets from his mother was dangerous, even for him. I guarded a few I hoped she hadn't learned, but I had no idea if he was doling them out to her when she got hungry for progress, or if he played his cards close to his vest with her, maybe especially with her —as he'd instructed me to do—and that meant hoarding my secrets until he could use them. The notion he might keep them without expectation...

It was a fairy tale, and I had never believed in those.

"The penthouse." I pretended shock. "*Ding, ding, ding.* Top floor."

His soft groan humanized him. "Are you enjoying yourself?"

"Immensely." I raced him into the hallway. "If it seems like I'm making fun of you, it's because I am."

"Really?" He pulled a keycard from his pocket. "I couldn't tell." After swiping it, he passed it over to me. "Keep this on you at all times. This is your ticket in and out. There are wards set to scan for keys."

"I got in without one this time." I wasn't arguing, just wondering how it worked.

"Hood let you in." He opened the door to his darkened loft but stood there obscuring my view. "He's the most mellow of the watchmen, but his temper can be short. Remember your key, and try not to talk to them."

"Are they like the guards at Windsor Castle?" I rose on my tiptoes to peek over his shoulder. "They can't talk or blink even if you hang from them like a monkey?"

"No." Linus thwarted me by blocking access to where I imagined the switches to be. "They've been known to eat visitors they don't like, and they're contractually permitted to do so."

"You aren't serious." Stepping into Linus's world was like strolling into one of those fairy tales I didn't believe in but felt realer by the minute. "Management would never go for that."

"Residents pay a premium for security, and it doesn't get safer than this. No one will harm you within this building, or they will be executed. The mingling of species requires harsher laws. That's why no humans are allowed. We all sign the same paperwork before buying or leasing in this building. We're all aware of the consequences if we—or our guests—misbehave."

"I can't believe your mother lets you live here," I squeaked, grateful Boaz wasn't here to call me on it.

"I'm shocked she does too." He glanced around the hall. "Every day." His gaze fell on me. "I think she hoped the terms and conditions would terrify me, and they did, but this is what I want." His half-smile was heartbreaking. "It's as close to freedom as I'll ever get."

Pity would earn me his anger, so I ignored the heartfelt sentiment and nudged him out of my way. I ran my hands along the walls in search of a switch, bumping art with my fingertips, and almost swallowed my tongue when illumination spilled throughout the room from the recessed lighting tucked in the flat spaces between thick, whitewashed beams.

"Grier..."

"Hush." I drank it all in. "I'm absorbing."

The far wall and the one behind us were hung with sheetrock and painted a soft greige color. The other two showcased original brick with plaster patches that softened the look. The floors were polished concrete and dazzled. A narrow staircase with glass panels in place of rails had been built along one wall. To maximize space, its interior had been hollowed out and transformed into a series of bookshelves overflowing with tomes. The elegant climb led up to the bedroom, a true loft space open to the rest of the apartment.

"There's something I need to tell you."

The wood and brick combination saved his home from being sterile, but the contemporary furniture and modern art pieces made me wonder if the space had come furnished. Since he had no eye for design, as evidenced by his support of my wardrobe, the magazine ad results probably bothered him less than they did me.

Or maybe this was more evidence of his chameleonic nature. Maybe this was his preference, and I was all wrong about how well he fit into the quirky vintage style at Woolworth House. But I didn't think so.

Drawn across the living room to the floor-to-ceiling windows, I stutter-stepped when movement caught my eye up in the loft bedroom, and I got an eyeful of a different view than the one I had expected.

An Asian woman lounged fully nude on the bed, her artful pose an invitation to gawk, and gawk I did.

"Hello," she purred, twining the silky ends of her ombre hair around a delicate finger. "I wasn't expecting Linus to bring home company." Her brilliant green eyes sparkled almost as brightly as the elegant emerald collar around her throat. "This should be fun." She wet her lips. "Do you want to be on top first? Or would you prefer to be topped first?"

Linus didn't spare her a glance as he wheeled my luggage to the base of the staircase. "Meiko, no."

Above him, Meiko climbed onto all fours and stalked down the length of the mattress. She hissed at him through needle-sharp teeth then leapt onto the floor. The resulting thud sounded more like a shoe dropping than a woman landing. About the time I got curious over what was happening up there, a furry leg banded with tabby stripes stretched for the topmost step.

"Um, Linus?" I felt my eyes widen. "What is that?"

"She's a nekomata, and my second familiar." He tapped his foot, waiting as the massive cat slinked down to greet him. "Meiko, Grier is our guest. No more pranks."

The cat stuck its tails, and there were two, in the air and twitched them once as if to ask *where's the fun in that?*

"Can she not talk when she's...?" I gestured to what appeared to be either a Maine coon on steroids or a runty bobcat, "...like that?"

"Meiko can talk in any form," he assured me. "She's being catty."

Literally in this case.

"You'll be staying in my room," he told me, and the cat yowled with indignation. "It's the only way you'll have any privacy. Meiko and I will stay down here."

"Where will you sleep?" The sleek, angular sofa looked about as comfortable as a cardboard box with a sheet draped over the top. "We can always pick up an air mattress and pump while we're out."

Ears perked upon hearing we didn't plan on sleeping together, the cat snapped her jaws shut then glanced between us, the light catching on her collar.

"I have a Murphy bed for guests." He indicated one of the built-ins I had assumed was an armoire to hide his television since I didn't see one mounted on the walls. "It's never been used." He pulled his luggage over and parked it at his new digs. "Now I can say it's been tested at least."

"I can stay down here. I don't mind. I don't want to run you out of your room."

"You're not. I'm offering it to you." He indicated one of two closed doors. "There's only one bathroom. We'll have to share."

"I can do that." I bet it was every bit as lavish as the rest of the space. It wouldn't beat the clawfoot tub in Maud's bathroom where I used to beg to soak, but I could make do. "I'll check in with Neely and see if he's arrived yet."

"All right." He took his suitcase into the bathroom with him. "I'll change."

Meiko exploded into sex-goddess mode as the door clicked shut. "So, you're Grier." Her eyes glittered. "Want to know a secret?"

Unsure what her angle was, I shrugged. "As long as you don't expect me to reciprocate, sure."

"Follow me." She crooked a finger in expectation I would trail her sashaying hips. "This is Linus's home office, broom closet more like it, but it doubles as an art studio." The door opened under her hand, and she flipped on a light. "Notice a theme?"

Gazing into his office was like staring into a mirror. On the back wall, hung above his desk, was an oil painting. The woman wore my face, but she wore it better than me. Happiness shined through her eyes, and a mischievous quirk lifted one corner of her mouth. She looked like she had a good secret and was seconds from sharing it if only you would lean close enough to hear.

This must have been his last memory of the girl I used to be.

"There are more," she confided. "You're his muse. You have been for as long as I've known him."

"How long is that?" I rasped, unsure what else I ought to be asking.

"Four years," she admitted. "Why he fixated on you when he has me is unfathomable."

"I shouldn't be in here." Viewing this without his permission was worse than Boaz thumbing through Linus's sketchbook in front of him. This was... More. A shrine—or mausoleum—where that past Grier remained entombed. "He won't want me to see this."

"Whyever do you think I showed you?" Delight rattled in the back of her throat. "Do you know what a nekomata is?"

"Not offhand, no." I backed from the room, and she followed, closing the door behind her. "Are you a true shapeshifter, or do you use glamour, like the fae?"

"You're a smart cookie." She tapped the end of my nose. "No wonder he wants to eat you up."

Heat flooded my face, part embarrassment over what she was telling me and part—I don't know what—at seeing his memorial. Though her diversion almost worked, I noticed she hadn't answered my question. "I'm guessing you trade in mischief."

"Right again, Cookie." Her husky chuckle, like she was sizing up how many bites that might take, made me uncomfortable. "I show people what they expect—"

"I did *not* expect a cat lady."

"Oh, Cookie, but you did expect a beautiful woman in his bed." Her eyes glimmered, the pupils dilating. "You must have put a lot of thought into his tastes in women." She raked her claw-tipped fingers through my hair. "I plucked the image out fully formed, no embellishment required."

"You're wrong." I backed away, but her fingers tightened on the ends of my hair to hold me still. "I have a..." *boyfriend* didn't feel like the right word, "...Boaz." Maybe if we had made it to our second date, or if he picked up a phone sometime, I might have had a different label for him. Right now, I wasn't sure what we were or weren't. Too much had changed that night in the Lyceum. *He* had changed. Given all that happened, it would have been impossible for him not to be altered. "Linus and I aren't like that."

"Yet." She twisted in on herself until a fluffy too-big-to-be-a-house cat sat at my feet. *"Brrrrrt."*

"Back at you," I mumbled, relieved when she padded into the kitchen. Antsy at being left alone in a strange place, I dialed up Neely for comfort. "Hey, where are you?"

"I just rolled up to a café on Peachtree Street Northwest. I couldn't remember where you said you were staying, and since you forbade me from hunting down my sugar lump, I figured I would fuel up while I waited."

A look down at my clothes had me second-guessing the need to change. Unlike Linus, I wasn't headed for a meeting, and there was only more of the same in my suitcase. With that reminder of why we had planned this outing in mind, I decided there was no reason to keep Neely waiting.

"Hold on." I located Meiko, who was busy lounging on a black mohair throw draping the couch, and waited while she decided whether to acknowledge me. "Can you tell Linus I left? That I'm going to meet Neely? He'll know who I mean." And since we hadn't nailed down our plans... "He's welcome to join us if he wants."

"He won't." Meiko yawned, baring a mouthful of teeth. "He's not a joiner."

"He did mention a meeting," I conceded.

"There you have it," she purred. "You best run along to meet your little friend."

"Grier?" Neely buzzed in my ear. "Are you coming or...?"

"I'll be right there." I checked my pockets for my debit card and room card. "Order me something hot and sweet to go while you're at it."

"Aren't you wicked?" He chuckled. "I'll see who I can rustle up."

"That's not what I meant." I pinched the bridge of my nose. "A drink, Neely. Not a person." I retraced my footsteps to the elevator. "I've got my hands full as it is."

"Do tell." His interest perked faster than a fresh pot of coffee. "I thought you were Boaz forever?"

"He's acting weird." Granted, he had plenty of reason for that. "I'm not sure what's going on there."

Rushing to my bedside made me think he was serious when he made his promises to me. Refusing to kiss me in more than a platonic way made me think he had changed his mind. Though I had just suffered an injury to my jaw, which made getting hot and heavy diffi-cult—and painful. But that still didn't excuse the lack of communica-tion since that night at the Lyceum. I didn't need a phone call a day, but maybe once a week. Or a text? An emoji? Something. Goddess, I was giving myself a headache.

"Well, the boy's got a reputation. I know you love him, that's obvious, but do you *love-love* him?"

I mashed the button for the lobby hard enough my pointer smarted. "I haven't figured out that part yet."

"Fair enough. Do I get to know who his competition is?"

"Competition isn't the right word." The elevator stopped somewhere in the middle of the building, and a couple entered the booth, deep in conversation. A tingle swept down my spine, alerting me to the presence of vampires, and I tightened my grip on the phone. "I don't have to choose."

"No, you certainly don't."

"Goddess, Neely, that's not what I meant."

Busy choking on his coffee, he couldn't answer.

"I meant I could stay single."

The woman noticed me, and her stare intensified until I stopped counting down the floors. Murky green eyes swept over me, and a furrow gathered on her smooth brow. The coil of red hair crowning her head glistened under the soft lights and complemented her smart black pantsuit. Her bolero-style jacket, studded with silver, was the only flash in her ensemble, but the overall impression was stunning.

The man was her mirror image, red hair and all. Equally well turned out, he wore black slacks with a matching button-down shirt and boots. The silver flash in his outfit came from the studs adorning the wide leather belt slung low on his hips.

The couple held still the way predators do while hunting, and the man flared his nostrils, drawing in my scent.

"Are you new to the building?" Butter wouldn't melt in her mouth. "I haven't noticed you."

Unsure if that was an insult, I kept my expression and tone neutral. "I'm visiting a friend."

"Some friend if he lets you wander unescorted," the man huffed. "The Faraday isn't a playground."

"I'm not a child." A clipped note sharpened my voice. "And I never said my friend was male."

"She does smell of female...and cat," his companion agreed. "That means she's to my tastes and not yours, brother."

"A pity," he allowed, smirking. "Although, I am quite persuasive."

"You didn't hear the last five things I said, did you?" Neely buzzed in my ear. "Should I call back later?"

"No," I all but croaked. "Keep talking."

Concern at my voice breaking overrode his annoyance. "Are you okay? I hear voices."

"A couple of Linus's neighbors are introducing themselves to me." I bucked up to keep them from closing in. "That's all."

The siblings recoiled at his name, their backs hitting the sides of the elevator.

The woman blanched as white as a corpse. "You're the potentate's guest?"

Holding on to the fragile connection with Neely, I nodded.

"Forgive our impertinence." Her brother slammed his gaze to the floor at his feet and kept it there. "We meant no offense."

"None taken," I assured them, though my palms still sweated. "It was nice meeting you."

The doors opened, and they huddled in their corner, allowing me to exit first.

Hubert looked up from behind his desk, spotted me, and charged across the marble foyer. "Are the accommodations to your liking, Dame Woolworth?"

Yep. He had spoken to the Grande Dame.

"Woolworth," the woman gasped as the elevator sealed the siblings away from me.

The numbers ticked up—not down. They had decided against joining me in the lobby or sinking lower, into the parking deck, assuming that's what the P button meant on the panel. For whatever reason, the combination of Linus's name and mine had spooked them back to their room.

"Dame Woolworth?"

Swinging my focus back to Hubert, I told the polite lie. "Linus has a lovely home."

"Are you going out? Alone?" Frantic to please, he trotted after me. "Shall I call your driver? Or would you prefer to use our car service? Only the best for our residents, and their guests of course."

"I have a driver, but I appreciate the offer." I picked up my pace to escape the lobby. "Still there, Neely?"

"Maybe? What I'm hearing on your end doesn't make a lick of sense."

"This is Linus's world." I shoved out into the fresh night air and sucked in lungfuls. "It makes no sense to me either."

This whole trip was beginning to make me feel like a country mouse to his city mouse.

Savannah's supernatural population averaged three necromancers to every vampire, which was to be expected in a city under necromantic control. But we didn't get much variety outside that.

Mom and I had always played human, so I hadn't come across more than the occasional necromancer or candidate for vampirism during our traveling years. We kept our heads down, settling in small towns and avoiding big cities. Even later, with Maud, we made social rounds together, and she kept to Society functions or human amusements like museums and libraries, things that fit the role she had carved out for me.

Linus was coaxing my eyes open to all the things Maud had hidden from me, starting with an education and ending with exposure to the world beyond the Lyceum and its rules. His break from Savannah ran deeper than I first realized. This wasn't a rebellion against his mother, this was him thinning ties with her and the Society. He truly was living his own life here rather than coddled in a Society enclave like me.

"This is the real world," Hood rumbled from his station near the door. "Your Society owns a chunk of it, but not all. Take a look around, Ms. Woolworth. What you see might surprise you."

Startled he had spoken to me, I nodded my thanks for the advice. "I'm working on it."

On my right, Cletus rippled into existence and evaluated Hood with a tilt of his head.

Hood's answering chuckle allowed me to exhale with relief that I hadn't inadvertently insulted him. "You do that."

The doorman melted back into the shadows, and I started ambling with no destination in mind. Mostly I wanted to escape the Faraday and its menagerie of peculiar residents before having my reality stretched thinner. Cletus stuck to me, allowing me to walk off some of my jitters.

"I'm putting you on hold," I warned Neely. "I have to call for a ride."

"Don't you dare." He clicked his tongue. "I'm halfway to the car. I'll pick you up."

"Thanks," I said thickly. "I could use a friendly face."

I located a MARTA bus stop and collapsed on the slatted bench where my right leg started bouncing like it was pumping a bicycle tire.

Neely arrived fifteen minutes later, and I sprinted for the passenger seat of his car with all the grace of an antelope a hairsbreadth from being dinner for a lion. With the door shut behind me, I buckled up and exhaled like I'd run a marathon.

"I need to call Linus." Severing the connection, even with Neely beside me, was hard. Vampires spooked me these days, a serious failing for a necromancer. "Maybe this wasn't such a great idea."

"You'll feel better after some retail therapy," he assured me. "I always do." He pressed a to-go cup into my hand. "Perk Up's hot chocolate isn't up to your Mallow standards, but it'll do in a pinch."

I drained half the cup before dialing Linus. "Hi."

"You left without telling me." A door slammed in the background, and a cat yowled with muffled rage. "What were you thinking? Did you listen to me at all?"

Never in all our time together had he used this tone with me, and it felt like a slap in the face. Perhaps a deserved one, under the circumstances, but that didn't lessen the sting.

"I heard your warnings." I stared at the ceiling of the car, wondering if Neely was aware there was a soda-colored stain in the shape of a giraffe up there. "I brought my keycard with me."

"Tell me exactly what happened from the moment you left my apartment."

"Yes," I feigned cheer. "I am with Neely, and we are going shopping."

"I see."

"You're more than welcome to join us."

"I planned on it," he clipped out. "I was changing so I could go with you."

Meiko was a dirty, rotten liar.

"Oh."

"Yes, oh."

"You mentioned a meeting. I assumed we were parting ways at the Faraday and would rendezvous at dawn." The temptation to fling Meiko under the bus was strong, but I managed to suppress the urge. "I didn't think you'd want to be stuck with us for hours and hours."

Neely nodded support in my half of the conversation. "Guys hate that."

"You're a guy," I pointed out. "Shopping is your number-one hobby. Probably two and three too."

His harrumph killed all support on that front.

"I don't want to trespass on your time with your friend," Linus said at last, "but this isn't Savannah."

"Yeah, I noticed." We zipped over asphalt marked with rubber skids and debris from accidents past, and I kept wishing for the *bump-bump-bump* of cobblestones. "How about we get started and you join us?"

"Let Cletus keep an eye on you." His sigh blasted over the line. "I'll be there shortly."

Given the fact his wraith was on guard duty, he didn't have to ask where we were going, not that I had a clue. Cletus would tell Linus, or show him. I wasn't clear on how their bond worked, if they conversed or traded thoughts, sensations, and images between themselves the same as Woolly and me.

Buildings whooshed past in a brick and metal blur. "What about your meeting?"

"I can make time, Grier."

Home for the first time in months, a meeting on the horizon, and he was prioritizing my vanity.

Being prioritized for a change felt…nice.

"Tell him to meet us at Haywood Square," Neely prompted me. "They have the best selection."

The mall was a Society holding, and it kept much later hours than the surrounding shopping centers. And Neely was right. Thanks to its investors, Haywood had the best of everything Atlanta had to offer in order to please its nocturnal clients.

"I heard," Linus informed me. "I'll see you soon."

I sat there after I ended the call, staring at the phone, the blacked-out display and its reflection of me.

"Girls do call boys these days," Neely suggested. "It's modern, not desperate."

I squinted at him. "What makes you think I'm waiting on a call?"

"Please," he huffed. "I haven't been off the market that long. I recognize that face. I used to see it in the mirror every time a cute boy forgot my number."

"Boaz has been busy." The defense sprang to my lips with ease. "He has a lot on his plate right now."

"How long has he been busy?" Neely cut his eyes toward me. "You've been wearing that expression for weeks."

"You've barely seen me," I argued. "Maybe you just caught me in a weak moment."

"You're a lot of things, Grier, but weak is not one of them."

Knowing he was thinking of Volkov, of the story I had spun about the vampire being a controlling boyfriend I had escaped with only a few bruises, made me think of him too.

He was out there, somewhere, locked in a cell I was certain lacked the amenities lavished on me. But bars or not, a cage was still a cage.

"Forget I said anything." Neely made the peace offering, but his eyes remained troubled, and it didn't escape my attention he hadn't asked about Amelie. According to our cover story, she was here in the city working an internship. Yet he didn't offer to include her in our outing. It made me wonder if he was avoiding the topic. Maybe he was hurt to have lost her too. "Tell me what we're shopping for and how much money I get to spend."

The budget was a good question. Too much would make him suspicious, but too little wouldn't get me the polish required to pass among High Society. I might as well get more jeans and tees while I was at it. I could use some underwear with elastic too. All mine had been stretched and washed past the breaking point. One pair I tied on over my right hip with the lacy detail unraveling from the waist.

"This asshat won't get off my bumper."

I checked out the mirror and winced from the bright lights. "Maybe they'll take the next exit."

"Maybe." Neely accelerated, nudging us a few miles over the posted speed limit as he took an overpass. "Let's see how he likes that." Flicking on his blinker, he changed lanes for good measure. "We've got two more exits until our next turn. We'll just chill over here and— *Grier*."

Metal screeched, and the car lurched sideways. I was falling, and then the seat belt yanked me back, its edge cutting into my throat. But we kept tumbling, over and over. Glass crunched and scattered, pelting my face and neck. An explosion whited out the corner of my eye—the airbag deploying—and Neely lost his grip as his head shot back.

Blood scented the air, almost indistinguishable from the hot metal smell permeating each breath.

Dipping my fingers in a gash across my cheek, I swiped a protection sigil on Neely's arm and then mine.

What damage had already been done was beyond help, but it might save us from breaking our necks.

Impact, harder than all the rest, made the frame surrounding us groan, and the car rocked to a stop.

I must have been screaming. My throat hurt like it did when I woke from the dream. Silence descended, a cocoon that wrapped my senses, the utter quiet only punctuated by Neely's too-sharp breaths. "Neely?"

A low moan was his only response.

With a grunt of effort, I reached out and mashed my thumb against his pulse. Quick but steady. That was all the energy I could scrounge together while my heart raced so fast my legs felt the burn.

Treading the familiar path to the door in my head, my consciousness locked me away from the pain.

"THE MASTER WILL KILL us for this," a masculine voice hissed from the shadows.

"The Master wants her," a woman answered. "Well, there she is."

The crunch of approaching footsteps shocked me back to my senses, and I forced myself to assess the situation.

Neely and I hung upside down, suspended by our seat belts. The car had flipped so many times the doors were bowed out and the glass had shattered in all the windows. Neely was alive, but hurt. I was alive, but so weak I must be losing blood. Or I had a head injury making me sluggish. With the ringing in my ears, I conceded that maybe it was a little bit of both.

"A salt circle won't keep out that wraith forever," the man warned. "We need to leave."

"We will," the woman soothed, "as soon as we have our prize."

The familiar tickle down my spine confirmed my worst fear. These were vampires, come to fetch me. Part of me had hoped I'd hallucinated the first part of their conversation, but there was no denying biology.

Fingers trembling from shock and fear, I wet my fingers against my cheek and started drawing.

Cletus might be out of action, but he was still broadcasting to Linus. Help was on the way if I could just hang on.

"Ah. You're awake," the woman crooned. "Fear not, mistress, we'll have you back where you belong in no time at all." Recognition kicked in a heartbeat later. The elevator. She was one of the siblings who'd panicked upon hearing my name. "The Master has been beside himself since you left. He forgives all your transgressions. He only wishes you to return home where you will be kept safe and cherished."

Returned to a gilded cage, that's what she meant. I would rather die than hear a lock turn at my back.

"Fuck." I dipped my fingertips in the blood running up my jaw and finished my sigil. "You."

"That's not very nice," she gritted from between clenched teeth. "I am here to serve."

"Linus is coming." I spoke with absolute conviction. "Leave now or suffer the consequences."

"We can't be here when the potentate arrives," her brother pleaded. "He'll kill us."

"We won't be if you'd get over here and lend a hand," she snarled. "Give me your knife."

Metal glinted in her palm as she reached through the busted window, blade aimed at my throat and the seat belt cutting into my neck. Light exploded in a blinding flash from the frame as the wards ignited, and the vampire howled in agony then fell on her butt in the gravel.

I shouldn't have laughed, goddess knows I shouldn't have laughed, but I did. I kept going until I hurt all over, but I couldn't stop. The manic relief bubbling up my throat kept spilling over until both vampires took wary steps away from me.

"She's unhinged," the sister lamented. "Do you think she was like this before?"

"I don't know, and I don't care," the brother countered. "Come on, Ernestine." Shuffling ensued, but all I could see were two pairs of black-clad legs tussling. "The wraith is like a beacon. The potentate will come for her."

"We'll never get another chance as good as this one," she argued.

"You'll never get another chance period," a new voice, dripping with ice, assured them.

The night came alive around us, shadows roiling, darkness rippling. A bone-deep cold pervaded the car until my teeth chattered from the sudden temperature drop. The hem of a wraithlike cloak swept into view, black tendrils whipping out, striking at the fractured light from the streetlamps overhead.

"We meant no harm, Potentate." The brother was quick to drop to his knees. "Have mercy."

There was no hesitation, no deliberation. "No."

Moonlight glinted off a wide blade as it completed its arc, and the man's head rolled to a stop against the car door. His disintegration was a slow, pathetic thing. He was new. Still juicy. Only the cast-iron stomach that came standard on necromancers kept me from spewing my hot chocolate.

"Frederick," Ernestine wailed. "You killed him."

"You almost killed one of mine," Linus snapped. "You would have returned her to her cage."

"The Master wouldn't have harmed her." She protested the second charge, knowing there was no wiggling out of the first. "She is his. We were doing as we were told."

"Grier belongs to no one."

Metal sang, and a second head joined the first. This one crumbled until the vampire was dust.

A distant part of my brain noted I had been wrong about them being siblings. Their deaths proved that much. Whatever game they had played with each other had been set into motion centuries apart, and it was done.

A familiar apparition peeled from the hem of the roiling cloak, and Cletus drifted over to me, running his skeletal knuckles across the wound on my cheek. Linus trailed him, the blanket of night sky unraveling as he approached, and knelt at my window, ducking until his forearms mashed into gravel, and we made eye contact.

"Thank Hecate," he breathed. "I got here as fast as I could, but I thought for certain I would be too late."

"Linus," I murmured, giving my eyes permission to close. "What are you?"

All the blood had rushed to my head, drumming in my ears. That's the only reason why I thought he replied *yours*.

ELEVEN

Suffocating pressure on my chest forced my eyes open, and I woke gasping for breath. "Meiko?" The hand I swatted the cat with weighed five hundred pounds. "Get off me. I can't breathe."

A heartbeat later, a nude woman stretched out beside me, her cheek propped on her fist. "My bad."

"Why are you always naked?" I sucked down gulps of sweet oxygen. "Don't you own any clothes?"

"I am how you imagine me to be." She walked her fingers up my arm, and I noticed I had been stripped down to my underwear. "At least give me lingerie. Something pink and lacy." She popped my bra strap. "I can Google it on your phone if you've never seen sexy underwear. Clearly, you've never worn any."

The snap radiated pain throughout my tender shoulder. For a second, I wondered why it hurt, but then I recalled the seat belt clenching taut. Quick as a blink, the wreck exploded with crystalline clarity in my mind.

"Neely." I shoved upright, wincing. "Where's Neely?"

"Relax." She pushed me back down then slapped me in the face with Boaz's oversized T-shirt. "And put this on."

"Where is my friend?" I shouted at her smug face. "I have to see him."

"He's at the human hospital where humans belong." Her rounded ears twitched like they wanted to flatten but couldn't in this form. None too gently, she yanked the shirt over my head. "He's got a broken nose, a fractured rib, and bruising, but that's it." She bared her teeth. "What does it matter if he dies today or in, what, five years? Humans are short-lived and—"

Body screaming from the strain, I fisted a clump of her hair and flung her off the bed. The expected thump of impact took longer than I anticipated, and that's when I grasped the situation.

This was Linus's bed, up in the loft, and I had tossed her down into the living room.

"Meiko?" I eased onto the floor then crawled to the edge and peered over. "Are you okay?"

A cat stood where the woman must have hit, fur standing upright over every inch of her, but she had landed on her feet. Ears pinned back, she slinked off, tails whipping through the air.

A wash of tingles over my skin had me eyeballing the door before it opened, and Linus entered with a stout vampire beside him. She wore scrubs a size too small, and a crossbody bag bumped against her hip when she walked. Her nostrils flared, scenting blood, and her gaze swung up to meet mine.

"What are you doing out of bed?" Linus strode forward, hand outstretched as if I were in danger of falling and he planned on catching me. "Are you hurt?"

"I, uh—" I raked my frizzy hair from my eyes, "—accidentally tossed your cat out of the loft."

Meiko chose that moment to yowl piteously, and he glanced between us. "I see."

"Hello, Grier." The doctor approached the stairs. "I'm Dr. Daria

Schmidt. I practice out of Gershwin Memorial Hospital, but Scion Lawson convinced me to make a house call."

"Oh good." I sat upright, folding my legs in lotus position until the room stopped wobbling. "I need to check the status on my friend. He was driving when the accident occurred."

"I just left Mr. Torres." Her smile was warm, her lips held tight to hide her fangs. "He's stable. His nose has been reset, his ribs wrapped, and his boo-boos kissed by a handsome lawyer."

"*You* were his doctor?" Shock made me borderline rude, but vampire doctors didn't waste time on human patients. "I apologize for my surprise."

After winking, she cut her eyes to Linus. "Mr. Lawson was very persuasive."

"I bet." His checkbook could persuade most anyone of anything. "How many zeroes did it take to convince you to treat a human patient?"

Linus stared me down. Up. Whatever. "Grier."

Schmidt guffawed, her feelings clearly not bruised. "Enough I almost ran out of fingers before I ran out of zeroes."

"Send me the bill," I demanded. "Whatever it cost, I'll pay it."

Linus developed a sudden case of selective hearing that tempted me to ask Schmidt to examine him.

"I'll come up to you," she said. "Could you get back in bed, please?"

"Sure thing." I grunted as I unfolded my limbs. "Just a sec."

Schmidt climbed into the loft while I rallied my battered legs into cooperating with me.

After setting down her supplies, she opened her arms, preparing to scoop me up and carry me. Her blue scrubs were a long way from pink satin and lace, but a vampire coming at me with arms extended kicked my hindbrain into high gear. I started backing away, not stopping even when my palms hit the edge.

"Step away from her," Linus commanded an instant before an icy hand clamped down on my wrist. He balanced with half his body on the stairs, half in the loft, and my back pressed flush to his chest. "Grier, I need you to calm down." He traded his initial grip for pinning an arm around my waist. "Daria isn't going to hurt you. She won't touch you if you don't want her to." His cool breath tickled my ear. "I can find someone else."

"I'm the best doctor in the city," she said defensively.

"I was..." I couldn't get out the words. They got stuck in my throat. "I was..."

"She spent five years in Atramentous," Linus told her, which wasn't what I had been about to confess at all. But, her being a vampire, I understood why he wouldn't want her to know about Volkov's—or the Master's—interest in me. "A vampire abused her." Truth told on an angle. "This was a mistake."

"You got me the best." I found my voice. "It's what you do." I inched forward. "Her being a vampire was secondary to you." I cast her an apologetic glance. "I meant no offense."

"You're Grier Woolworth," she said, dumbfounded. "I should have put it together sooner when Linus Lawson requested me to treat his friend Grier, but it's been a long night."

A deadly calm settled across Linus's features, and the memory of a black tattered cape tickled the back of my mind. "Will that be a problem, Doctor?"

"My clan is pro-Coalition, so that's a no." She leaned against the wall, as far from me as she could get, while I crawled back on the bed, Linus at my side. "I have no interest in political jockeying. Whatever this nonsense movement is selling, I'm not buying."

Once I situated myself against the pillows, I waved her over to me, feeling slightly ridiculous to have her at my beck and call. "Do you have a name for the clans splintering from the Undead Coalition?"

"No." She proceeded with caution, moving slowly so as not to spook me. "I didn't watch the news when I was human, and that hasn't changed. Any particular reason why you're asking?"

"No." Her no-nonsense attitude helped me relax. "Living in

Savannah, so close to the Lyceum, you hear things and wonder. That's all."

Her noncommittal noise told me she knew there was more to it, but also that she was smart enough not to investigate. Letting the matter drop, she confirmed her story that politics wasn't her bailiwick.

Some girls have all the luck.

"Can you lift your shirt, please?"

I peeked at Linus, but he had already turned his back.

"You're healing well," she said as she started my exam. "I don't see any wounds consistent with the blood on your face, throat, and hand." She checked with Linus. "I assume that's your work?"

"Yes." Using touch to guide himself down, he sat on the floor at the foot of the bed. The ceiling was too low for him to stand without bending. "I treated her while the EMTs worked on Mr. Torres."

"I almost feel bad for taking your money." She put away her supplies then winked at me, not looking sorry at all. "She's bruised and tender. She's going to be sore for a few days, so make sure she takes it easy. Light exercise is okay, but nothing strenuous." She pulled down my shirt then slung her bag over her shoulder. "You can give her another pass in the morning if she needs it, but you've repaired any major damage. Her body can handle it from here." Edging past Linus, she nodded to us. "I'll let myself out."

We watched her go, neither of us speaking until the door shut behind her.

Linus cocked his head to one side. "Are you decent?"

Swaddled in Boaz's shirt, I was as decent as I was getting. "Yeah."

He twisted around, seeming to finally notice Meiko's choice of nightgown for me. A frown gathered across his forehead before he caught my look and erased the telling lines. "Do you want me to call anyone for you?"

"No." I shook my head. "Odette most likely knows. She's good at gleaning me in other people's futures. Woolly would demand I come home. Amelie will tell Boaz, and I..." I toyed with the hem of my—*his*—shirt. "I don't want them to worry."

As much as I had enjoyed Boaz rushing home to check on me, I was tired of bonding with him over near-death experiences. Part of me wondered if I would have heard from him at all if not for my jaw. Sure, he had seemed like his flirty self during his visit, but how much of that was reflex?

Relationships were built on communication. That much I knew. So, was this the point where I told him I deserved more? Or was that being too needy? Would the wrong word send him running? Clearly, something had him eyeballing a new pair of sneakers. Why else would he avoid me?

Linus nodded like he understood the things I hadn't said. "I called Mathew."

I blanked on the name. "Oh?"

Not fooled for a minute, Linus chuckled under his breath. "He'll want to spar with you to gauge your skill level. On Dr. Schmidt's recommendation, I've invited him to Savannah next week rather than facilitating a meeting on this trip."

Oh, yeah. Mathew. The self-defense instructor. "That makes sense."

He scanned my face as if my capitulation surprised him. "Are you up for answering a few questions?"

"Sure." I curled on my side to see him better. "Fire away."

"Did you see your attackers?"

What did it matter since he had killed them both? "Yes." I picked at a wrinkle in the cover. "I met them in the elevator on my way down. They got spooked when I mentioned I was your guest and fled when Hubert used my title. I was going to tell you about them tonight but..." I rubbed my face. "After everything, it's hard for me to tell if I'm overreacting or if my paranoia is justified. I misjudged them. I should have brought them up when you called."

"They were reckless." Linus wrapped a hand around one wrist

and pulled until he could see my face. "This wasn't your fault. We had no reason to think they would risk harming you to capture you."

"What changed?" A memory of the knife in Ernestine's hand winked in my mind's eye. "They weren't gentle about getting what they wanted."

Linus studied me, waiting for a reaction. "How much did you see?"

"I saw their heads separated from their bodies."

Lips twisting, he grimaced. "I wish you hadn't."

"You saved me."

"You give yourself too little credit." He lifted his hands, exposing reddened skin blistered up to his elbows. "You were holding your own."

"Goddess." I leveraged up onto my elbow. "What happened?"

"Your sigil happened." He twisted them to and fro as he examined the damage. "I tried to pull you out, but you set a ward inside the car." He made fists then flattened them, watching the skin flex. "It took me fifteen minutes to break it, and I'm convinced it only failed then because you smudged a line to let me in."

"What sigil did I use?" Trauma had softened those edges to a comforting blur. "I'll have to remember it for next time."

"I have no idea." He huffed out a laugh, a surprised sound. "I've never seen anything like it."

"Where will they take Neely's car?" I wondered. "Do you think we could get a picture before they do whatever they do to it?"

"It's at an impound. Neely needs to speak with his insurance company. They'll have to come out and take pictures before it's scrapped." He reached behind himself and produced his phone. "Is this what you had in mind?"

"You're sneaky." I accepted the phone when he tossed it and traced the lines of the sigils with a fingertip. It resonated, even though I had no memory of drawing it. "I should have known you couldn't pass up the opportunity."

"I couldn't risk leaving it behind." He leaned against the nearest wall, making it easier for me to see him from this angle, and stretched out his long legs. "I took photos in case you wanted them, and I burned out the rest of the design."

Fire was a good, if absolutely destructive way to negate magic. Water was best, but it wouldn't wash blood out of fabric, and we couldn't risk leaving behind stains.

"The photos are for me, huh?" I couldn't resist teasing him. "I'm sure you haven't doodled the design or backed these up for your own records."

The promise of a grin fluttered along his lips. "I might have sketched it once or twice while waiting on Dr. Schmidt to finish her rounds."

"That's what I thought." I took the opportunity to forward the images to my cell, and I heard a distant ping announcing its success. "Ah. My phone lives on."

"It fell out of your jeans when I removed your..." Ears bright red, he rubbed the sting from them. "I had to see how extensive your injuries were before I could repair them."

"I understand." His flush seemed to be spreading into my cheeks. "I trust you not to take advantage."

Trust must have been the magic word. The sound of it snapped his gaze back to mine, and a desperate hope transformed his navy eyes to blackened pools of endless longing before he tucked away his emotions.

I had told the truth. I trusted him.

I trusted Linus Lawson.

That faith in him might damn me, but... He had saved me. He kept saving me.

He was not the man I'd thought he would be. He was not his mother's creature. I had seen his dizzying array of masks, one for every occasion, and I had peeked beneath them.

He wasn't a stranger to me any longer. He was Linus. He was... my friend.

"I put it on the counter in the kitchen." He jerked his chin toward the living room. "I can fetch it if you like."

"Is that wise with Meiko padding around?" I was only half joking when I asked, "She won't accidentally knock it into the garbage disposal, will she?"

His mouth opened, but then he turned his head. "Paws off her phone, Meiko."

A pissy yowl echoed up to us. I wondered if the notification had captured her attention, and if we had headed her off before she could act. "We haven't covered dual familiars in our lessons. When were you going to tell me about her?

He tipped his head back. "Never?"

"Taking on a second familiar, a sentient one, that has to be rare."

"It is," he agreed. "Both the act and her breed."

"You didn't think I would ever come here to see her?"

He angled his face toward me. "Was I wrong?"

"Odds were slim before you started tutoring me, yeah, but I like to think we'll keep in touch after this."

His eyes drifted closed. "I like to think that too."

Taking a moment, I studied his profile and pronounced him exhausted. "How did you come by her?"

"A student of mine lost his childhood familiar to cancer. His girl-friend, a vampire, procured what promised to be a rare and powerful replacement." Laughter moved through his shoulders. "Imagine her surprise when she visited his dorm and found a naked woman curled around him while he slept."

Incoherent noises fell out of my mouth. "Meiko told me she shows people what they expect."

"Meiko lies. It's a hobby of hers." He linked his hands at his navel. "Her kind tend toward mischief, and she enjoys a vicious sense of humor. Her favorite pastime is watching sparks fly, and she knows a beautiful, naked woman in bed with a man in a committed relation-ship will do the trick every time."

From where I sat, she was lucky no one had snatched a knot in her tail yet. "So why manifest in your bed when I arrived?"

"To embarrass you? To annoy me?" He cracked open his eyes. "The possibilities are endless."

Shock and awe made sense unless he'd told her to expect us. In that case, she knew he was bringing a guest home with him. More than a guest, she had anticipated *me*. That meant her exhibition was calculated to gauge my reaction. She wanted to see if I would pass or fail her test. After years of watching him draw me, she must have wondered if I was equally drawn to him.

"The benefits must outweigh the burdens," I decided. "She performs an important function for you?"

Otherwise, another owl or other familiar would have sufficed. Even I would prefer Julius 2.0 to a Meiko.

"Yes" was all he said, and his tone ended that line of questioning.

"What happened with your student?" I was not going to ask the obvious question. It was none of my business if he snuggled up to Catwoman each night he spent in the city. Served me right for comparing him to Batman. "Better yet—why did you keep her?"

"The student, who was mortified, called security. The guards escorted Meiko out to the quad, where she shifted and fled. I got called in after numerous complaints about both the cat and the woman." He looked tired just recalling the incidents. "She was bred to be a familiar, though it's against the law to bind a sentient creature that way. She had no pride to take her in, no education, and no means of supporting herself. I didn't know what to do with her, and she was so traumatized from the familiar bond breaking she remained a cat for the first two years after I brought her home." He frowned. "At the time, it didn't seem odd keeping her as a pet. She let me forget she was more than a house cat."

"And then one day she was a beautiful naked woman again." Evil as it was to bait him, I couldn't help myself when he blushed that way. "Can't put one of those out on the street, either."

"I can't win this argument, can I?"

"Nope." All his talk of familiars did make me curious. "How does Julius feel about her?"

"Julius was not impressed with her and chose to live in the atrium at Strophalos rather than share the loft. I gave Meiko away six or seven times during those early years to peers I felt could handle her brand of magic and provide her with a comfortable home." He wiggled his fingers at me. "The problem with a shapeshifting cat are thumbs."

"She came back each time."

"I don't know why she stays. I'm rarely home. She's alone all day."

"What I'm hearing is free room and board in the safest building in the city under the protection of the man responsible for keeping it that way." Poor Linus. I would have thought him above manipulation tactics considering who raised him, but...gorgeous nudist. "She's playing you, and she's going to keep on until you change the locks."

"I can hear you two," a shrill voice called up to us.

"No one cares, Meiko," I yelled back before pegging Linus with a look. "More than anything else, this tells me there's no woman in your life."

"I am female," Meiko growled. "I am in his life."

"Still don't care," I hollered then got back to Linus. "No woman would put up with *that*."

"You could have asked me if I was involved with someone." His auburn lashes kissed his cheeks as he closed his eyes. "If you were curious."

"I didn't mean—" I pulled the covers up to my chin. "That's not—"

"You're such a little liar," Meiko spat, her tone growing as coarse as a cat's tongue.

"Meiko." A sigh moved through him. "No."

"I am not a dog to be given orders," she hissed.

Glass shattered, a concussive blast, and loud purring revved her engine. No doubt a vase had met its doom, smashed against the concrete floor after she accidentally swished her tail too hard or licked her paw the wrong way while sitting next to it.

Briefly, I wondered if I could barricade the narrow staircase for the night. "Are you sure it's safe for you to sleep down there?"

"She won't hurt me." He massaged his hands. "She'll tire herself out soon."

Plink. Crack. Smash.

Those weren't the sounds of a cat giving up on revenge. "Do you want to hang out with me until she winds down?"

Eyes opening, he held out his arms. "Toss me a pillow?"

"Not until I examine you. You're still rubbing your fingers like they ache." I shoved upright and ordered him to take a seat beside me. Once I gathered his hands in my lap, I got a good look at what my sigil had done to him. His palms were blistered, his elegant fingers raw and swollen. From wrist to fingertip, his hands appeared sunburnt. "Why didn't you treat this? Or ask Dr. Schmidt for ointment?"

"I did treat them," he said quietly.

"How much worse?" Stomach plummeting into my toes, I caught him by the chin when he didn't answer. "How. Much. Worse?"

Inky tendrils filled the spaces between his pupils and irises, flooding his eyes until blackness pooled from corner to corner. "To the bone," he said at last, his gaze fixed on me. "I was charred to the bone."

And yet he had challenged the ward, battered it until I relented and let him reach me.

"Goddess." Releasing his chin, I threw my arms around his shoulders and yanked him close. "I never meant to hurt you."

"That ward saved your life." Linus was about as cuddly as an ice sculpture in my arms until he started melting against me in slow increments. "I'm proud of you, and you should be too. You defended yourself and Neely until help arrived."

"That part does not suck," I allowed. "Do you have a pen handy? I want to try something."

Linus raised one hip and produced his pen, which he offered to me. "What do you have in mind?"

"The sigil that hurt you was mine, drawn in my blood." I reached out, and his hand closed over mine. He cocked an eyebrow, waiting on an answer. "I'm going to need that hand back." I wiggled my fingers where they gripped the cap. "If I draw this on with my left hand, goddess knows what might happen. I don't want your hand to explode or—" given the sigil responsible in the first place, "—ignite."

His sudden release plopped me back on my butt, but he steadied me with a hand on my shoulder. "Which sigil do you have in mind?"

"That's the *something* part." I squirmed under his regard. "I figure if instinct got me into this mess, then instinct can get me out again."

"All right." He shifted closer, extended a hand, and waited. "I'm ready."

"You're not worried I'll maim you?" I cradled his palm in mine. "A necromancer's hands are their livelihood."

"I trust you." He gave my words back to me. "Besides, I won't exactly be destitute with or without them."

"There is that." I snorted a laugh. "Okay, here we go."

Closing my eyes, I gave myself free rein to design. Pretending his skin was no different than the pages of my grimoire, I followed the tug in my gut to dictate each curl and swoop. A flush warmed his fingers, and my eyes popped open. I was terrified I had managed to set him on fire for real.

The angry redness in his hands disappeared, fading along with the feverish heat, until I held his cool fingers in mine, his skin smooth and flawless. Well, except for the charming freckles I suspected covered every inch of him.

And that was not a helpful thought to have while sitting on his bed.

"All better." I capped the pen and set it on the mattress to prevent more accidental touching. "See for yourself."

"This is remarkable." Linus examined each knuckle and nail,

crease and fold, and his proud smile was blinding. "*You* are remarkable."

"I bet you say that to all the girls who maim and then heal you."

"I mean it, Grier." This time when he flexed his fingers, his face didn't pinch with hurt. "Do you think you could teach me the sigil you used?"

"Probably not." I nibbled on my bottom lip. "No offense."

"I understand." His fingertips rubbed together as though reacquainting themselves with one another. "We all have trade secrets."

"It's not that." Good thing he was into self-experimentation. "I don't know what I did. I wasn't looking."

A laugh shot out of him and ricocheted through the loft, startling a growl out of Meiko.

"Where's your phone?" I searched the bed, unable to remember if I had returned it yet. "We can snap a few pictures of what hasn't flaked off and recreate it when we get home."

Home.

Savannah was home. For me. This—Atlanta—was his.

Yet another reason not to get attached to him.

"It's in my back pocket." Linus shifted his weight to one side. "Can you reach it? I don't want to risk scraping off the ink."

Careful not to cop a feel, I pinched his phone between my fingers and tugged it free. "Unlock it, please." I rested it on his thigh then angled my head away to give him privacy, but he didn't budge for concern over flaking. "Do you need help?"

Fingers outstretched, he glanced up at me. "Do you mind?"

"You'll have to reset your password after this," I teased. "Who knows what secrets I could unearth if I dug around on your phone long enough?"

"You can look if you want." He held still while I took a series of shots, with and without the blinding flash. "I don't mind."

I got the sense he wanted to prove something to me, that by sharing the contents of his phone—which, for most people encapsulated their whole lives—he was entrusting part of himself to me. It was the kind of act that begged for reciprocation. *You show me yours, and I'll show you mine.* But I wasn't ready for that.

"I don't want to invade your privacy." That sounded polite and not panicky. "There are things on my phone I wouldn't want anyone else to see. Selfies mostly." I passed him back his device. "I've been trying to replicate this winged eyeliner thing Neely does, but it's beyond me. Pretty sure he busts a gut laughing at my attempts when I text them to him."

"Why the sudden interest in makeup?" Linus scratched his hands where the dried ink pulled his skin. "I don't remember you wearing it except on special occasions." He answered his own question. "Boaz."

There was no point in lying. I had wanted to look nice for him once upon a time.

"Yeah." I shrugged. "I gave up on it, though. I would rather beg or bribe Neely into glamming me." A pang rocked through me when I recalled how pale and broken he'd looked hanging there from his seat belt. "Cruz must have lost his mind when he got the call," I said softly. "Neely is his whole world."

"I'll take you to see him tomorrow before we meet Reardon," Linus promised.

"Thanks." My jaw, which must have finished healing thanks to all the magic Linus pushed through me, didn't twinge when I yawned. "I apologize in advance for my nightmare waking you. If it gets too bad, just toss a pillow up here at me or something. I don't want to get you in trouble with your neighbors."

"I etched soundproofing sigils into the floors. You won't bother anyone."

A shiver tickled over my skin, the idea of no one hearing me scream if Meiko tried to off me in my sleep as much of a relief as it was a worry. "Except you."

"I'll use earplugs if you don't want to be disturbed." A slight rise in his eyebrows left it to me to decide.

As if I would be the one bothered by hearing my screams or watching my thrashing.

"That would probably be for the best." I rubbed my arms, sheepish. "If you wake me up, I'll only go right back to where I left off in my dream. You can't save me from it."

His lips parted like he wanted to argue, but he wisely closed his mouth. I wasn't interested in sigils or in sedatives. Enduring the dream sucked, I had to agree there, but it's not like it stuck with me after I woke. All I had to do was survive the day. Easy-peasy. Sure it was.

"Sleep well, Grier."

Not likely. "Good luck."

Linus took the stairs down, and I got comfortable in his bed. Sleep forced me to chase it, but eventually, I caught it with both hands.

TWELVE

He has a new girlfriend. His third one this week. Just as mundane as all the rest.

Why not me? Why won't he ask me? I would say yes. He knows I would say yes. Maybe that's the problem. Maybe I should play hard to get. Maybe then he would see we were meant to...

The carpet squishes under my feet, and cold slime seeps between my toes. I shiver, confused, my anger at Boaz forgotten. The smell hits me then, copper and rose water and thyme.

Maud.

I collapse to my knees beside her and scoop the icy blood back into the gaping hole in her chest.

"Maud?"

The sobs start, and I can't stop them. I'm working as fast as I can, but her heart—her heart—it's missing.

"Wake up. Please wake up. Please, Maud. Wake up. Please."

Shivers dapple my arms, and my teeth chatter, but it doesn't matter. None of it matters if she won't open her eyes. I'll be alone again. All alone. Maud is all I have, and she's...

She's gone.

She's dead.

Dead.

Using her blood for my ink, I start drawing a sigil, one I've never seen in any textbooks.

"No, Grier," a voice pleads behind me. "Stop before it's too late."

I woke screaming her name.

Maud. Maud. Maud.

Throat raw, lips chapped, I panted through a panic attack while I adjusted to my surroundings. I was tucked so deep in the crack of the wall, the sloped ceiling rested on top of my head.

Snatches of conversation, too faint for me to remember, too devastating for me to forget, echoed through my head, pinging off the walls of my skull then bouncing into oblivion as I woke fully.

What had I dreamed? What had I dreamed? What had I dreamed?

Already, the fine details eluded me, leaving behind vague dread and fresh grief.

"Are you finished?" a brassy voice snapped. "My ears are ringing."

Climbing from my hidey-hole, I crawled to the edge of the loft and peered down at a flurry of activity.

Racks of clothes had been wheeled in and pushed against the walls. Boxes of shoes towered in one corner while purses and other accessories cluttered the couch. Wafer-thin women dressed to the nines fluttered between piles, cooing and flattering Meiko, who presided over the affair from the center of the room.

The scene wrecked me with its familiarity, and a sour taste flooded my mouth.

I'm safe, safe, safe.

The similarities proved too strong until all I could hear was that last conversation with Lena the night I executed my escape from Volkov, and the Master.

"Have you put any more thought into what I should wear tomorrow night?"

"I do have some ideas." She hesitated, uncertain if I actually cared about her opinion. *"Would you like me to show you?"*

"I want to look my best." I offered her my hand. *"I might need help getting back in bed, though. Do you mind?"*

"Not at all." She carried me back to bed and propped me up with pillows. *"Wait just a tick, and I'll be right back with my top choices."* Her smile widened. *"Then we can talk about accessories."*

The clothes. The bed. The flitting helpers. It was all too much. I hated all of it until my eyes crossed.

Linus. I needed Linus. Where was he?

"Cookie, Cookie." Meiko sneered, her cherry lips curling. "Are there crumbs in his bed?"

"Why not ask him," I said, aware I was being nasty but too stung to curb my tongue. "What is all this?"

"Your new wardrobe." She cocked a silk-clad hip and planted a manicured hand below the chain mail belt cinching her emerald dress tight. Clothes. She was wearing clothes. And, of course, she looked as good in them as she did out of them. The fabric was the exact color of her eyes. "That was the purpose of last night's debacle, was it not?"

"Yes."

She tapped one toe made viciously sharp by her glittering pumps. "And your mission was unsuccessful, correct?"

"Yes."

Tired of waiting for me to make the connection, she shrugged. "Then I don't see the issue."

Woozy. I was getting woozy. So woozy.

I told myself it was the height, but I knew it was memory warping the scene before me, twisting it into a nightmare tableau where vampire guards might storm the room and haul me before the Master at the slightest provocation.

"I'd heard you were broken." She dismissed the others with a wave. "I suppose even rumor mills are bound to churn out the truth now and again."

"I'm not broken." Catwoman wasn't snatching a morsel of progress from me. "I'm...mending."

"Prove it." She trailed a fingertip down the sleeves of the shirts on the rack nearest her, showcasing the department store she had brought to me. "Either you wear your past, or it wears you."

A sick certainty knotted my gut. "You know."

About Lena. About the clothes. About polishing me until I shined.

"Linus was right about me." Her plump lips smashed together. "I am a liar." She picked invisible lint from her gown. "Although I wasn't lying when I said I can pluck your worst fears from your head."

Meaning she had been taunting me with the naked-woman routine, but this... This was designed to hurt. "That's comforting."

"Believe it or not, I was trying to behave since you'll be gone in a couple of days." Her tone promised she would never see me again, and it made me question what Linus had told her about his long-term plans. "You're not worth upsetting my applecart over."

Again, I wondered what role she filled in his household, and again I reminded myself it was none of my business. "So, what's all this about then?"

"Why go to the shops," she said, smirking, "when we can bring the shops to you?"

"You don't get it." I sat down before toppling face-first over the edge. "Part of the fun—okay, actually *all* of the fun—was the experience of going out with my friend." Buying the clothes was necessity. Goofing off with Neely would have been the only highlight of the experience. "He's got an eye for this kind of thing, and I haven't seen him much lately. This trip was going to be an apology for being a lame friend."

"Your human is unavailable." She clipped each syllable shorter than Boaz kept his hair on the sides. "That doesn't change the fact you need clothes. I saw what you brought with you when I located your pajamas. Do you really want to step foot on Strophalos soil dressed in rags?"

"Jeans and T-shirts aren't rags," I grumbled, ignoring how many holes frayed each of mine.

"Linus has a reputation to uphold." Her nose wrinkled. "For that matter, so do you. Do you want people to associate the Woolworth name with grunge rockers from the nineties?"

"No?"

"I've wasted enough of my time on this." She tipped up her chin. "I'll be back in an hour, and we'll talk lunch. Make sure you've picked out at least a dozen outfits. It's not much, but it's a start."

"A dozen? Outfits?" That was like—I did quick math in my head —thirty-six or more individual pieces. "I don't know what to choose. You've seen what I wear."

A calculating smile curved her pouty lips. "That's why I pre-coordinated each piece here. You cannot go wrong. The palette is traditional. Whites, grays, blacks, and reds. These are the colors your adoptive mother wore, the shades associated with your family and your station."

Surprise left me speechless. This was...a kindness. Meiko didn't do kind.

The odds of her suffocating me in my sleep jumped by twenty-five percent.

"I'll do your hair and makeup," she informed me. "Fashion is armor where you're going."

The sentiment was visceral in its accuracy and yet... "Why are you doing this?"

"The sooner you accomplish your goals, the sooner you'll go home."

"He's coming back to Savannah with me." The taunt popped right out of my mouth without permission.

"This is his home," she purred. "He belongs here, with me." Her smile sharpened. "You'll break his heart. You're already half in love with someone else, and when you crush him, he'll finally understand you don't care about him. Don't you get it?" She laughed, all sly venom. "I'm helping me, not you. He needs to let go of this fantasy of you. Make your choice, and put him out of his misery. You might not love him, but surely you care enough to want what's best for him?"

"Linus doesn't care about me that way," I said, hearing my own uncertainty.

"You saw his office." A grimness tightened her eyes as she plucked her keycard from her cleavage. "You know the truth. Run from it if you like, deny it if you must, but remember this: There's nothing wrong with lying until you start telling them to yourself."

The door clicked shut on her heels, and I was left alone with a loft full of clothes and the budding certainty I might not have been the only one nursing a teenage crush.

Meiko might be a liar, but her hurt over his rejection rang all too true.

PARTLY TO SPITE MEIKO, and partly to cut myself some slack since I had no idea what I was doing without Neely, I chose two. Five pieces of clothing total. Three baubles. Plus, one pair of shoes—flats— guaranteed to earn me a lip curl when she spotted me wearing them.

One of the most valuable lessons I learned from being a Haint, besides breathing was optional, was comfortable shoes trumped beauty every single time. There was a reason we dressed in full Southern-belle regalia, hair and makeup just so, but wore coordinating sneakers instead of the heels that were period accurate.

When the door opened an hour later and Meiko sashayed in to survey the results of her ultimatum, I stood as tall as one could in black flats. The black slacks emphasized my thinness, but the ruffled front of the white blouse gave the illusion of cleavage. A strand of red glass beads hung around my throat, and I paired it with a matching bracelet at my wrist. The coordinating jacket, also black, hung over the back of a chair, the red embroidery on the lapels peeking out just a touch. Makeup wasn't happening, I would end up looking like a runaway clown if I applied it myself, but I had put a little effort into my hair.

After pulling the frizzy mass into a ponytail and deciding that wouldn't do, I sacrificed a sock to the cause. I trimmed off its toe and scrunched it down until it formed a donut. From there, all I had to do was thread my hair through the hole, tuck as I rolled it down against my scalp, then secure the sleek bun with bobby pins. Not too shabby.

"You look...decent." Meiko prowled a circle around me. "Where are your other selections?"

"This and that," I said, indicating my second outfit, "are all I want from you."

"It's your money." She twitched an elegant shoulder. "What do I care how you spend it?"

"Wait—my money?" Nails bit into my palms when I formed fists at my side. "How do you figure?"

"I used the debit card from your purse when I called in the order." Smugness lent her beautiful face a cruel edge. "All of this is yours. Keep it, wear it, or burn it. I couldn't care less what you do."

While I didn't mind paying for my clothes, I had no intention of stuffing a closet full of pieces handpicked for me by her.

"This is what we're going to do," I told her, slow and polite. "You're going to return everything but what I'm wearing and the one other outfit I showed you." Her lip peeled over her teeth, but I kept going. "Anything that's nonreturnable will be tallied and billed to you. Not Linus. You."

"You can't be serious." She fisted the sleeve of the nearest garment. "Have you seen the price tags on these pieces?"

"Oh, I'm sure they were the most expensive clothes you could have delivered on short notice. Just another way to stick it to me. Don't worry, I get it. But here's the thing. The money you spent? It's mine. It's not yours. I'm not Linus. I won't allow you to play with me or my things, and I won't let you spend my money as if it's yours when I've bled and grieved and almost died to earn it."

Meiko sharpened her scowl into claws she raked over me. "I was wrong about you."

In a fit of pique, she shrank into her cat form and stalked off without finishing her thought. No doubt she hoped to leave me in suspense, but I didn't care about her opinion of me. Not before this moment, and certainly not after it.

But I did wish we had put off this confrontation until after lunch.

Most days I did a good job of acting like the old Grier. Enough so people didn't stare, didn't ask what was wrong. But new Grier lurked beneath that thin skin, and she wasn't someone I wanted off her leash.

Anger simmered in me, even when I laughed, even when I smiled, and one day it would devour me from the inside. What emerged would be the truth of what was left after Maud, after Atramentous, after Volkov. That Grier would make a merciless Dame Woolworth, a matriarch the Grande Dame would adore, and that more than anything had me tucking her deeper and deeper within me until I could act like everything was okay again.

While I waited on Linus, I texted Amelie a heads-up about Meiko's prank. As my financial advisor, I didn't want her to have a heart attack when the bill arrived.

Guilt tempted me to fess up about the accident while we chatted, but she would be livid I hadn't confessed sooner, and I was too tired to face a lecture. A suffocating weight pressed on me every time she explained how much losing me had cost her, and her brother. When I was feeling uncharitable, I asked myself if they realized how much losing the old Grier had cost *me*. But mostly I was just lonely for the simplicities of that life.

The front door opened, and Linus entered wearing charcoal slacks with a matching jacket over a white button-down shirt. His dark auburn hair had been combed back and gathered at his nape, and he had slung a black leather messenger bag across his shoulders that matched his shoes. His glasses completed the look, and I had to shake my head. "I see why Meiko is such a smitten kitten."

"Hmm?" Linus wasn't listening. He was staring. At me.

Not about to renew the sentiment while he was looking at me that way, I said, "We're having lovely weather."

"Are we?" He sounded distant, thoughtful. "I haven't noticed."

"You're giving me a complex, here." I snagged my jacket off the back of the chair and shrugged it on as insulation between me and his intense focus. "Nothing's hanging out? All my buttons fastened?"

"Apologies." Linus wet his lips and tore his gaze from me. "This isn't what I expected."

"I wanted to look nice." I smoothed my hands down my pants. "Now I see I was right to worry. You're all GQ over there. Do you really teach dressed like that? Do you have a janitor assigned to your room just to mop up the drool between classes?"

"Thank you." Swaths of red highlighted his cheeks. "I think."

"Are you ready to go?" I grabbed my purse, checking for my debit card and room key before tucking my phone inside and zipping it closed. "We're still visiting Neely first?"

"Yes." He cleared his throat. "I just spoke to Dr. Schmidt. We're cleared for a half-hour visitation window, but that's all they're allowing for nonfamily members."

Eager to go, I hustled out into the hall to wait while he locked up behind us. "Where did you run off to?"

"I rescheduled the meeting I missed last night for dusk." He guided me onto the elevator. "The timing allowed me to add the identities of the vampires who drove you off the road into our database."

As the numbers counted down, I couldn't suppress a shiver. A database full of vampires who were out to get me. Not exactly how I imagined reemerging into Society. "Did you learn anything new?"

"I reviewed the security footage." He shoved his hands into his pockets. "They left within minutes of you exiting the building. We can only assume they made calls in the privacy of their room then followed the orders they were given."

"Have you located their cells?" Cellphones were modern-day diaries, after all.

"They were recovered along with the bodies. They got greedy, sloppy. Hopefully, they left clues behind in their apartment for us to find." Linus hadn't been gone long enough to perform a search, so he must employ a team. Though, I suppose even Batman had his Alfred Pennyworth. "I doubt the Master would allow anyone so reckless in his inner circle, so odds are good we won't unearth anything of consequence."

"Have they lived here long?" I grimaced with the knowledge there were likely others whispering my secrets, camouflaged by the sheer volume of residents. "Did you recognize them?"

"They had been living here for two months." He adjusted the strap on his bag. "I never met them. I'm sure there are others, but good luck to us finding them until they make a move. There are too many residents, too many variables."

"The Faraday ought to introduce tougher screening protocols for vampire applicants." As soon as the words left my mouth, I regretted them. "Scratch that. Discrimination is not the answer." There were thousands of law-abiding vampires across the country who had done nothing to deserve yet another restriction on their undead lives. The whole community shouldn't be punished for the actions of a few, and certainly not on my behalf. "I'm just thinking out loud."

"We'll figure it out," he promised.

"*We* as in you and me or *we* as in you and...?" I was genuinely curious. "Don't potentates work alone?"

"We do, in the field." A slight hesitation tipped me off as to how rare it was for him to talk about this aspect of his life with others. "I have a team that helps me. I couldn't do it all alone. They're all safe behind their desks."

Interesting. "Will I meet them at Strophalos?"

"They're kept anonymous for their own protection." Regret darkened his eyes. "It's dangerous working for a potentate. It's twice as dangerous working for the Grande Dame's son."

I saw where this was headed. "Three times as dangerous when he's friends with me, huh?"

"Yes," he agreed, lightening the sting with a faint smile.

The lobby was empty when we hit bottom, and I grabbed him by the wrist to haul him outside before Hubert could insert his nose in the crease between Linus's butt cheeks. Rather proud of our escape, I grinned brightly until Hood planted himself in my path.

Cletus drifted down, his tattered cloak tickling my elbow.

"Evening, Ms. Woolworth." Hood skimmed me from head to foot, eyes golden. "You're looking much better than the last time I saw you." His nostrils flared. "You were covered in blood, and not all of it yours."

"All thanks to Nurse Linus." Noticing I still held his wrist, I released him. "He patched me up as good as new."

"Glad to hear it." He inclined his head toward Linus, almost in gratitude. "Enjoy your evening, folks."

"You too," I replied awkwardly, like standing guard was the thrill of a lifetime.

Within seconds, our ride pulled up to the curb. Ignoring us, Tony kept chugging his energy drink.

Behind us, Hood chuckled darkly. I turned and saw him lifting his phone to capture Scion Lawson, the Potentate of Atlanta, climbing into a grungy van driven by a human dressed in days-old pajamas. I narrowed my eyes at him in warning, which tickled him all the more.

"Do you remember what I told you about the watchmen?" Linus asked once the van merged with traffic.

How could I forget? "That they eat people who annoy them."

"And?" His lecturing voice was in the on position. "Anything else come to mind?"

"Hood's the one who keeps initiating conversations. It's not my fault he's gabby around me. Which is worse? Responding to him or ignoring him? I don't want him to eat me for being rude."

"Honestly, I'm not sure." The city beyond the window caught his eye, and he noted each lamppost and street sign like it would be a long time before he saw them again. "The gwyllgi don't chat up residents. They barely condescend to acknowledge me. I'm not sure why Hood is fascinated with you."

"Maybe he's just curious." Though not as intrigued as I was about his true nature. *Gwyllgi* sounded Welsh—fae—but that was impossible. "You've never brought anyone home, right? He might wonder what earned me the invite."

"Perhaps," he conceded, though he didn't sound convinced.

The drive to Gershwin Memorial was loud and...fragrant. Our driver grew more pungent by the day, his natural cologne a mingling of armpit funk, unwashed feet, and pepperoni. Try as I might, I couldn't think of a polite way to point out there were free bars of soap and mini shampoo bottles in his hotel room, and that he maybe ought to think about using them.

Linus didn't complain, though he did breathe through his mouth. I patted his thigh in solidarity.

After missing the turn three times, Tony dropped us off under the portico. From there, Linus led the way straight up to the third floor to a room marked *Private*. He knocked once, and Cruz emerged, looking like someone had taken a sock full of quarters to him. His brows crashed down when he spotted me, and the bruises under his reddened eyes made my gut twist.

Careful not to make a sound, he eased the door shut behind him to bar the entrance. "What are you doing here?"

This was not going to end well. "I came to see Neely."

Cruz measured me and found me wanting, more so than usual. "You almost got him killed last night."

Hating he was right, I still fumbled for an excuse. "Another car—"

"I saw the footage from the traffic cameras." Much like Linus, Cruz must have contacts all over the city. "The driver of the other car pulled out of the parking deck at your building within thirteen minutes of you leaving. She was gunning for Neely from the moment he picked you up at the MARTA stop. That tells me what happened wasn't an accident. She intended to do harm." A quiver in his jaw warned me not to push him. "Who could her intended target have been?" He pretended to consider it might be Neely for, oh, all of about zero seconds. "My husband, who has never so much as jaywalked in his life, or *you*?"

Cold sweat beaded down the small of my back. "What are you saying?"

Neely had no idea who or what I was beyond his struggling-to-get-by friend Grier, but Cruz...

According to Linus, Cruz worked for the Society, managing their human interests, whatever that meant. Over the course of three years, he was smart enough to have figured out there was something hinky about the work he was doing and his wealthy clients. Intelligent enough not to question a good thing as long as the work he did was legal and the deposits arrived like clockwork. But he must have wondered, maybe even fit pieces of the big picture together.

How much did he know? Or think he knew? And how much protection would his job title afford him?

"The accident wasn't Grier's fault." Linus waded in, playing peacekeeper. "She's a victim here too."

Victim. The word made me flinch. I hated it more than all others combined.

Cruz noticed me recoiling. From the darkening of his scowl, I bet he had mistaken the reaction for guilt.

"The auto claims adjuster sent me pictures of the car. I saw the blood in the passenger's seat. *Your* seat." His knuckles popped at his sides under the strain of his fists. "Yet you weren't admitted. You walked away while Neely—" His voice broke, jagged edges that cut me. "He's..."

The urge to reach out and soothe him almost overcame my common sense. "He will recover."

"Neely told me about your boyfriend. The one who knocked you around. That stunt with the detective in Savannah—Russo—was that about this?" When I didn't answer, his eyes brightened, a predator scenting blood. "Whatever hot mess you got yourself tangled up in almost cost Neely his life. Stay away from him."

Throat tight, I forced myself to swallow. "You're telling me what Volkov did to me was my fault?"

"Fuck." Cruz rubbed his face while he breathed in deep. "I didn't mean that. I'm not victim blaming."

Linus cupped my elbow and pitched his voice low. "We're drawing too much attention."

Nurses and visitors alike stood frozen in the hall, watching the fireworks, while a matched set of security guards approached us slowly, careful not to alarm the patients.

"Tell Neely I stopped by," I rasped as Linus guided me away. "That I hope he's feeling better."

He didn't agree to pass on the well-wishes, but he didn't tell me to jump off a cliff either. So, progress?

Linus escorted me past the security guards, who gave me the stink eye, to the bank of elevators, trading his grip on my elbow for an arm around my waist when my knees wobbled. "None of this is your fault."

"Yes, it is." Leaning into him, I wiped tears from my cheeks. "Neely is in this hospital because of me."

"Neely is in this hospital because vampires knocked his car off an overpass with you both inside it." Linus rested his cool cheek against my temple as we rode down. "Your quick thinking saved his life, and yours."

"This is just the beginning." The wider the Master cast his net, the more factions learned about me. "It's only going to get worse." A shuddering exhale rounded my shoulders. "Cruz is right. I should stay away."

"Let Neely decide." Linus ushered me through the quiet lobby out into the night air. "You're his friend, it's his choice." The featherlight brush of his lips across my temple registered as he withdrew. "Neely is tougher than Cruz gives him credit for, and his husband is about to be reminded of that fact."

"I wish I had never come to Atlanta," I said softly, and Linus flinched as if I had struck him.

"Neely—"

"It's more than that." I withdrew from him, unable to stomach hurting him again. "I've felt upside down since I arrived, like you brought me to an alternate universe instead of North Georgia."

Maybe this trip had been a mistake. Maybe I had needed more time to adjust to my freedom before trading the comforts of home for an adventure in the city. Or maybe I had grown too used to enclosed spaces and silence to appreciate the noise that came from wading into a sea of humanity. Inhumanity, in the case of the Faraday.

Neither of us spoke after that, and I decided I was wrong about silence.

I hated it, hated how unspoken words hung suspended between us, hated how he angled his body away from mine. Most of all, I hated the mask he wore to hide whatever he was thinking instead of sharing his concerns with me.

The long, dull drive had me ready to comment on the weather to get him talking again.

"Perhaps this will make the trip worthwhile," he said as he opened the door on a world of possibilities built from brick and writhing with magic. "Welcome to Strophalos University."

THIRTEEN

Towering red brick buildings, each laid out in a square and open to a central courtyard, cut an imposing figure on the manicured lawn. A clock tower rose from the centermost building, its face engraved with archaic sigils rather than numbers, and magic pulsed in subtle waves as the second hand chased its tail.

Gardens so lush they might have inspired Maud when she designed the ones at Woolworth House had me gaping after them. Some of those flowers... I had never seen the like. I didn't have species, let alone names, to call them. I took a step toward the enclosure, only to be halted by Linus's hand on my elbow.

"Reardon is waiting for us," he reminded me. "I promise you the full tour tomorrow."

While I watched, he slid another mask into place, this one shades of the quiet academic I had come to know from my nightly lessons mixed with the rigidity of Scion Lawson. He was approachable, though you might think twice before you worked up the nerve. The flatness of his full lips implied you better have a darn good reason for talking to him, and an even better excuse for believing your time was worth a second of his.

The posture was looser, more slouched, but not normal. Comfortable, but not himself. The clothes were nicer than what he wore in Savannah except when visiting the Lyceum, but not so ostentatious you marveled that a professor would dress so well. The glasses and the crossbody bag made him more relatable, but I saw them as camouflage. Props meant to help him blend in with the faculty. Accessories that screamed *scholar* and hid the predator lurking beneath his polished exterior.

After Fredrick and Ernestine, there could be no doubt lethal magic prowled beneath his skin.

With Linus as my escort, we strolled down one of the many winding paths landscaped within an inch of its life. Guys stood taller as we approached while girls tittered behind their hands after we passed. Linus appeared oblivious to it all, but I couldn't read him with that mask on, and eventually I stopped trying.

"Reardon's office is this way." Linus indicated a domed building on the outer fringes of the campus. "Are you sure you want to go through with this after last night?"

"I'm a necromancer." I exhaled through my parted lips. "I can't avoid vampires forever."

"No," he agreed softly, sounding more like himself. "But you can avoid this one."

"I need answers." And I would face a vampire to get them. "Amelie can't live bound to me forever."

Settling my concern on her made it easier to forget my own life hung in the balance.

"We won't know for certain if the effects are permanent until she's free to leave your house." He let me consider that before shaking his head. "She might be fine away from Woolly, out of the protective circle of the wards. Or she might remain susceptible to your magical influence. There are too many variables."

Leave it to Linus to force me to voice what I was already thinking. Dreading, more like it.

"This affects my ability to practice—" to *live*, "—and I want that."

The Grande Dame might have plans for me, but I was starting to imagine a future for myself too.

All I had to do was survive. So pretty much business as usual for me.

"I understand." Linus gentled his voice as he ushered me in the building.

A frazzled man greeted us in the hallway with a chewed pencil tucked behind one ear, and the *zing* of otherness skated over my skin. His shaggy hair, a muddy brown color, hung in his green eyes. His tan corduroy pants were tailored, and so was his short-sleeved shirt. The white button-down was wrinkled beneath his chocolate and mocha striped sweater vest. When he spotted Linus, he grinned from ear to ear, but the tips of his fangs lent his expression an edge.

The aggressive display had me bumping into Linus to put distance between Reardon and me.

"The fangs?" Reardon mused, raising a lip to tap one. "It's rude to flash them at visitors, I know, but I wasn't made in a controlled setting. I have..." he gave it some consideration, "...quirks."

"I should have warned you." Linus rested his hands on my shoulders, his cold a soothing presence at my back. "My apologies."

"A heads-up might have been nice," I allowed then addressed Reardon. "It's a pleasure to meet you."

"My young friend tells me he has a puzzle for us to solve." He focused on where Linus touched me until the latter removed his hands. "Are you assisting him in this matter?"

Relegated to the role of assistant once again. "Yes."

Reardon grinned at Linus, his smile no less alarming for his assurances. "Does Meiko know?"

"Oh, yes." I beat Linus to the punch. "She's done everything short of scent marking him since I arrived." I rolled a shoulder. "I also suspect she tried suffocating me in my sleep."

There was no other reason to wake with all fifteen or so pounds of her pressing down on my chest.

"You've met her?" His shock conveyed a few things. That he

knew Linus kept Meiko as a pet, and that if I had met her, then I had been to Linus's loft too. On second thought, I should have kept my mouth shut. "Not many have had the pleasure."

"Yesss." I drew out the word, hoping Linus would rescue me from myself. No such luck. He was too busy pinching his lips together to avoid laughing. "Hey, that woman has claws, and I'm not talking about an acrylic manicure. I'm afraid to close my eyes to sleep around her."

This tidbit succeeded in digging my hole deeper. Reardon now understood not only had I seen the apartment, but I was staying there.

"She blushes," Reardon mused. "How lovely." He smirked at Linus, who was starting to look a bit pink himself, thanks to his pale complexion. "What a handsome pair you make."

"We aren't a pair," I informed him, then immediately regretted my decision when his smile revealed fangs.

"The reason we're here—" Linus casually nudged me behind him, "—is a delicate matter." He reached in his bag and withdrew a white metal box with KEEP REFRIGERATED written down the side. "Here is the sample we discussed. I gave my word that it wouldn't leave my sight and that we would destroy all traces after you conduct your tests."

"Interesting," he said, his gaze fixed on me, almost like he could smell the magic in my blood. But that was silly. Paranoid. He hadn't opened the container. There was no basis for comparison. It wasn't even my blood. And yet...

Clearly, he scented something on me. Perhaps he was old enough to have known one of my kind, or clever enough to grasp I wasn't what I appeared to be. Either way, I didn't want him drawing any connections between me and what he might discover.

"I need to use the ladies'." I clutched the strap on my bag. "Can you point me in the right direction?"

Reardon indicated the hall adjacent to this one, and I kept my stride casual until I rounded the corner. Maybe this wasn't such a great plan. I had a theory about how to conceal my scent, but it might not work, and it might still land me in hot water later.

Once inside the restroom, I turned the lock and reached in my bag for the modified pen. I had no reason to hope it would work, but I closed my eyes and focused on the idea of a sigil that might do the trick, letting my hand follow the path mapped by instinct.

With that done, I lifted my wrist to my nose and inhaled. I smelled nothing. Perfume wasn't my thing, so it might be best if I tried the one spot where artificial fragrance clung. Yes, my armpits. I sniffed them. Not one single whiff of the aerosol I'd sprayed on earlier lingered. The sigil had masked my scent entirely.

Triumph welled in me, and I allowed myself a short happy dance before capping the pen and returning to Reardon's office. The man himself greeted me at the door, and I caught him leaning in to sniff me as I walked past him to join Linus.

The frown tipping his welcoming expression toward annoyance made the gamble all the better.

So maybe I would never have moves like Taz or encyclopedic knowledge like Linus, but I had one thing in common with Maud I never expected to claim. I was an innovator. An accidental innovator, sure, but an innovator nonetheless.

A pang of sadness pierced my heart that Maud wasn't here to see what I had done, what I had the potential to do, but she must have suspected. It was thanks to her I was in this position in the first place.

"Forgive us," Reardon said. "We got started without you."

The box lay open on the counter, and a vial of bright blood had been slotted into a sleek machine that whirred happily at having been fed.

"Linus failed to introduce us." He pulled out a stool and nudged it closer to me. "I'm Reardon McAllister."

"I'm Grier Woolworth." I offered him my hand, which he flipped over in an elegant move, exposing my wrist to the ceiling. He bowed low and pressed his lips against the network of veins, and I saw his chest expand as he inhaled. "Linus and I grew up together."

There was no harm in telling him that since my last name would ring all kinds of bells for him.

Chair legs scraped behind us as Linus rose. "Reardon."

"Fascinating," he murmured. "May I continue to blame my poor manners on being shoddily made?"

"You're old enough to know better," I answered, "and smart enough to know how dangerous it is to provoke a necromancer."

"An assistant." He fed my title back to me, and it took every ounce of strength I had to keep from flinching. "You're not quite so deadly as my friend here."

"I wouldn't be so sure." Linus extracted me from Reardon's grasp and urged me onto my stool, drawing his beside mine. "I wouldn't provoke Grier if I were you."

"Oh?" Interest sparkled in the vampire's eyes. "Why is that?"

Squirming on my seat, I pretended I was getting comfortable, but what I was really doing was wondering why the heck Linus would dangle that kind of carrot in front of a vampire.

"She's got a temper." He traced the perfect line of his nose. "She broke this once."

Laughter exploded out of Reardon, and the tension in the room shattered around us.

"I confess, I've wanted to do that a time or two myself." At Linus's arched brow, he explained, "Linus is so very good at everything. He makes for an annoying friend." His smile turned wicked. "Especially when I'm trying to impress a pretty girl."

A flush brightened my cheeks. I would have scrubbed them to cease the tingling, but it would have made things worse. Nothing like blushing to draw a vampire's attention to the fact you're a walking, talking blood bag.

"Ah, there she goes again," Reardon murmured. "You have stumbled across my greatest weakness."

Referring to my earlier thoughts, I blurted, "Food?"

Laughter pelted the air once again, and he couldn't seem to wipe the smile off his face. "Humility."

"Reardon," Linus warned. "Perhaps we should return to the matter at hand."

Tearing his gaze from my glowing face, Reardon resumed his position at the counter across from Linus. Using a dropper, he began several tests on Amelie's blood that left me puzzled as to their purpose.

Heads bent over their workstation, the pair discussed what Linus hoped to learn and the sample's origin.

Past that point, they might as well have been speaking a foreign language. I had no clue what they were discussing, only picking up one familiar word in ten. Chromosome. Platelets. Antibodies. Thankfully, science appeared to be Reardon's true love, and he forgot all about me once she took center stage.

I didn't mean to doze, but that didn't stop me from jerking awake seconds before the dream took me.

One minute, I was resting my forehead on my stacked arms. The next, I was catapulting backwards from my stool, tripping over its legs, and falling on the tile hard enough to bruise my tailbone.

Not even the fear twisting cold knots in my gut over what they might find had kept me from dozing.

Fed a steady diet of terror, I was too full to make room for more.

I sprawled there, panting and mortified, while I caught my breath.

Reardon knelt at my side as the scream died in my throat. "Are you hurt?"

"Only my pride, and there wasn't much of that left." I winced up at Linus, whose eyes had bled full black, and only a fool would have refused the hand he offered me. "I'm good, really." I flashed them a weak smile that lingered on Linus, on where he still held my hand. "Serves me right for falling asleep in class."

Linus smiled at the joke, faintly, but puckers gathered across Reardon's forehead.

"There's a coffee shop on campus. No hot chocolate, but their mocha lattes are popular. Cletus can show you the way." Linus released my fingers after a beat too long. "Why don't you go get a drink and stretch your legs?"

"I'll take you up on that." I resisted the urge to massage my aching tailbone. "You guys want anything?"

"My usual," Linus said with a straight face.

"I'll take a tall black coffee." Grinning, Reardon reached for his wallet. "I like the smell."

"My treat," I assured him. "You guys enjoy your science while I'm gone."

Outside, I chose a direction and started walking. At a fork in the path, I stopped to read a sign that might have been helpful had I known Lindbergh Hall from Heinemann Hall. Just as I was wondering where my promised guide had gone, Cletus joined me with a moaned apology for his lateness. Or so I imagined.

"Take me to your coffee shop," I beseeched the wraith.

With a clack of his nails, Cletus billowed in the opposite direction from the one I had been heading.

Busy admiring a stone amphitheater sunk into the earth, I wandered off the path. A small gathering sat on the curved seats that functioned as steps to reach the floor, and each took turns reading from a book of poetry they passed around and around.

Distracted by their laughter, I almost missed the long shadow prowling across the quad in my direction.

Not everyone is out to get you. Not every shadow is nefarious.

Just to be on the safe side, I let Cletus usher me back on track with a gnarled hand on my shoulder.

Ignoring the twitching skin beneath my tattoo, I hit the coffee shop, where a flirty barista who knew how to earn a tip filled my order. Still smiling at her outrageousness and the stack of phone numbers jotted on receipts peeking from her skirt pocket, I experienced a pang on my way past the campus bookstore.

"Really, Cletus? You couldn't have told me that was there?" I glared into the whirling darkness where his face ought to be. "I could have picked up a shirt or a keychain, a *souvenir*. Now it's too late to browse."

A low moan I interpreted as an apology had me sighing. I could always come back tomorrow.

"Cheese and crackers," a high voice squeaked. "What is that thing doing loose?"

Glancing over my shoulder, I spotted a young man wearing the designer equivalent of my usual duds. Jeans, shirt, sneakers. His blond hair curled around his face in a mass of artful twists. His pink cheeks made him downright cherubic, and I wondered if many people asked to pinch them.

Clearly mothering a six-year-old ghost was having an effect on me.

"He's tame," I teased. "Don't worry. He won't bother you as long as you don't bother us."

"How can you be sure?" Squinting, the necromancer studied me. "You're not bonded. Who does he belong to?"

I blamed his curiosity on his panic and figured telling him would calm him. "Linus Lawson."

"Professor Lawson's back?" His eyes lit up like stars in a moonless sky before crashing to the earth in meteoric indignation. "He loaned you his wraith?"

The ease with which I chatted openly with this guy about Linus and his wraith drove home how foolish I had been to ignore the early-warning signs with Amelie. There was just too much history there, too much unhappiness. It had been easier to avoid the cracks in the façade of friendship than face what was happening. But there was nothing for it now, and this guy wasn't going anywhere until I answered his question, judging by the look on his face.

"Yes, he did." I lifted the tray of coffees. "Nice bumping into you and all, but I need to get back."

"I'll come with." He grabbed for the tray and frowned when I didn't hand it over, but I didn't want to explain about the empty cup when he tried passing out the drinks. "Where are you headed?"

"To Professor Reardon's office."

"Have you had him yet?" The guy groaned as he fell in step with me. "He's a GPA torpedo."

"I'm not a student here." I saw no reason to lie. "Though I did fall asleep listening to him bat theories around with Linus. I fell off my stool and busted my butt, the whole nine yards."

"You came here *with* Professor Lawson?" Any rounder and his eyes might pop from overinflation. "As in, you're *with* him?"

"Well, thanks for chaperoning me." Ignoring his question, I picked up my pace to a near sprint until the squat building came into view. "I've got it from here."

"Let me get the door." He rushed ahead and held it open. Darting in on my heels, he jogged past me on his way to Reardon's room. With an apologetic look flung over his shoulder, he hammered on the wood. "Your hands are full."

"Thanks." This kid had a serious case of hero worship. He was giving me flashbacks of me at my most obnoxious, when I would have done anything to catch Boaz's eye. "You've done your good deed for the day." I smiled tightly. "You can get back to what you were doing before Cletus and I derailed you."

"Cletus?" The guy divided his attention between me and the door. He was worse than a dog pawing to get out when he had to pee. His focus snapped into place when Linus appeared on the threshold. "Professor Lawson."

Arching a brow, he glanced between the two of us. "Do I know—?"

Linus didn't finish asking before the guy swung out his arm, metal glinting, and sliced a thin line through the shirt over his chest. Stunned by the sudden violence, Reardon froze. Or perhaps it was the scent of fresh blood that immobilized him.

Determined not to freeze too, I pried out the tall black coffee, flipped off the lid, and flung it at the back of the guy's head. He screamed, twisting to look at me, but didn't lift a hand to stop me as I splashed my mocha latte in his face.

Arm swinging in protective arcs, he kept Linus back while he dried his eyes on his sleeve, but his face was a mottled red, and his vision was shot. He cranked his head back toward the doorway, squinting to relocate his target, in time to intercept Linus's fist across his jaw. He took the hit and crumpled to his knees.

Tossing the tray and empty cup aside, I used Taz's favorite move and kicked him so hard in the ribs, I felt the reverberation through my aching tailbone. He slumped onto the floor, hand fisting the knife, fingers twitching on the handle.

I took a healthy step back, not out of fear, but to escape the seething fury in Linus's limpid, black eyes.

Strolling forward, he stepped on the guy's wrist, applying pressure until his fingers flexed open, and the knife clattered onto the tiles. He kicked it away before squatting near his head, forearms resting on his thighs. Black wisps pooled around his ankles, the hem of a cloak that climbed up his shoulders in a creeping fog that had the man babbling for mercy.

The wasteland of eternity shadowed his eyes. There was no mercy to be found there.

With the attacker subdued, Reardon turned his back on us and focused on deep-breathing exercises that did nothing to bolster my confidence in his ability to not eat me.

"Who sent you?" Linus demanded, his voice as hollow as a tomb and just as resonant. "Who escorted you onto school grounds?"

Trembling, looking anywhere but at Linus, at that living fabric, the guy kept his mouth shut.

"Are you willing to die for your secrets?" His tone hardened. "Who. Sent. You?"

"Linus," I whispered, unsure what I was asking, if I was asking anything at all.

"The punishment for treason against your potentate is death." He cradled the man's skull in his elegant hands, the ones capable of producing such beautiful art. "Speak now, or your sentence will be carried out where you lie."

Tears pricked the corners of his eyes, but he locked his jaw.

"Justice is served," Linus murmured. "May the Goddess grant you peace."

The crack of vertebrae splintering was deafening, and my ears kept ringing long after Linus lowered the man's head gently back onto the floor.

This violent side of him I had, on an intellectual level, known existed. A new mask. One I had yet to see how well it fit. He was the champion of a city, the Society's own law made flesh. Enforcing those rules would come at a cost. What I hadn't expected was the cold light that gilded him the moment he decided the man's fate or the indifference that smoothed his features as the spark went out of his eyes.

While Linus arranged for a cleanup crew, a service I shuddered to realize must be on most necromancers' and vampires' speed dials, I sank to the floor in the farthest corner of the room. Knees tucked against my chest, I had the phone in my hand before making a conscious decision to call Boaz.

"Hey, Squirt."

"Hey back," I rasped. "You got a minute?"

"Sure," he said, distracted. "What's up?"

"I'm having a bad day," I confessed. "Two bad days, actually."

"You okay?" A hint of his usual warmth surfaced. "Where are you?"

"It doesn't matter." I rested my chin on my knees. "Where are you?"

"My location is classified."

"Yeah." I exhaled, long and slow. "Yeah."

"Talk to me, Grier."

The brutal mask of executioner Linus had slipped on moments earlier shook me, and I couldn't pinpoint why, but that coldness had seeped into me. "Have you ever killed anyone?"

"Yes."

"A lot of someones?"

"Yes."

"During your army days?"

"And as an Elite, yes."

As the tension in me uncoiled, I realized this was what I had wanted to hear. Proof that black and white were myths. That only shades of gray existed. That good people did bad things, accepted malignant stains on their souls, when all other choices were stripped from them.

Linus was as much a soldier as Boaz, even if his battlefield was defined by city limits, and I had no right to judge either of them unless I picked up arms—made those same life-or-death decisions —too.

"You sound off." A throaty horn that reminded me of a container ship blew in the distance. "Where's Linus?"

"He's disposing of a body."

"Not funny." A car door slammed, cutting off the background noise. "I'm serious."

Tears threatened. "So am I."

"Grier?" Linus called, and I sniffled before lifting my head. "Are you ready to go?"

Knuckles white, I clutched the phone like a lifeline. "We're leaving. Call me later?"

"Sure."

I signed off without saying goodbye, not seeing the point when I could hear the lie in his voice.

"Amelie?" Linus asked after I got to my feet. "How's Woolly doing?"

"Boaz," I corrected him.

The cleaners, whoever they were, worked fast. No signs of a life snuffed out marred the tiles. The corpse had been moved, and the floor glistened where it had been polished to a high shine.

Reardon, the coward, had escaped at some point. Vampires his age, made poorly or not, ought to be in control of their bloodlust. That he wasn't had me questioning if this was his refuge or his prison.

"Ah." Linus locked the office behind us then turned and painted a series of warding sigils on the door.

My jacket, splashed with coffee, bothered me, so I tossed it in the trash. "We're done?"

"You are." He paid the crumpled jacket more attention now than while I was wearing it. "Are you all right?"

"You beheaded two vampires last night." I hadn't meant to blurt it out quite like that, but there you go. "You executed a necromancer tonight." I unclasped my red accessories and ditched those too. "Your life here isn't how I pictured it. You—as this person—is not how I imagined. I'm not sure what to think."

"I warned you." Disappointment rang out loud and clear. "I explained there was a cost."

"You did." I owed him that much. "But this..." the killing, the darkness, "...it's not you."

"How can you be sure?" His honest curiosity made my heart ache. "Maybe this is who I am."

"No." I refused to believe this was the core of his apple. "This is a thing that you do, not who you are."

"The city is unsettled." The abrupt change in conversation left me no wiggle room to get us back on topic. "Part of that is due to my absence."

"And the rest is my presence."

"Yes." He didn't sugarcoat the truth. "Whispers about a goddess-touched necromancer are spreading faster than the Society can contain the rumors."

The elegant neckline of my blouse might as well have been a noose. "I won't be locked in a cage."

Confinement made the most sense. It would be the next logical step once the streets became too dangerous for me to roam freely. Though Cletus negated that. Free wasn't free when you were watched and reported on every second you spent outside your house. Still, it was a pretty illusion.

"It won't come to that," he vowed, and I believed him.

Holding tight to that hope, I had to ask, "Why did he attack you and not me?"

Hindsight, as always, brought clarity. The shadow near the amphitheater. Goddess, I should have asked Cletus to investigate. Going for coffee had given the would-be assassin a few precious minutes to bump into me. But there had been no time to mention the incident to Linus. Everything had happened so fast.

"I've been asking myself the same thing. He isolated you. He could have taken you at any time. There was no reason to confront me. Unless he was afraid of the wraith. But it doesn't track that he wouldn't fear me more. And yet he did escort you to the classroom." Linus touched his chest, where blood stained the front of his shirt. "Incapacitating me appeared to be his top priority. Any designs he had on you were secondary."

The bull's-eye was still painted on my back, though. Not his. "He went out of his way not to harm me."

"I wish I had a better answer for you," he said, sliding a look at me, "but I don't know."

Unable to glance away, I couldn't hide the truth from either of us. "All these deaths are on my head."

Linus stopped in his tracks, and I paused at his side, glancing around the quad to see what he'd spotted that I hadn't, but he turned to me and framed my face between his cool palms.

"None of this is your fault." His thumbs stroked my cheeks, and I should have cringed away, the death still so fresh on his hands, but I couldn't move. His open expression, all masks removed, held me rapt. "I killed those people for the choices they made, the actions they took. Their blood is on my hands." As if realizing he meant it in the literal sense, he dropped them to his sides and left my face tingling. "The Society wants you seen as untouchable. For that to happen, an example must be made of those who try and fail to obtain you." His dark blue eyes held mine. "I'm happy to provide that example."

Heart crumbling around the edges, I linked my arm through his and led him to the parking lot in time to watch Tony cut off two cars and bump his passenger-side wheels on the curb. He raised his eyebrows and mouthed *what* before turning up his can of energy drink.

Linus and I didn't speak during the drive back to the Faraday, and I hoped the silence wasn't becoming a habit with us. He helped me out onto the curb, and I eased around him while he tipped the driver. I was making time toward the entrance when the spectacle unfolding in front of the building pulled me up short.

A frazzled man was being assaulted by one heck of a pissed-off woman. The pair blocked the front door, and Hood, who peeled from the shadows where he had been content to watch, seemed to notice this too.

"Take your domestic issues elsewhere," he growled. "You're blocking the entryway."

"He pays your salary," the woman sniped. "We can fight wherever we damn well please."

A warning rumble pumped through Hood's broad chest.

"Vi," the man soothed. "This isn't the time or the place. Let's go upstairs and talk."

"Upstairs?" She jabbed a finger toward one of the higher floors. "I saw that hussy napping on your bed. *Naked.* How could you? You better not have bought her that collar. Those were real emeralds, Ian."

Oh, goddess. There had to be more than one collared hussy in the building, right?

Surely Meiko didn't spend her days amusing herself by popping up in bed with Linus's neighbors.

Then again...

"Ah, excuse me." I hated to butt in when things had gotten so heated. "About the naked woman?"

That was as far as I got before the crazy lady whirled on me.

"Are you another of his girls?" Her fevered gaze swept over me. "How many are there?"

"Move aside," Hood ordered, lumbering toward us. "Or I will clear her a path myself."

Reaching the end of her rope, the woman swiped out with her arm, claws shining on her fingertips.

Our proximity allowed me to knock her hand aside without Hood getting shredded in the process.

Taz would have been proud of my quick reflexes.

Gently, he ushered me out of his path until he loomed over the woman. "This is your final warning."

Sucking in a lungful of air, she screeched, *"Bite me."*

Magic washed up his legs in a red wave that splashed onto his shoulders, climbing until it tickled his jaw. When the viscous liquid drained away, Hood did too, melting into a muscular form that was half bull mastiff and half Komodo dragon. His rust-colored fur gave way to heavy scales in strategic spots. Needlelike teeth filled his mouth, and his bloodcurdling bay as he challenged her raised chills down my spine.

The man turned on his heel and ran faster than any necromancer had a right to move.

I took one step back but froze when Hood swung his blocky head my way, and I rasped, "Good boy?"

Snorting out what might have been a canid laugh, he resumed his hunt.

After knocking the shrieking woman onto the ground, he clamped his wide jaws on her thin shoulder and bit down until crimson stained his mouth. He slung her between his paws until she fainted from sheer terror. With a disgusted huff, he released her then padded over to me.

A cool presence materialized at my elbow, but Cletus made no move to intervene. I was hoping that was a good sign.

Out of the corner of my eye, I spotted Linus, but he too remained still. Tension lined his face, but he was absent his tattered cloak, telling me he hadn't hit panic mode yet.

Ignoring the wraith, Hood snuffled my palm where it rested

against my thigh until I lifted my hand. I gave his massive head a hesitant pat, and he licked me, smearing gore and drool from the wrist down to my fingertips.

"Oh, ick." I flung my hand. "Are you serious?"

Chuffing under his breath, he walked off wagging his tail, leaving the woman to bleed out on the sidewalk.

An ambulance pulled curbside within seconds, and Hubert exited the building in a huff. Two paramedics jumped out with a stretcher hung between them. They checked the woman's vitals, scooped her up, and vanished all in the time it took me to remember how to shut my mouth.

"Hubert would have called them once Hood got involved," Linus told me. "A precautionary measure."

"Hood savaged that woman." I held up my arm, crimson drool stringing between my fingers. "He could have killed her, and no one came out to stop him. No one told him no. They just watched."

I had watched, too terrified I might be next to intervene. But as the adrenaline ebbed, the excuse felt flimsy to me.

"The Faraday has its own laws, and she broke them." Linus cast the darkest shadows a wary glance before guiding me into the lobby. "I've seen Hood do far worse with much less provocation." His cool fingers brushed the small of my back, and he guided me into the lobby. "I'm not certain why he finds you so interesting, but it's for the best that we're returning to Savannah tomorrow."

Savannah, not *home*. This—this topsy-turvy mess—was his haven.

"Thank the goddess." I wiped my hand on my pants. "I take back what I said about wishing I had never come here. I'm glad I did. I was chafing against the bonds holding me in Savannah, and this cured me of that. I'm more of a homebody than I imagined."

This side of Atlanta was not a facet I ever needed to see again.

Linus shuffled me into the elevator. "Do you still want to tour the campus before we go?"

"I'm good." I waved away the offer with a sticky hand. "Maybe some other time."

"I ruined this for you." He shoved his hands into his pockets. "I wanted to show you the best of my city, but it seems determined to only show you its worst. *My* worst."

"Hey, I meant what I said." I caught his eye. "We can try this again after things calm down." I smiled to make sure he understood I wasn't laughing at him when I added, "But next time I'll be getting a hotel room across town."

"I hoped you might see a different side of me," he said softly. "Not this one."

"Don't all those sides get confusing?" I bumped shoulders with him. "Can't you ever just be the real you?"

"Real is an abstract concept. Are we ever ourselves, our whole selves, except when we're alone?"

Once, I told Boaz that old Grier was a shirt I pulled on when I expected company and warned him that eventually it wouldn't fit me anymore. One day, I would be forced to wear a new one or remain exposed. I had never considered that the alternative might be investing in a closet full of new shirts to wear when the mood struck me. Not until I glimpsed Linus's wardrobe.

"I want to believe we can all find at least one person to show our true faces."

Curious, he glanced over at me. "Boaz is that person for you?"

"Sometimes." I mulled over my answer. "I show him the best of what's left, but he's seen the worst too. We've known each other forever. It's impossible to hide your whole self from someone for that long. You can keep corners of your heart secret, but that's about it."

"Hmm."

The flashing number slowed as we reached his floor. "What does that mean?"

"I envy you," he confessed. "I don't have that. I have too many secrets to be open with any one person." He followed me into the hall. "You're the closest I've gotten."

"Oh, come on." I forced a laugh to shatter the quiet moment.

"You can't tell me you and Meiko don't do the pillow-talk thing. I've seen your pillowcases. They're covered in cat hair."

Card in hand, he hesitated. "I'm not sure it makes any difference, but I want you to know that Meiko and I..." A flush rose up his pale throat. "She might appear as a woman when the mood strikes her, but it's an illusion. Beneath her magic, no matter how real she might otherwise appear, she's anatomically a cat."

Embarrassment flared in my cheeks, because I was mortified to realize it did matter. "I'll admit I was curious."

"I've long believed that's how her favorite game developed," he admitted. "She was gifted, or cursed, with higher awareness, and she wants to be more. She wants to be human, or something like it."

"She got someone hurt tonight," I reminded him. "There's no excuse for that behavior."

Smile curling his lips, he huffed out a laugh. "I'm open to suggestions."

"I'm willing to design wards to keep her out of your apartment," I said sweetly.

"Don't tempt me." He let me into the apartment. "I must return to Strophalos. A few of the tests we initiated earlier will be ready by now, and Reardon can't enter his office until I remove the wards."

"I can entertain myself," I assured him. "I brought a book to read. I might go soak for a while and lose myself in a small town where only a postal worker and her dog can unravel the mystery of who is killing the people on her route."

His eyes sparkled. "Sounds riveting."

"Don't mock me," I said primly. "I'm expanding my intellectual horizons."

"You'll have to loan it to me when you finish. Perhaps I'll pick up some sleuthing tips."

The reminder of his job curdled my stomach, but I tamped down the roiling so as not to wound him.

"I'll do that." I did a cursory check of the loft and found it empty. "Can you do me a favor?"

"Name it."

Sucker. "Can you keep Meiko busy for a few hours so I can enjoy some peace and quiet?"

"I'll bring her to Strophalos with me." He pinched the bridge of his nose. "I can set up temporary wards to prevent her from escaping my office. Her magic nullifies mine, so I can't promise how long it will last."

It was on the tip of my tongue to ask what good a familiar that nullified rather than amplified magic was to him, but every second the door stood open was an opportunity for her to snake between his legs and ruin my relaxation time. "Your sacrifice is greatly appreciated."

"Cletus will remain in the area, and I'll check in before I return home in case you need anything."

"That sounds perfect." I cheered up on the spot. "Be thinking about food." I rubbed my hands together, stomach growling. "I vote you pick up takeout on your way back, and we binge on cartoons until dawn."

And pretend today never happened.

"We can do that." He ducked his head, but it failed to hide the curve of his cheek. "Enjoy your evening."

"You too." I waved him off then got down to the business of bumming around. The one thing missing from my stash was bubble bath, but shampoo would do in a pinch, and I had no doubt his was top-drawer. "Relaxation, here I come."

While the tub filled, I gathered pajamas and toiletries. Stripping out of Meiko's selections made me feel lighter. It wasn't, I assured myself, because of what Linus had confessed. With a hiss, I sank into the hot, fragrant water and allowed its warmth to lull me. Aches and pains deep in my muscles, reminders of the accident, had flared up during the scuffle with the guy on campus, and the heat felt delicious.

I closed my eyes long enough to gather my willpower to not think about what Boaz was doing that was so much more important than calling me, but when I opened them, darkness shrouded the room.

"Meiko," I growled. "This isn't funny. Turn the light back on."

Aggravating cat must have given Linus the slip and sneaked back up to the loft to torment me.

"Meiko?"

A rattling noise curved my hands around the edges of the tub. Thanks to my keen night vision, I could tell the doorknob rattling wasn't the one in here, but that meant...

Someone wanted in the apartment.

Meiko had a keycard. I'd seen her brandishing it earlier. Otherwise, she couldn't come and go as she pleased while under residential protection. And if she hadn't answered the door, that meant she wasn't here.

There was no love lost between us. I had no doubt she would swing it wide open if a vampire horde descended upon the Faraday in search of me. Her absence erased any hope the lights might be a trick. The power had either been cut to the apartment or to the entire building. Not good.

Quick as I dared, I stood and toweled off, yanking on my pajamas and twisting my wet hair into a soggy bun I secured at my nape. I sucked in a deep breath and cracked open the door, exhaling when no one jumped out to grab me.

On tiptoe, I crept up into the loft where I kept my bags and pulled out the travel kit I used to bring Eileen, ink, brushes, and the modified pen and its parts with me. I shoved them into my purse, swung it over my shoulder, then climbed back down to hide in the maze of clothing racks Meiko had yet to return.

The rattle escalated to a fist pounding on the door in a steady beat that set my pulse hammering.

The same wards that kept sound from escaping must not work in reverse since I heard it all so well.

Whoever—*whatever*—was coming, I had to get out of here.

The front door was the only way in or out of this apartment that I had seen, but that couldn't be all. Linus was too paranoid for that. But first, I yanked on the pair of flats I'd discarded earlier and picked a knee-length jacket to shrug on over my pajamas. There was no time to change. I had to move. At least this would keep me modest if I lucked up and managed to hit the street.

"Cletus," I hissed. "Where are you?"

Viscous darkness whirled on my periphery as he took form on the other side of the window.

Fiddlesticks.

I had forgotten he was banned from the building.

Hand pressed to the glass, I peered down at the sheer drop to the alley below. "How do I get out of here?"

The wraith indicated the latches and made a flipping motion.

"I...don't think that's such a good idea." Wood groaned and splintered behind me. "Okay, so maybe I'll give it a try."

Once I wedged open the window, Cletus drifted closer, beckoning me to join him with a curl of his fingers.

"I can't fly." I gulped as the warm breeze whipped stray hairs in my eyes. "You get that, right?"

A moan sounding suspiciously like a sigh moved through him as he pointed down.

"Yeah, I don't want to go down." I sank my nails into the windowsill. "Down bad."

Quicker than I could escape his chilly grasp, Cletus circled his bony fingers around my wrists and yanked me out the window.

FOURTEEN

I screamed bloody murder for a solid thirty seconds, even after my knees slammed against a metal grate. An invisible metal grate. Linus must have applied obfuscation sigils to disguise his fire escape. Even knowing it was there, feeling it under my palms, I had trouble seeing past my panic well enough to bring it into focus.

Wasting precious time, I took out my pen and drew amplification sigils across my forehead.

A beat passed as they battered against the illusion and then shredded it to ribbons. I could see the metal landing where I sprawled as well as stairs zigzagging down, down, down. After pushing to my feet, I hit the first step, gripped the rails in both hands, and ran as fast as I dared.

Cletus drifted in front of me, forcing me to acknowledge him, then pointed up at the window.

"You're going to hold them off?"

The wraith nodded as he began to rise.

"Be careful."

There was no point in calling Linus. The connection he shared with Cletus meant he had been notified the second the wraith grasped the situation. Linus could perceive through their bond, which meant he ought to have an idea of where I was headed. It also gave him an opportunity to catch a glimpse of my would-be attacker.

Panting hard, I started tasting blood in the back of my throat but didn't slow. I didn't dare. I kept up my downward momentum, leaping over stairs, using my death grip to keep me on my feet when I stumbled on impact.

An eternity later, I jumped from the last platform, hit the pavement hard enough to jar my bones, and rolled my ankle.

Allowing myself a second to catch my breath, I drew an obfuscation sigil across the back of my left hand to make it difficult for others to see me then scribbled a healing sigil on my ankle while I was at it.

Just as I straightened, ready to bolt for the busy street ahead, a furious roar belted out the window above me, and a massive body hit the fire escape with enough force to buckle the metal.

Ankle barking with each step, I ran up the alley. The end was in sight when a hulking shadow crossed my path, tipping its nose skyward.

Hood.

A bone-rattling growl reached out to tickle my hindbrain, and it was all I could do not to scream when he rushed me.

With no weapons and nowhere to hide, I flung myself to the side, smashing my shoulder against the brick wall as he barreled past. Expecting him to slide into a spin and come at me again, I was stunned when he hit the fire escape and started climbing.

Cletus brushed my cheek with cool fingers, shocking me back to myself, and I sprinted for the sidewalk and the cover of sweet, sweet pedestrians.

Dialing Tony was out of the question. I didn't have time to wait for a pickup, and I didn't want to embroil another human in our world. Figuring the next best thing was a good old yellow taxi, I flagged one down as it passed.

I was belted in and headed for Strophalos within minutes, leaving the chaos at the Faraday in my wake. The one thing I hadn't considered was the fact humans can't see the campus, let alone enter it. And, I remembered after paying my fare, neither could I without a staff member to get me inside the wards.

Fingers shaking, I dialed Linus and waited for him to answer.

He didn't.

"Cletus." I ended the call and started dialing again. "Fetch Linus."

The wraith rippled in the air, ignoring the order to leave my side as my second call connected.

"Grier?"

"Boaz." I bit the inside of my cheek. "I don't suppose you have any friends in Atlanta? Or friends at Strophalos?"

"Yes to both."

"Friends who might be persuaded to let me in and hide me for a bit?"

"What the hell is going on?"

"Someone tried to break into Linus's apartment while I was there. I escaped, but I wasn't thinking, and I came to Strophalos, but I can't get through the wards without a faculty member." I was rambling, my tongue tripping over every other word. "I called Linus, but he's not answering his phone, and I don't know what to do."

"He left you alone?" Boaz growled. "I thought he was smart."

"It's not his fault. I should have been safe at the Faraday."

"The Faraday?" A moment of stunned silence followed. "Of course that's where he lives."

"Can you help me or not?"

"Don't budge. I'll use your phone to pinpoint your location. We've got a guy on the inside. He's posing as a janitor. He can let you in and keep you safe. Don't leave his side until Linus comes for you."

"Okay." I bobbed my head like he could see me. "I can do that."

"Talk to me, baby," he coaxed. "Quiet on your end makes me want to kill things."

"You called me baby."

"Did I?"

"Yes." I kept sweeping the area for signs of my escort. "When a guy calls a girl something as unflattering as Squirt, she notices when he mixes things up."

"Ah, but you'll always be my Squirt." His rough chuckle had me rolling my eyes. "What are you wearing?"

"Really?" I laughed and felt better for it. "That's what you want to know right now?"

"I have to tell Victor what to look for," he lied smoothly.

Glancing down, I fessed up to my wardrobe choices. "Pink pajama shorts with white polka dots, a pink camisole, and a knee-length charcoal pea coat. I'm also wearing what used to be white ballet flats, if that helps."

"Grier?" He sounded far too reasonable in that moment. "How would he see your pajamas to ID them?"

"I never belted the coat." I didn't much see the point now. "My taste in sleepwear is on display for everyone to see." A husky groan rattled in his throat, and I flushed. "I miss you growling at me."

"I miss growling at you too." A soft curse fell from his lips like he hadn't meant to say that, but he came back at me, all business. "There's an elderly man wearing a navy uniform walking your way. He's pulling a trash can on wheels behind him and wearing an Atlanta Braves ball cap. Do you have a visual?"

"No. Wait." I bumped into Cletus, who seemed more substantial than ever, trying to get a better view. "Yes. I see him."

"I'll stay on the line until you're inside the wards."

Throat going tight, I admitted, "That's more than I thought I'd get."

"I'm always here for you, you know that."

"It hasn't felt that way lately." I took a chance and told him the truth. "I need you."

His voice broke on my name. "Grier..."

"Ms. Woolworth?" The janitor—sentinel?—grunted in my direction. His stooped shoulders and the graying hair frizzing from under his cap made him look old, but the way he moved... "Young lady, belt your coat. You can't walk around campus flashing your goods. It's not allowed."

"Give me a break. The disguise isn't that good." Boaz snorted. "He's nineteen and still wet behind the ears."

"That Boaz?" Victor, the sentinel janitor, asked while digging in his pockets.

"Yes," I told him, ignoring Boaz. "Would you like to say something to him?"

"A janitor using a student's phone would look far more suspicious than one letting a student in who forgot her keycard. Trust me, I do this all day. I can't remember the last time I touched a bag of trash. I might as well wear track shoes and let them call me the concierge." He reached through the wards, taking my hand in his. "Stop side-tracking me, whippersnapper."

One big step got me through, but Strophalos had been compromised too. There was no safety to be found here. "Thank you."

After releasing my hand, Victor tipped his can back on its wheels and started rolling. "This is a hell of a lot more interesting than what I would be doing otherwise."

"Poor newb," Boaz tsked. "He's tired of babysitting rich geeks. He doesn't get that's ninety percent of the job."

Pretending the jab at the High Society didn't hurt, I asked, "Why don't you tell him?"

"And ruin all the fun?" I heard a smile in his voice. "He'll become a disillusioned soldier all too soon. Let him enjoy the fantasy. The reality will never measure up to what he's got cooking in his head. See, he was a voluntary enlistment. He really does want to be out there saving the world one necromancer at a time."

"He still yammering?" Victor kept his voice pitched low and added a creaky note to it now that we were on campus. "Goddess knows he loves to hear himself talk."

"I was wrong," Boaz deadpanned. "Tell him the truth. All of it. About the early mornings starching uniforms and shining boots, the hours standing statue-still at assemblies while fighting for your life not to fall asleep and face-plant in front of our charges, the crap pay and constant travel, being at the beck and call of every necromancer with a shred of power and the ability to pick up a phone and dial in an order for their very own sentinel."

"Your bitterness is showing," I teased to snap him out of his anti-High Society rhetoric. "Tuck it back in before your superior officer notices."

He didn't snark back or laugh or give any of the responses I expected, and that made my stomach churn.

"We need to talk," he said. "Soon."

Full-blown cramps tightened my gut. "This isn't good news, is it?"

"You need to get somewhere safe, and I..." He bit off the thought. "We'll talk soon. I promise."

Boaz ended the call before I could thank him or say goodbye, and I was halfway to dry heaves wondering what he meant. *We need to talk* was code for *this isn't working* in relationships, but we had barely gotten started. How could he know this was a bust when we hadn't gotten to try? Maybe slow and careful wasn't how the race was won, but if he wasn't willing to pace himself, then we never had a chance.

"I thought you were a myth," Victor murmured, keeping his head forward to make it look a little less like he was shadowing me. "To hear Boaz tell it, you're the ideal to which all other women should aspire. And yes, he used those words. Must be the wearing-pajamas-in-public thing. I can see how that would appeal."

"Yeah." Not really feeling it, I put away my phone. "That must be it."

Picking up on my weird mood, he tucked away the personal questions. "Where are we headed?"

"Professor Reardon's office." I checked with Cletus. "Linus is still there, right?"

The wraith bobbed in answer.

"Who are you talking to?" Victor lowered one hand to the slight bulge next to his hip. "You put your phone away."

Leaning forward, I examined his cap. "Do you have eyes in the back of your head?"

"Answer the question."

"Linus assigned a wraith to me. They share a bond, so I was double-checking his location."

"It's damn creepy knowing those things are flying around and not being able to see them."

"Boaz can." Cletus was one of the few entities most necromancers could see without aid.

"I'm the next best thing to human. Boaz doesn't have much juice, but he's got more than most of us. That's why he gets all the fun jobs."

Until this exact moment, I'd had no idea Boaz had *any* juice. Amelie would have burst a blood vessel trying to manifest if she had any hope of there being real power in their bloodline. Unless...

Maybe that explained her obsession with the haves and have nots of magic, and Ambrose too.

Carefully, I tiptoed around what I wanted to know. "How long have you known him?"

"Eight months, more or less."

How could a recruit who met Boaz eight months ago know more about him than me?

"Seems to me he's been getting more and more fun jobs lately." I poured a dollop of pouty girlfriend in the mix. "I never see him these days. He's always off on a mission."

"That's messed up if they won't let you guys spend time together."

"He visits when he's able."

"Still, he's stationed in Savannah. Why force him to stay in the barracks when he could live at home?"

I tripped over my own two feet and almost went down, would have if Cletus hadn't caught me in his arms. The fact a wraith could support my weight ought to worry me more than it did, considering his teeth and claws should be his only substantial features, but I had gone numb.

Boaz was stationed in Savannah. *Savannah.* How was that possible?

That would explain...a lot, actually.

The container ship horn I overheard on our earlier call had been exactly that. He must have been standing near River Street, maybe haunting the *Cora Ann* for old time's sake, while we talked.

All the brownie points I had awarded him for showing up when I needed him most tasted like ash. The trips home I imagined him making on a plane from all over the country had been made on foot or in a cab. How could that be? Why would he lie? How long had he been hiding the truth?

Stumbling across him while hunting the dybbuk was one thing. Learning the Society had kept him local? That he hadn't told me? It stung. All of a sudden, the calls to Amelie made more sense. She knew. She had to have known. And she hadn't said a word. He must have pulled strings to stay close to her. Fine. Okay. Boaz had a protective streak a mile wide. But why hide it and leave me the odd woman out?

As much as I wanted to blame a vow of silence, like the one the Grande Dame had extracted from Linus, if Boaz had told Amelie—even if she figured it out on her own—they had colluded to keep his whereabouts from me.

Desperate to distance myself from his truths, I tried outpacing him. "I can take it from here."

"Not happening." Victor blocked the path with his can. "My orders are to pass you off directly to Scion Lawson."

The title felt odd considering everyone on campus called him *Professor* Lawson.

Another face, another title, another facet to a man who might as well have been a twenty-sided die.

"That would be me," a grim voice announced behind us.

Sweet relief spiked my bloodstream as I glanced over my shoulder and spotted Linus standing there.

For the first time in our reacquaintance, he was the one who initiated a hug. The cold of his body pressed into mine gave me a surface layer of numb to go along with the deadened sensation spreading through my chest. His hands trembled on my back, and his hold was awkward, like he had no idea how to comfort someone. Or maybe, since he was the one wrapping me up tight, he had no idea how to take comfort either.

"Thank Hecate you're all right," he breathed against my ear before tucking his face in the damp curve of my neck. His heart raged, a pounding drum trapped between us, as if he had run the whole way. "The wards I placed on the door to keep Reardon out of his office sealed the room behind us." He withdrew, a few inches at least. "There was no cell reception. With the building warded against wraiths, I didn't know you were in danger until we concluded our latest experiment, and I stepped out to check in with Cletus."

"He saved the day." I forced out the words. "He almost gave me a heart attack by pulling me out the window, but mostly he was golden." I had to give credit where it was due. "Hood kept the intruder busy while I escaped. I didn't get close enough to tell if I was being attacked by a vampire, but that's a safe assumption. Hood also gave me arrhythmia, but it's all good." I smoothed trembling hands down my sides. "I'm here in one piece. That's what counts."

"Thank you for escorting her." He addressed Victor for the first time. "I'm in your debt."

"There's no debt, sir." Victor puffed out his chest. "This is what we do."

The urge to pull off his cap and ruffle his hair almost overwhelmed me. He wasn't that much younger than me, but goddess, I felt old where it counted. His youthful optimism, his dedication to his job, made me wish the sentinels had a dozen more just like him. Maybe then my time in Atramentous wouldn't be kept wedged behind a wall to protect me from remembering all the ways bored sentinels entertained themselves with people society, and the Society, had forgotten.

Wheels squeaking behind him, Victor started rolling away, donning his ancient-janitor persona.

"Is Meiko with Reardon?" I rubbed the base of my neck. "Or did you confine her to your office?"

"I couldn't find her. I had to leave and hope for the best." His sheepish admission colored his pale cheeks. "I wouldn't worry about her, though. She's smart enough to have found a safe place to hide until the lights come back on."

"Good." I gusted out a sigh. "We'll never be BFFs, but I don't want her to get hurt."

I had enough blood on my hands without dipping them in hers.

"I'm taking you home." Linus hefted a file. "I've got enough information to get us started."

"Home?" I flinched away from him.

"To Savannah," he clarified. "To Woolly."

Relief melted my bones, and I closed the gap between us, allowing my head to fall against his chest. Holding it up on my own wasn't happening. I was too exhausted. "That's the best offer I've heard all weekend."

The door swung open behind us, and Reardon burst onto the lawn with a manic energy about him.

"Linus," he pleaded, clearly picking up on an earlier conversation. "See reason. We can continue the project here. We have the facilities and the library at our disposal. There's no reason to take half an answer back with you." He noticed me and wet his lips. "The sample you brought me—"

"No." Tentatively, he stroked the back of my head, his fingers tangling in the strands of hair. "There's nothing more to be learned in twenty-four hours, and I have obligations in Savannah I can't neglect."

"You mean Grier," he surmised. "That's what's keeping you there."

"The Grande Dame herself issued my orders." The use of her official title told me Reardon was digging his hole deeper, that Linus had run out of patience. "I have no choice but to obey."

Though the tender way he cradled me made me wonder if maybe he didn't hate that he had been called back.

"Your mother would extend your leash for another week surely." Reardon cut his eyes to me, to how I leaned on Linus's strength, and that was enough to have me straightening. "Your charge is here. What harm can come to her by your side?"

"Multiple attempts have been made on Grier's life," Linus murmured, frowning at the distance I put between us. "There are those who oppose the Grande Dame's ruling, those who believe Grier is guilty of the crime of which she was convicted. It's best if I get her home where she is safest."

The misdirection wasn't a lie, it just wasn't the truth as it applied to this situation.

Fingers a gentle cage around my elbow, he guided me away from the eager professor.

"I thought you trusted Reardon." That's how he'd justified bringing me with him.

"I do." He cut me a look. "Within reason." He bypassed the parking lot and led me through a small garden. "He hasn't discovered that the magical remnants in the blood he finds so fascinating is yours, or he would have pressed harder. As it is, he's salivating for another sample to run more tests."

"A salivating vampire does not sound good." I hoped he meant metaphorically, but it was hard to say given Reardon's behavior.

"I've known him for years, and I've never seen his control slip. His lapse around you at the first sign of violence makes me wonder if made vampires are affected by your presence to some degree."

"I really, really hope not. I've got ninety-nine vampire problems, and I don't want him to be one."

"He can't leave the campus." Linus kept going, almost dragging me into a massive building filled with trophies and awards that spit us out on a sidewalk leading deeper into the city. "You're protected beyond the wards."

The farther we walked, the less familiar the landmarks. "Where are we going?"

"We need a safe place to wait while I arrange for transportation." He slowed when he noticed I was out of breath. "I sent Tony home. It's too dangerous for him to stay here. Having him pick us up again might cost him his life."

Proving I was thinking along the same lines, I admitted, "That's why I took a cab."

Approval warmed his eyes. "How did that go?"

"I've had more fun, but I managed. The pants-wetting terror helped."

The next corner we rounded announced our destination. On the lowest floor of a high rise, a sprawling shop with flickering neon signs announced *The Mad Tatter, We're All Inked Here*. He shoved into the shop, bell jangling over our heads, and bypassed the counter. The bored girl perched on a stool behind it kept reading her magazine as he led me to a cluttered office tucked against the far wall.

The low thrum of necromantic magic brushed against my skin, too powerful for the practitioners at their stations. Residual maybe? Magic was in the blood, and while Clorox might bleach away any crimson stains, power was harder to erase. "We're here to meet Mary Alice?"

"Yes." He tapped a finger on the particleboard desktop. "She's around here. Somewhere. She practically lives here."

"This is an expensive corner to set up shop," I observed, curious about this mentor of his. "She must be very good at what she does."

"Oh, she is, just not tattooing. She can't draw a stick figure, but Mitch—her husband—was a master." A wry twist bent his lips. "Mary Alice is an information broker. The shop is her cover."

"Tatter is some kind of black market hub?" And the potentate of Atlanta was elbows deep in its secrets.

"Mary Alice is High Society without a drop of magic in her. She married into the Low Society, but she has valuable connections through her family. Without magic, she had to carve out her own place in the world. Mitch was happy to help. He saw it as a team effort. He kept their noses clean enough for anyone who looked, but the real action was always in the back room." He nudged me toward a chair opposite the battered desk. "I went to her for information once, months after I moved to the city, but she refused to sell to me. I was High Society, and the law, and she wanted to protect her sources. I kept going back until Mitch accused me of scaring off his clients. He joked that I might as well work for him since I spent so much time there." He smiled. "I took him up on the offer."

"I wondered what drew you to tattooing." I should have known that his reasons would be multilayered.

"You could have asked," he pointed out. "I can't tell you every-thing, my position won't allow it, but I could have told you that."

Shame, that was shame curling through me for not being more interested in his life, his past. Friends asked questions, and they paid attention to the answers. So far, I had done neither.

"I'm asking now. You started an internship to get street cred and make your own contacts. Smart." According to TV, cops brokered with snitches all the time. For a man with deep pockets like Linus, I could see the information trade being lucrative. "But you liked it, or you saw its potential applications, and you stayed on to claim a chair."

"No," he corrected me. "I loved it from the moment I put needle to skin."

"Is that why you covered yourself in art? Or was it camouflage?"

"I'm one of the few necromancers dabbling in permanent sigils anchored on the body. Mitch introduced me to a field where I can break new ground with each discovery, and that's exhilarating." His cheeks flushed as he warmed to his topic. "Every sigil on my body is designed for a purpose. I try to make them beautiful, to create art, but it's secondary to my goal."

The brutal planes of his stomach, all lean muscle and ink, flashed in my mind before I could slam shut whatever mental vault stored such memories. My curious fingers had traced those smoky whorls, those shaded loops, and his cool skin had pebbled beneath them.

"You succeeded on all counts," I assured him, blinking clear of those images.

"Wait here." He reached for the door. "I need to find Mary Alice."

"Now that you've parked me, I'm not moving." Feet, calves, knees, and thighs all burned. "I'm all out of gas."

Linus paused on the threshold, one foot in the shop, but rocked back inside the room with me.

"I'll be fine," I promised. "I'll scream bloody murder if I need you."

With a tight nod, he strolled out at a clipped pace, rounded a corner, and vanished from sight.

Through the open door, I glimpsed yet another of his facets, this one the least expected of all.

The gleaming black-and-white-checkerboard pattern to the linoleum floor reminded me of a retro diner until I spotted the lobby, where leather couches and chairs had been upholstered to resemble giant white-capped mushrooms with red spots. The toadstool foot-stool was my favorite piece.

Artists' stations lined two walls opposite one another, each with segmented chairs that reclined. They called to mind dentists' offices and popped in the same bright red. The few clients lounged on those, a mix of college-aged kids and seasoned ink collectors, necro-mancers and humans. The walls behind each station depicted a different scene from *Alice in Wonderland*. Some drawn, some painted, some color, some black and gray. All lovely and original pieces of art.

Despite the ache in my limbs, I was drawn to one of the empty stations and the colorful mural behind the chair.

A garden scene spilled over this section of wall, stylized, yes, but as familiar as the back of my hand. I had played in that garden throughout my childhood. And peering around an arbor wreathed in climbing roses, a young girl with wide eyes and a sharp chin watched as a white rabbit thumped his hind leg on the grass.

The girl...was me. Dressed as Alice. At about six or seven years old. The likeness was stunning.

Forcing my hand to lower before I touched the paint, I examined the rest of the space.

A drafting table of some kind filled a nook obscured by my previous angle. The surface was backlit and glowed softly, illuminating the face of a teenager as he doodled absently, his head bobbing along with the music pumping into his ears through an electric-blue headset. The cord was in his mouth, and he was rolling it between his lips. When he paused to trade out for a new paper, a huge smile spread at whatever he saw. He spat out the cord, tossed the headset, and leapt to his feet.

Linus approached from a different direction than when I last saw him, and the teen trotted over, all gangly limbs and enthusiasm. He must be the Oslo to the Mary Alice he was hunting.

Mary *Alice*.

Clearly someone had a sense of humor.

This shop must be her own private wonderland. Well, that or a clever marketing ploy.

Oslo initiated a complicated handshake that I could never reproduce but Linus kept up with just fine. Having passed some test, the boy leaned in. "Did you bring them?"

"I did." Linus shoved his hands in his pockets. "I left them at my place, though. I'll have a courier deliver them Monday."

"Why did you come if you didn't bring the drawings?" The teen laughed awkwardly. "Let me try that again—I'm glad you're here, but why the visit?" He blasted out a sigh. "You know what I mean. I fail at social interactions. Don't make me keep going. It's only going to get worse from here."

"Official business," he said smoothly. "I need to speak to Mary Alice, if she's around."

"She stepped out back for a smoke." He mimed taking a drag. "It's going to kill her one day. Statistically speaking."

Linus patted the boy's shoulder, met my eyes, then left out the back.

The glance didn't go unnoticed. The boy followed his line of sight, spotted me and then waved. "Hey."

"Hi there. Oslo, right?"

"You must be... No clue. Linus keeps his private life private."

"I'm Grier." His candor made me laugh. "I'm a friend of his from Savannah."

"Visiting the big city?" His grin widened. "How does it compare?"

For me, it didn't. "I won't be packing up and moving here anytime soon, if that's what you mean."

"Eh. It's not for everyone."

Keeping it polite, I smiled. "I'm sure the same could be said for my hometown."

"I would rather donate my eyes to science today than give this up." His mouth flattened. "But I'm sure it's great. There's got to be something decent there to keep Linus's attention." He wiped a hand across his mouth. "I'm going to stop there. Trust me, it's for the best."

A booming feminine voice rang out from the back, and a woman who appeared to be in her late fifties power-walked into the office I had vacated. A well-preserved sixty-seven indeed. She waved Linus and me in, then shut the door in Oslo's face before he could join us.

"This is her?" she demanded. "You can't be serious, Doodlebug. Sneeze, and she'll blow away."

"Why is it open season on my weight?" I folded my jacket over my chest and the boobs that required no bra to fight gravity. "Trust me. I miss my curves. I'm working hard to get them back."

"Curves don't vanish," she scoffed, indicating her rounded hips. "Trust me. I've fad dieted off and on for four hundred years."

"Maybe you should try prison." Chin up, I sank into the chair across from hers. "It worked wonders on me."

"Shit," Mary Alice snarled at Linus. "This isn't just—" she made air quotes, "—a friend who needs help."

"I never said—" he began.

"This is Grier Motherfucking Woolworth." She shoved him hard in the chest. "Do you know what a hot-ticket item she is right now? Word on the street is there's a bounty on her head that would buy me this whole block."

Dizziness settled around me as the blood drained from my head. "Since when?"

"Yesterday." Her frown sliced through me. "I had no idea Doodlebug brought you here. I'm guessing that's the only reason you're still alive. Not many would square off with the potentate in his own city. All bets are off once you leave, though. I hope you've got someplace safe to go."

"Can you get us transportation?" Linus pressed. "Nothing fancy. A van or SUV if you've got one."

Huffing out a sigh like he'd asked for her firstborn grandchild, she snagged a pair of keys off a hook by the door. "Take my ride. There are spare plates in the trunk. Folks might be looking for an Atlanta tag."

"Thanks." He bent and kissed her cheek as he accepted the keys. "I'll have it returned to you Monday."

"You do that." She straightened his collar. "You sure this girl's worth the trouble?"

"I'm sitting right here." I waved at her in case her eyes had gone bad. "Can you not talk over me?"

Mary Alice continued ignoring me. "Well? Is she?"

"Yes," he said without hesitation.

"All guys think that right before the truth smacks them between the eyes." She flicked a dismissive glance my way. "That wraithlike waistline won't last forever. The looks won't keep either. There's no good reason for a kid your age to settle down. Let alone with this one. She's going to get you killed or end up dead herself. Still think she's worth it?"

My gaze clashed with his, black and endless, and held longer than a simple yes or no required.

"Yes," he told her, his voice raw in a way I had never heard from him.

"She gets it, okay?" Mary Alice plonked down behind her desk. "You're willing to sacrifice your life for hers. Blah, blah, romantic sentiments, blah, blah, death wish, blah. We got it." Her scowl carved her wrinkles even deeper. "Take care of yourself. Don't make me give up your chair, okay?"

"I earned that chair." Lips twitching, he cut his eyes to her. "I don't want anyone else using it until I get back."

Mary Alice grunted and settled in to start filing her nails. "Every day it sits empty is a day I lose money."

Linus studied the ceiling like he might find patience there. "We'll talk about my return later."

"If there is a later," she grumbled, dismissing us.

Linus helped me to my feet then showed me through the emergency exit into the alley that ran behind the building. The air stank of old cigarettes, and I wondered why no one had suggested Mary Alice switch to vaping since the hookah-smoking caterpillar was an iconic Alice character.

We started walking toward a parking deck a block down, our footsteps the only sounds. The booth was unmanned at this hour, our trek up the incline to the second level uncontested. Flickering lights gave the concrete tomb an eerie effect, and I stuck close to Linus as we searched the short row of marked spaces labeled for Tatter employees.

A throaty rumble echoed through the deck, reverberating in my bones, and my ankle buckled. Tiny hairs lifted down my nape in a warning prickle, the skin between my shoulder blades itching as I regained my balance. "You heard that too, right?"

"Keep walking," he said, soft and calm. "Pretend nothing is wrong."

Clicking sounds, like claws on concrete, came from all directions.

"Where's Cletus?" I scanned the cavernous space for wisps of black more alert than all the rest.

"The garage is warded." Linus held his laser focus. "I can break them, but it takes time we don't have. I keep them muted while I'm home, but I didn't bother for such a short trip."

"Okay." So, we were on our own.

"Mary Alice drives a silver Dodge Grand Caravan," Linus said, attempting to distract me. "There are stickers all over the back from her grandkids' schools and activities."

"Okay." The row assigned to Tatter employees wasn't *that* long, and I wasn't seeing any van, but I was hearing steady panting. "Any local warg packs?"

"Yes." Reaching back, he took my hand and hauled me behind him. "Three, actually."

"Okay." Me and my big mouth. "New topic."

He cast a glance back at me, an unreadable expression sharpening his features, but then he set his jaw.

Woof.

The single huff got picked up into a song that echoed all around, converging on our location.

"We're not going to make it," I said, jerking on his hand. There was no point in pretending. "We need to lock ourselves in a warded circle and find out what we're up against."

"We don't have time for that." Linus scowled at the rows of vehicles fanning in all directions, none of them the silver van we had been promised. "They'll be on us the second we stop moving."

"I used a protective sigil on Oscar that night aboard the *Cora Ann*. It held the dybbuk at bay. Would that work?" I started fishing in my bag for my pen. "We could swipe those on and then risk stopping to draw a circle?"

"It's worth a try." He angled us toward a covered stairwell. "This ought to hold them long enough to give us a fighting chance."

No hands meant they either had to shift to open the door or smash it down with brute strength.

Three heartbeats later, Linus and I stood on the third-floor land-ing, and the dull thud of flesh against metal told us which option our pursuers had chosen. I wasted no time drawing the rune on top of his hand. Once I finished with him, I did the same for myself.

The wards we'd used to trap the dybbuk had been his work, and I wasn't certain I could replicate those from memory, but I had a brush and ink. I could follow his lead. We could tag team again. He could start the wards while I acted as a distraction.

"Keep moving." He led me out into the parking deck once more. "We don't want to get trapped in the stairwell if they break through before we can finish." He froze when I pressed my ink pot, made with Maud's blood, and a brush into his hands. "What are you—?"

"You need time. Find an out-of-the-way corner and start working. I'll jog around the first two rows and lay a false scent trail to distract them when they get up here."

Linus strained forward, the urge to snatch me back to him twitching in his fingers, but he forced a nod, his knuckles tightening around the supplies I'd given him. "Be quick, and be careful."

"I will." I had no intentions of becoming a chew toy for whatever hunted us.

Clearing the first row winded me, and I was already flagging, but adrenaline gave me a healthy boost when I heard the padded echo of my movements. Not daring to hold still long enough to find out if these creatures could retract their claws to hunt silently, I pumped my thighs harder.

An all-too-familiar baying noise ricocheted off the concrete pylons in response to my burst of speed.

I would never forget that sound for as long as I lived, or the needlelike teeth that went along with it.

"This can't be good," I panted. The watchmen were contracted to the Faraday. Why the heck were they hounding me? I was the guest of a resident, and the resident himself was busy drawing a barrier to keep us safe from our would-be protectors. After skidding around the corner, I started running flat out for the spot where Linus knelt. "Incoming."

Hot breath fanned the back of my left thigh, and a cold nose brushed the bend of my knee as teeth closed over the hem of my coat. The beast behind me skidded to a halt, yanking me back with such force I hit the ground on my tailbone. Impact shot a burst of lightning zigzagging up my spine, and I cried out in pain.

Noticing my abraded palms, sliced open when I braced for the fall, I used my own blood as ink. Instinct guided me to finger-paint protective sigils down my exposed legs, and I kept repeating the pattern until my wounds clotted on me.

Magic, old and rich, snapped into place around me, locking me in a bubble I couldn't see but sensed in the way air moved slower through the barrier.

A yelp resounded behind me, and I turned to find a massive dog-lizard thing pushing off the ruined fender of a nearby truck where the punch of energy had flung it away from me.

"Linus." I twisted toward him. "Raise your circle. *Now*."

Agony pinched his eyes as he obeyed. A shiver rode my skin in response to his magic, and I thanked the goddess we were both safe and sound. For now. The way the beast snarled his upper lip had me questioning how long our good fortune might last.

"What do you want?" I yelled at it. "What have we ever done to you?"

In response, it tipped its head back and howled a message I had no doubt went something like *Soup's on!*

Before long, answering calls alerted me to the presence of two more of the things.

Just how many watchmen were there? I had only ever seen Hood. Had that been by design?

Unsure how much they understood in this form, I tried again. "What's your deal? Why are you chasing us? Did we forget to get our parking validated or something?"

The other two closed in on the one in the middle, sniffing and licking until content it was mostly unharmed. With a huff, it liquefied into a reddish puddle before spraying several feet in the air like a geyser that poured into a humanlike form. The curtain of magic dripped away until a petite woman with sleek blue hair and sharp green eyes stood before me dressed in workout clothes like she had just left the gym. Or enjoyed a wicked sense of humor about how she got her cardio.

"Grier Woolworth."

"That's me." No point in denying it when they'd tracked us this far. They had our scents in their noses.

"I'm Lethe Kinase." She sighed when the larger of the two remaining beasts stalked toward me. "Hood you know." The third creature padded over to her and leaned its head against her thigh. "This is my brother, Midas."

"Nice to meet you." I poured enough sugar into my voice to sweeten a family reunion's worth of iced tea. "Thanks for the introduction. It's always good to know your enemies by name." When Hood nosed closer, I hissed at him. "Traitor."

The soft whine in his throat made me feel like I was the one who had betrayed him. How, when he was the one chasing me around like an M&M rolling across a counter, I had no idea.

"We owe you a boon." Her fingers curled in Midas's ruff. "No one has successfully infiltrated the Faraday in the history of its operation until tonight. How it was accomplished is still under investigation, though I imagine we'll discover a resident missing a keycard at best. A resident with malicious intent at worst. Neither scenario changes the fact we were remiss in our duties, and you almost died as a result."

The sweet edge of relief threatened to swamp me, but my luck wasn't this good. "It's no problem. Really. You guys can go back to whatever you were doing, and we'll get back to whatever we're doing. No hard feelings."

Red magic splashed against my barrier as Hood shifted forms. "*You* are what we're doing."

"Hard pass." I pulled my coat tighter around me. "I'm not that adventurous."

Lethe's husky laughter brought my attention swinging back to her, but she was eyeing Hood like he was listed as a prime cut on a menu only she had been handed. "I'm glad you feel that way." Her lips quirked as their eyes met. "He's mine, and I don't share."

"Oh" seemed like the best answer, so I stuck with that.

The third dog-lizard thing dissolved and reformed into a gilded version of Lethe that made me wonder if his spun-gold hair had earned him his name. From a distance, he was heartbreakingly beautiful, his features hewn from granite, his skin kissed by the sun. But upon closer inspection, he was too gaunt, with scars crosshatching his forearms, and his eyes, a rich aquamarine, held an edge of sorrow that was as likely to slit his throat as yours.

"It's an honor debt," Midas informed me, his voice rasping like speech hurt. "You were attacked on our watch, and that means we're in your service until the threat has passed."

"What about the Faraday?" *Please let there be a non-compete clause.* "I don't want to cost you your jobs."

"Our pack will see that the Faraday is well protected," Midas assured me. "This was our mistake, and we will see our honor restored."

That sounded an awful lot like he wasn't willing to take no for an answer.

"I'm going home. To Savannah." I shrugged apologetically. "You'll have to restore your honor another way."

"We'll come with you," Hood decided after exchanging looks with the other two.

"That's really not necessary." I shot Linus a panicky glance. "Right?"

"The watchmen seldom offer their services to individuals and never for free." Linus stood within his circle, arms crossed. "Hood has shown marked interest in Grier from the moment she arrived. There's more to this than you claim."

"Her scent reminds me of a young woman to whom I owe a blood debt." Hood bowed his head. "I couldn't save her, but perhaps this might help me balance the scales."

There was more, I could tell the story didn't end there, but I understood too well how much easier it was not to talk about the past. "How about you come with us then? Just you."

The fewer, the merrier, I always say. When it comes to slavering dog-lizard things.

"We are kindred." Midas shook blond hair into his eyes. "His debt is ours."

"Our bond doesn't allow for separation," Lethe explained. Leaving her brother, she approached us, pausing in front of Hood. "I almost lost him once. I won't risk him again."

"I was a pup then." Hood cradled her face in his palm. "I'm not so breakable now."

"Still." She leaned into the touch. "We go with you. Always."

Hood smiled, all teeth, and brought her in for a bruising kiss. "Always."

Turning away, I resisted the urge to fan myself. At least someone had their relationship all figured out.

"You own enough property to give them room to run," Linus said thoughtfully. "They sleep outdoors, so Woolly's wards won't be an issue." His smile was calculating, far too amused, when he said, "Boaz did suggest you hire full-time security."

But he meant handpicking Elite loyal to him, not adopting dog-lizards who would answer only to me.

Hmm.

Maybe Hecate did listen to our prayers. This unexpected boon would certainly answer one of mine.

"You think this is wise?" So far I had an undead parakeet, a dybbuk-possessed bestie, and a ghost child living under my roof. The roof belonging to a sentient house. And Linus lived next door. Those things I could handle. But adding three watchmen into the mix?

Even if they kept me from relying on sentinels? "How certain are you on a scale of one to ten?"

"An eight." He shrugged. "I subtracted two points for the cost of feeding them and the maintenance required to clean up after them."

I palmed my forehead. "Are you really telling me I have to buy sides of beef and shovel-sized pooper scoopers to make this work?"

A smile quirked his lips, and the others laughed like I had told the best joke ever.

"We'll only follow you if you don't agree," Lethe confessed at last. "Hood's peace of mind is worth more to us than your permission."

Thinking of ninety percent of the people in my life, I sighed. "Then you'll fit right in." The trio shared a triumphant howl that made me nervous coming from human-looking throats. "You're not going to eat me if I erase my wards, right?"

"That would be counterproductive," Hood said, amused.

"Still, it's been a long weekend." Growing longer by the minute. "Humor me."

"I vow we won't bite you." Hood grinned at me. "We won't even nibble."

Midas joined the others, and Lethe hooked her arms around their waists. "You won't notice we're there."

"Okay. Fine." I erased my sigil, and the protective barrier dissipated. "Do you want to ride with us?"

"Nah." Lethe's eyes sparkled as she rested her head on Hood's shoulder. "Race you?"

An interested sound moved through his chest. "What do I get if I win?"

"The better question," Midas interjected, "is what do I get when I win?"

The trio melted and reformed as scaled hounds, the smaller male taking the early lead while the other two bumped shoulders and watched him go before sprinting after him. Hood and Lethe embodied matehood in the same way that Neely and Cruz exemplified marriage. They personified ideals and made such lasting bonds appear as the only logical step when you couldn't breathe without the person next to you.

Maybe that apparent ease was what made their unions burn so bright from the outside looking in. Maybe that kind of love *wasn't* simple. Maybe it was a goal you strove toward every single day for the rest of your lives. A peak you never reached, but that was okay as long as you kept climbing.

Silence reigned in the parking deck, and I breathed a sigh of relief as Linus appeared at my side. "I was so put out at Strophalos."

He shoved his hands into his pockets. "Oh?"

"I didn't see the bookstore until after the coffee shop. I missed my chance to browse for a souvenir." A tired laugh rocked my shoulders. "Be careful what you wish for, huh? Looks like I won't go home empty-handed after all."

He started walking, and I fell in step with him. "These aren't the kind you keep."

"I wish I had your faith." I beat him to the stairwell and held open the door. "Midas said 'until the threat has passed,' and we have no clue how long that will take."

His silence left me wishing I could peek into his head and see what thoughts put that look on his face.

With time on our side, Linus texted Mary Alice, who forgot to mention a customer had taken her usual space. She had been forced to park on the opposite side of the level, which explained why we hadn't spotted her van on our first pass.

Linus, who I had never so much as caught with a crust of sleep in his eye, stifled a yawn as we located our ride.

"I'll drive." I held out my hand for the keys. "You look beat."

"I am tired," he admitted, brow gathering as if the admission surprised him too. "Thank you."

We got in, and I familiarized myself with the cockpit. I captained Amelie's sedan once in a blue moon, so I wasn't a total washout when it came to driving vehicles that required seat belts. But it was never as comfortable for me, even when I was a teen. And after Atramentous... Yeah. I much preferred the open air to any type of confinement.

Taking it slow and easy, I checked the mirrors to make sure we weren't being followed as I eased out into traffic. Linus kept watch too, though his eyelids drooped lower and lower. "You never told me what the initial results on Amelie's blood yielded." I decided to nudge him along by talking his ear off. "Did Reardon pinpoint any magical anomalies in her blood?"

"Yes," he murmured. "That's why he was so insistent we continue our research." He reclined his seat a notch and crossed his hands at his navel. "Heinz wasn't wrong when he compared Amelie's symptoms to that of a strained familiar bond." His blinking slowed until his reddish-blond lashes rested against his pale cheeks. "There are unmistakable markers in her blood put there by foreign magic, but I misdirected him, let him believe any peculiarities were due to the dybbuk bond. Possessed subjects are rare, so he has no basis for comparison."

Meaning I would live under the sword of Damocles until Linus finished collating his data.

"You mentioned exorcism as the only cure." Ambrose was glutted with power from his kills, Linus warned me that night in the elevator, and Amelie would die if he attempted to separate them before the energy dissipated. "Does this mean we'll have to wait until Ambrose weakens to get our answers?"

"No," he breathed, mouth barely moving. "Design a tattoo. For me. We can test for magic transference that way."

Traffic be damned, I whipped my head toward him. "Forget it."

"I will act as the control variable."

"We don't know for sure what the first one did yet, what the dangers are to the wearers. Until we figure that out, I'm not going to let you ink yourself. Plus, you're bonded to a wraith. You're hardly control variable material. We can't risk... Linus?"

A faint snore escaped his parted lips.

"Who did this to you? What made you believe you're disposable?

You're an heir, a scion, a professor, an artist, a potentate. Those are all positions of power." I kept going, thinking it through. "Do you think you didn't earn those first titles? That you must keep proving yourself? Heaping on more and more of them? Will it ever be enough?"

His only response was the slackening of his fingers as they slid onto his lap.

"You are worthy, Linus Lawson. You hear me?" I reached over and squeezed his chilly hand. "Don't die proving it to yourself."

With him sleeping soundly beside me, I pointed us toward home, sweet home.

FIFTEEN

L eft unsupervised, I might have broken a few speed laws during that last thirty-mile stretch. Or was it forty? Fifty? Who was counting? Come dawn, I wanted to collapse in my own bed instead of a borrowed one, and I was willing to pay a few tickets to make that happen.

Grinning like a loon, I swallowed a squeal of delight when I spotted Woolly. The van whined as I gunned it up the driveway, and it groaned as it bounced to a stop in front of the garage.

"We're here." I reached over and shook Linus. "Wake up, lazybones."

A faint moan escaped him, and I chewed my bottom lip while debating my options. Sleeping might be like eating for him. I had never actually seen him do either, but he must at some point. For him to be out like a light, he must be exhausted.

"I'm going to let them know we're here." I couldn't sit still another minute. "I'll be right back."

While Linus snoozed, I ran up the stairs and embraced the nearest pillar like I was part kudzu.

Woolly shrieked with glee, her voice a smoke alarm's piercing bleat. Beneath that, a symphony of magic burst in my head, the tempo as light and fast as a frantic heartbeat. All the curtains started flapping in her excitement, and the front door swung open, waving back and forth as she ushered me in.

"I have to wake Linus." As far as I was concerned, the luggage could wait. "I can't leave him out here."

The wards solidified as I hit the lower step, and I bounced off them before my foot touched the ground.

"Woolly," I sighed, leaning against the railing. "He'll get a crick in his neck."

"I thought I heard someone." Amelie skidded into the foyer with a wide grin. "You're home early."

"Dirty pool," I chided the old house, certain she had called for Amelie to lure me in without a fuss.

Amelie tackled me, almost knocking me back out onto the porch, and wrapped her arms around my waist. Over our heads the crystals in the chandelier tinkled merrily at our reunion, and the door snicked closed.

With my eyes shut tight, Amelie a familiar comfort in my arms, it was easy to forget what she had done.

Pretending nothing had changed, that things were as they always had been between us, was so much easier than holding on to the betrayal, the guilt, and the fear. But vigilance had kept me alive this long. A clean slate wasn't given, it was earned, and Ame still had a long way to go until she won forgiveness.

"I was gone forty-eight hours," I grunted, unable to resist slumping against her, allowing my old friend to support me for a change. "You couldn't have been that bored."

"Boaz told me what happened." Hurt throbbed beneath her words, and I tensed, forgetting which *what* she meant. "He said there was trouble at the Faraday?"

"You could say that." I let her drag me down onto the couch with her. "The Master is tired of waiting for a chance to make his move." I sank into the plush cushions, so much comfier than the ones on Linus's couch, and groaned with the simple pleasure of being in my own place, among my own things. "Turns out there's a bounty on my head."

"A bounty?" Amelie clung tighter. "How do we get it removed?"

"Other than surrendering me?" I tipped my head back. "No clue."

"You're home now." She exhaled with relief at that. "You're safe."

Home.

Safe.

Two of my favorite words.

"What have I missed?" I smiled at Amelie, who vibrated with pent-up energy in need of an outlet. "Any more attacks?" I did a mental check with Woolly, who swelled with pride over her pristine wards. "Any more fainting spells?"

"No and no." She curled up beside me, resting her elbow on a fraying cushion, and propped her chin on her palm. "Do you think those incidents were related to the bounty? Do you think hunters are responsible?"

"Seems likely." I hadn't had a spare moment to consider a connection until now. "They must have decided it was easier plucking me off the street than stealing me from behind the wards."

Our trip to Atlanta might have failed on some fronts, but it had lured my enemies away from my home.

"Vampires with a direct line to the Master, or to Volkov, would have heard the news first. They could have learned how he weakened your wards last time too. Some of the dumber ones might have hoped you didn't bother patching them yet. They might have been willing to gamble even if it gave them away."

Enough money would tempt all kinds. Not only vampires. "Mary Alice implied there are a lot of zeroes attached."

Amelie's forehead wrinkled. "Who?"

"Linus's boss at the Mad Tatter." I grunted out his name as I remembered where I'd left him. "It's her van we borrowed to get home." Shoving against the squishy pillows sucking me down, I hauled myself back on my feet. "Speaking of Linus, he's still buckled in. Poor guy slept the whole way home."

The locks snicked into place on the front door before I got close enough to touch the knob.

"Come on," I groaned. "I can't leave him out there all night."

"I wish I could help." Amelie released a sigh. "I'd kill to walk barefoot in the grass right about now."

A reflexive cringe hiked my shoulders up around my ears before I forced my muscles to relax.

"Poor word choice." She drew her legs to her chest and wrapped her arms around them.

Forcing my body into calm lines, I noticed our missing guest. "What about Odette?"

With any luck, Oscar, who was also absent, was recharging his batteries and not playing in the forbidden basement.

"She left about an hour ago." Tension strained her voice at the mention of the seer, but I was at a loss as to what could have happened between them. "One minute she was repotting the herb garden she planted for you in the kitchen, and the next her eyes glazed over." Head down, Amelie flexed her toes like she could imagine the tickle of grass blades between them. Or like she didn't want to meet my eyes. "When she snapped to, she muttered about being allergic to dogs and called Woolly a halfway house for broken dreamers."

"That sounds about right." I pressed my hand flush against the smooth door. Not so long ago, I'd had to beg her to let me out for work each night. I didn't want to go back to that, for both our sakes. "Woolly, I'm just going to the van. It's parked right in the driveway. I'll take Cletus with me, and Linus is already out there. It's going to be fine. I'll shake him, wake him, then come back to fill you in on my weekend."

And drum up some goodwill for our new security team while I was at it.

Maybe she would agree that every ghost boy needed a dog or three?

The overhead lights dimmed as she pouted about not getting her way, but she turned the first lock. Sure, snails have moved faster, but she was working with me. That's what counted.

In the time it took the Apollo 11 to get Neil Armstrong ready to walk on the moon, Woolly finished unlocking the door and opened it a crack for me. Huffing to wedge it wider, I sucked in my stomach and squeezed out onto the porch. From there, I tread the stairs gingerly, pausing with one foot above the ground to test the wards. When I didn't stub my toe on hardened air again, I took a leap of faith, holding my breath in case Woolly clung at the last moment. Much to my surprise, she behaved and allowed me out of her protective sphere.

The music of her wards changed from bright and energetic to a dirge, and I smothered a laugh under my breath. Woolly was such a drama llama. Sheesh.

Back at the van, I spotted Linus, still sleeping, and my gut started twisting with a sense of wrongness.

I rapped on his window with my knuckles, but he didn't stir. So I popped the locks, opened the door, and rested my hand on his shoulder. I half expected him to startle awake, for his tattered cloak to burst into existence, but he kept dozing.

"Linus?" I gave him a shake. "We're home. Well, I'm home. In Savannah. At Woolly." Nothing. "Wakey-wakey."

Warning tingles speared down my spine, and I sucked in a breath to scream, but it was too late.

A wide palm that smelled like old pennies slapped over my mouth, while a muscular arm snaked around my waist, cinching my upper arms flush with my sides. The vampire yanked me back against his hard chest with a husky chuckle in his throat as he drawled, "Remember me?"

The familiar voice, the taunt, caused my heart to jackrabbit.

My stalkerpire, the first vampire to attempt to bring me into the Master's fold, had returned.

All this time I had hoped—prayed—he was killed in the estate massacre.

"Volkov should have controlled you when he had the chance. A Last Seed's ability to mesmerize necromancers is a mercy." His breath skated across my throat, far too close to tender skin. "He could have convinced you that you were a happy couple until you started believing the lie without his influence." The tips of his fangs raked my neck. "Now you're going to be wide awake for what happens next."

Twin points of agony pierced my throat, and I raged against his hand, biting down until I tasted his blood. I spat a mouthful down the front of my shirt, thanking my lack of boobs for once. With my arms free from the elbows down, I had enough movement to reach up and dip my fingers in the stain. I painted the same protective sigil I'd used against the watchmen on the back of my left hand.

Magic in the necromantic markers in his blood reacted, blasting out around me in a protective bubble, and the vampire was blown off me. Confident the ward would hold, I turned back and drew the same design on Linus's cheek to protect him while I dealt with the vampire. As soon as Linus was as safe as I could make him, I shut his door and faced my attacker.

"You're right about one thing." Fury trembled in my voice. "I'm wide awake now, and I'm never going under again."

"Big words, little girl." He stood from a crouch, looking exactly as he had the first day he introduced himself, and he straightened as he licked his lips. "The Master is tired of waiting on you to come home."

"What is that psycho's deal?" I scanned the yard for signs of backup, but Taz was nowhere in sight, and I had no idea how long it would take the watchmen to arrive. "Home is here, and he's not welcome in mine. Neither are you."

Amusement glittered in his eyes. "You don't remember at all, do you?"

"I remember being snatched off my porch and driven to an estate where vampires played dress-up with me like I was some kind of freaking doll. I remember being promised to Volkov like a prize mare ready for breeding, except that's not the type of procreation he had in mind. I remember thinking one of the best days of my life was when I left that place, and him, behind me."

"I warned him." He tsked. "I told him you were too young when your mother ran, that necromancers don't imprint on their elders the way vampires do, but he was convinced a hybrid would carry more vampiric traits than not. He believed you would remember your nursery, filled with all your dollies, but you didn't. You didn't even remember your nursemaid. It broke Lena's heart."

"What crazy are you spouting now?" The thunder of my pulse in my ears made hearing impossible. "I'm not a hybrid."

"The necromancers use a much more egotistical term. I'm sure you've heard it bandied about by now." His mirth swelled. "Goddess-touched, I believe is the term."

No, no, no, no, no.

Maud would have...

Stupid, stupid, stupid.

When would I learn? Maud would have done whatever she felt would protect me. Even lie to my face.

"I see you running the calculations." He chuckled. "You never knew your father. You barely knew your mother. The Master is all the family you've got left."

"You're lying," I rasped. "Hybrids don't exist. Goddess-touched necromancers are—"

"Abominations," he informed me with a smile. "They were wiped out centuries ago. By your people. Given the chance, you think they won't try again, starting with you?"

"The Society doesn't waste resources." I was one, whether I wanted to be or not.

"Your guardian died protecting your secret. Your Society murdered one of its own to get to you."

"No." Once I started shaking my head, I couldn't stop denying it over and over. "It's not possible."

Maud had been invincible standing within Woolworth House, her magic at its apex while in her home.

And yet, she had fallen. And yet...and yet...and yet...

"You gotta learn to lie better than that if you want to survive this world." His teeth glinted. "Your power is young, but the knowledge in your blood is ancient."

A buzzing started in my ears. He knew. About the magic. About the sigils in my head. About *me*.

"Come with me." He held out his hand. "Let me show you who you are. Let me take you where you belong. Let me protect you from the machinations of your mother's people." He curled his fingers in a c'mon gesture. "Stay with them, and they will own you. Once they grasp the breadth of your power, they will control you, or they will make certain no one else can."

"How is the Master any different?" Fury swirled hot through my blood. "You're all the same. You all want the same thing. I would rather trust the devil I know than the one who kept me drugged and locked in a room. At least the Society grants me the illusion of freedom."

"An illusion is all you've got. The Grande Dame's son lives on your property. His wraith shadows your every move." The truth in his words cut deep. "But by all means, keep deluding yourself."

"Oh, Goddess," Amelie moaned from the safety of the doorway. "*Grier*."

"Don't you dare," I growled when she darted onto the porch. "Stay inside the wards."

"*You* get inside the wards," she screamed, clutching the railing. "*Now*."

Risking a glance back at Linus, I swallowed as my heart lurched at his still form. "I can't leave him."

"He's not worth—"

"I won't abandon him," I snarled at her then whirled on the vampire. "You're not taking me. I won't be caged again."

"The Master has been patient." His fist clenched as he lowered his arm. "He wants you to come home."

Anger erupted from my core, whiting out my conscious mind, and a new language unfurled in my head. Sigils passed through genetic memory from others like me. How else could they be branded in my mind?

The punctures in my throat had started healing, so I scratched at the scabs to reopen them, dipping my fingers in the sluggish blood. The ward separating me from him formed a thin shield of compressed air, magicked into impenetrability. The principle was the same as what Woolly used to insulate her doorway from uninvited guests.

I didn't stop to wonder if I could do it, if it was even possible. I simply did as those instincts dictated, let that tug in my gut guide me as I drew a sigil in the air before me, right on the shield. And then I smacked it with my open palm.

Power blasted from the sigil in a wave that knocked him to the ground. "What did you do to Linus?"

There was no graceful landing this time, no crouch or mockery. Blood poured from a gash on his forehead and smudged the corner of his mouth. "You didn't wonder why that student attacked Linus at Strophalos?"

"He wanted Linus out of the way," I said, and heard the hollow ring to the words as I spoke them.

The pointlessness of the attack had left a bad taste in my mouth. The assassin lacked the skills to best Linus. I had given him the element of surprise by bringing him to Reardon's classroom with me. Otherwise, he wouldn't have gotten close enough to Linus to scratch him, let alone skewer him with that blade of his.

A hairline scratch across Linus's chest was all the guy managed before Linus gained the advantage.

The exchange began so suddenly and ended even faster. But had it been too quick? Too easy?

"He was an acolyte. He performed tasks for me, hoping to earn his immortality." The vampire spat clotted blood on the grass. "He wasn't a fighter, but he didn't have to be. His blade was dipped in a slow-acting poison." He struggled to his knees. "Your protector is dead. The toxin has been in his system too long. No one can save him."

A pit opened in my gut, and rage howled through the abyss. I had to finish this, and fast, if I wanted to save Linus. I couldn't believe the vampire, that it was hopeless. I had to try. "Where is the Master?"

The vampire cocked his head, listening. "What is that?"

The howls weren't all rage as it turned out. Or at least they weren't all mine.

The watchmen had arrived.

"Tell me where he is," I bargained, "and I'll call them off the hunt."

I had no such power, but he didn't need to know that.

"This isn't over." He pointed at me. "You can't stay inside your wards forever."

Lip curled up over his teeth, flashing fang at me, he ran for the trees bordering the property.

As much as my thighs twitched to pursue him, as much as I could taste the answers I would scrape off his tongue, Linus was more important.

A scaled beast with a golden ruff sped past me. Midas. Two more followed, allowing him the lead.

"Take him alive if you can," I yelled after them, but they gave no sign they'd heard.

Blocking out Amelie's frantic screams and the watchmen's joyous baying, I yanked open the van's door and did a quick examination of Linus. As a necromancer, I knew zip about healing from a medical standpoint. We were taught the signs of death so that we could encourage them in our clients to hasten their resuscitation, but not how to counteract them, and Linus was ticking off all the boxes.

Sluggish pulse. Poor color. Faint breaths.

"You're going to have to trust me." I gripped the front of his shirt and ripped it straight down the middle, sending buttons pinging off the dash. "I have an idea that I think might work." With the fabric untucked from his pants, I parted the halves of his shirt to expose the planes of his inked chest and the smooth rounds of his shoulders. For this to work, I wanted the largest canvas possible. "Okay, here we go."

Strange magic licked over my skin, and the ward surrounding me burst like a balloon punctured with a needle. A sharp point wedged between the knobs of my vertebrae, stunning me into stillness, and I sucked in a shocked breath that hissed through my teeth as that power burrowed into my blood.

"Hello, Grier."

Careful to keep the movement slow, I dared a glance over my shoulder. "Eloise?"

"Not quite." Her eyes were sharper, her face harder, and she mocked me from a greater height. "I'm Heloise Marchand. Her twin. And don't get me started on the rhyming names. Our mother did it to bind us tighter than she was to her sister." A mocking smile curved her lips. "It's a pleasure to finally meet you, cousin."

Twins?

Sloppy of me not to have dug into Eloise's past after she appeared on my doorstep, but I had turned her on her heel and sent her packing. The skeletons in her closet were her problem. Not mine.

Well, until now.

Learning Mom had a twin should have jogged my memory that fraternal twins run in families.

Heloise's smugness forced out one burning question. "How did she beat the wards?"

Woolly would have never allowed Eloise in if she had treacherous thoughts in her head.

"Vain, aren't you?" She clicked her tongue. "With Maud as a mother figure, I expected as much."

Maud's blood, and my sweat and tears, had seeded the foundation for those wards, so yes, I was proud of them. I had constructed them to protect me, to keep Woolly safe, and it was a blow to my ego to learn I had failed us both. Again.

"Ellie has no idea I'm here," she said when I didn't rise to her bait. "That's how she beat your wards. Ignorance. Or innocence. Depending on how charitable you're feeling. That house read no ill intent from her, so it allowed her entrance."

"She left that first night, didn't she?" I thought back on it. "You were the one waiting for me at Mallow. You had done your research and knew where to find me." I hissed out a curse. "The grape. Eloise is the one who's engaged. That's why you weren't wearing the ring."

Heels or flats could have explained away the difference in their heights, but the rest was all on me.

"An oversight, I admit." Her lips flattened. "I had to gamble you wouldn't notice. Or, if you did, that you wouldn't feel it was your place to ask."

Society training did have that effect on people. Polite to a fault up until the moment they buried a hatchet in your back. "What's your angle?"

"I was Eloise's first stop after she overheard the conversation between Grandmother and Madame Lecomte. I encouraged her to track you down, to make contact. An infamous relative fostered by one of the most famous necromancers of all time. How could she resist?" Her smile was wrong on Eloise's gentler face. "I wanted an in with you, a reason why you might accept an invitation if I asked you out for coffee. I could have cold-called you, but you struck me as a cautious person, and I was proven right by the wards on your home. That's why separating you from Woolworth House was paramount."

"You're the one who attacked the wards?"

A shrug rolled through her shoulders. "I jabbed them a little to see what makes them tick."

All of a sudden, the random images Woolly had shown me made more sense. A fallen branch, from my family tree. A starburst, like the giant ring on Eloise's finger. Two peas, these had shared the same pod.

"You followed us to Atlanta." That explained why the issues stopped after we left.

"I thought your disappearance might be more open to interpretation if you got lost in the city," she admitted, "but I underestimated how badly your grandfather wants you returned to the fold."

The Master was...my grandfather?

A scream of denial welled in my throat, but I swallowed it down.

No time to dwell on what this meant. I could melt down in the safety of my bedroom later.

Replaying how everything that could go wrong on the trip had, I gritted my teeth, fury igniting in my blood. "The accident?"

Cruz had been adamant about a woman being responsible, but Ernestine had been the instigator between the two vampires, and I assumed that meant she had been the driver. I assumed wrong.

"I admit, it was rather impulsive of me, but the vampires were too close for comfort." A growl entered her voice. "They still beat me to you. Though I can hardly complain given the outcome. The potentate of Atlanta was prepared to raze his own city to protect you. I find that quite interesting."

The mention of Linus had me tasting bile. I had to buy us more time, but his was running out, and the odds of a rescue were looking slimmer by the minute. "You orchestrated the infiltration at the Faraday."

Finally, the escalation in violence made sense. Even impatient, the Master wanted me unharmed. Clearly, the Marchands weren't as particular about the shape I arrived in.

"It was easy with inside help." Her smile was pure delight. "Meiko sends her regards, by the way."

That backstabbing little beast. "He will never forgive her for this."

"I know that, and you know that, but..." Heloise twitched her shoulders. "Meiko thinks in straight lines. Cat logic, if you will. Linus is her person, and she refuses to share him. Much like a cat knocking a glass off the counter because it can, she determined you were an obstacle to her happiness and removed you."

Cat logic had failed her. The Faraday operated by its own rules, and she had broken the golden one.

"You executed your trap well," I admitted. Isolating the weakest link, she used Meiko's petty jealousy and vanity to achieve her own ends. "I can admire that, but you hurt one of my friends in the process. That I won't forgive."

"I don't need your forgiveness," she scoffed. "You will return home with me and take your place among the Marchands. Your mother was disowned. You are simply a recording error in need of correction."

The scope of Dame Marchand's foresight in forming this loophole made me warier than ever of that side of my family. Before they had been a nebulous nonentity. Now... They had declared themselves my enemies.

"Grandmother is strict," she said, digging the metal into my spine, "but she won't punish you as long as you cooperate."

A shiver coasted down my arms as a new possibility surfaced, one that filled in a few of the cracks spiderwebbing over my heart.

Neck aching from cranking my head around, I looked to Linus for a heartbeat, let myself watch the rise and fall of his chest. "How did you nullify my wards?"

"An artifact from the family vault made by the last goddess-touched necromancer from our bloodline, more than seven hundred years ago."

A family trait. I swallowed. This was a legacy that originated in my mother's blood. It explained how she knew to run when she fell pregnant with me. It might also explain why she accepted the disownment rather than turn me over to her mother.

The Marchands owned a goddess-touched artifact. What else

might they have in their arsenal? What knowledge might they possess about my condition? Did they know how to sever the thread binding me to Amelie? And would they ever share that information with me without shackling me to their will first?

"Let me save him," I bargained. "Let me heal Linus, and I'll go with you."

"We don't have time." Heloise searched the darkened yard. "Your pets will return soon enough."

"You can't let him die." My voice went hoarse. "Please."

A gunshot pierced the night, and the sharp pressure at my spine vanished.

I whirled as my cousin collapsed on the grass, her mouth gaping in mute surprise. A red dot smudged her left temple, but the right side of her face was missing.

Heart pounding in my ears, I searched for the shooter and found Taz limping toward me, dragging one leg, leaving a trail of blood shimmering wetly on the grass behind her.

"Sorry I'm late," she grunted. "I was tracking the vamp when I triggered a circle." Her eyes blazed when they fell on Heloise's crumpled form, a wildness in them screaming she wished the deathblow had been dealt by her hands and not her weapon. "I would have still been trapped if she hadn't also shot me in the thigh and left me to bleed out. Took a while, but the blood erased her sigils, and the ward fell."

The parallels between what happened to her tonight and her brother's fate so long ago made me heartsick. Heloise had been family —blood—and she was a monster.

One halting step was all I managed before figures dressed in black fatigues bled from the shadows.

The cavalry had arrived, and the Elite sentinels swarming the night were armed to the teeth.

No familiar platinum-blond head towered over them. No chocolate-caramel eyes sought mine. No Boaz materialized to lead the charge.

"Freeze," the man in front barked at her, clearly not recognizing Taz, a mistake that might prove deadly. For him. "Put your gun down."

"Fair warning," Taz growled, lowering her weapon. "Shoot me, and I'll shoot back."

With Taz disarmed, he set his sights on me. "Step away from the van, ma'am."

A split-second decision had me putting my thin acting skills to the test. Dropping to my knees beside the body, I feigned shock. "My cousin." As I bent to check Heloise's pulse, I leaned over her corpse, using the motion for cover as I pried the goddess-touched artifact from her clenched fist. There was no time for an examination before secreting it away, but I got the impression of age-worn wood with a tapered end. "She's dead."

"Step away from the body," he barked. "Move away from the van."

Wiping my bone-dry cheeks with a hand I trembled for effect, I did as I was ordered, turning just enough to hide the movement as I slipped the artifact in my pocket.

Sadly, my theatrics had exposed Linus, and the sentinel bristled in response, his finger on the trigger.

"Sir," he boomed, "I'm going to have to ask you to exit the vehicle."

"Are you serious? He's unconscious. He can't exit the vehicle. He can barely breathe." Huffing out a laugh that bordered on deranged, I reached up and scratched the scabs at my throat until fresh blood trickled down my neck, then wet my fingers. "I don't have time for this."

"Ma'am," the Elite tried again. "We got a call—"

"Let me tell you who you can call." I stepped aside and gave them a good, long look at who reclined in the seat. "This is Linus Lawson, Scion Lawson. Dial up the Grande Dame and ask her how she feels about her niece being held at gunpoint while her only son and heir dies from poisoning."

The man lowered his weapon, his cheeks paling as the blood drained from them.

"Note to self," I muttered. "Name-dropping is the new Kevlar."

With two fingers, I drew a double-lined healing rune that stretched from Linus's collarbones to his navel. Bright crimson whirls smeared over the art covering his torso. Eyes crushed shut, I listened to that inner voice and followed its instructions to the letter. Instinct guided me, calling for more blood, more pain, more sacrifice to bring him back.

Please, bring him back.

I sent up a prayer to Hecate as I closed the final loop with a flourish.

Magic, rich and potent, coated him from head to toe in a shimmering veil of incandescence. His entire length jolted hard once, and then again, and then again.

The spell was working as a defibrillator, jump-starting his heart with magic.

The sheen beading his forehead gave me hope the poison was being expelled.

"Come on," I chanted. "Come on."

One last blast illuminated his skin before the glow seeped into his pores. In the stillness that followed, the impossibly long seconds where nothing happened and I was certain I had failed him, his eyelids started twitching in what appeared to be restless sleep.

A kinder woman might have given him a moment to recover. I was not that woman.

"Linus." I grabbed him by the shoulders and shook him. "Wake up. Let me see your eyes."

Cletus materialized in the driver seat, almost giving me a heart attack.

Well, that explained why the wraith had been absent. Linus had been so close to death their bond must have faded until he did too.

"Can you hear me?" I rechecked his pulse. Steady. His lungs were expanding fully, so that was good. But was it enough? "Linus?"

"In all the...stories," he rasped, eyes slitting open, "the prince...is awakened...with a kiss."

"Linus Andreas Lawson, are you flirting with me? Maybe I zapped you too hard." I pinned him in his seat while his limbs spasmed. "Besides, you've got it wrong. It's the princess who gets kissed. Didn't your mother ever read you storybooks when you were a kid?"

"No." His teeth started chattering. "What...happened?"

"The vampire who helped Volkov kidnap me got an acolyte into Strophalos. The guy who cut you used a poisoned blade. Since I'm an idiot, I didn't realize you weren't sleeping and left you out here until you almost died."

"Not your...fault."

That's not how it felt. "I ditched you to go say hello to my house."

Heavy footfalls yanked my attention to a commotion across the yard.

A second unit, more heavily armed than this one, jogged in from the direction the watchmen had gone. Two men peeled off toward the driveway with a mangled body strung between them. The others melded into the group facing us down, and a man stepped from the middle of them.

"What the hell happened to that vampire?"

Stomach roiling over the carnage, I didn't register the speaker's identity at first. When I did, a new type of sickness uncoiled through me, and I almost wished I had kept my focus on the maimed vampire.

Boaz might have looked good enough to eat, but he acted mad enough to spit nails.

"Security...team," Linus panted. "Don't harm...the...pack."

"The pack?" Boaz flexed his bloodied hands at his sides. "There are no warg packs in Savannah."

"They're not wargs." And I was under no obligation to tell them more than that. Boaz maybe. This gaggle of gun-toting zealots with itchy trigger fingers, not so much. "I appreciate the assistance, but your presence isn't necessary." I folded my arms across my chest.

"I've got things handled here. You can run along back to wherever you've actually been the last few weeks."

A slow whistle rose from the back of the crowd, and I spotted Becky wincing like she wished a hole would open up and swallow Boaz before I buried him in front of his men. When she noticed me, she waggled her fingers in a weak *hello*, but I was done playing nice.

"You heard the lady," he called over the murmurs. "Clear out."

Neither of us budged until the yard was empty except for the three of us, and I was pretty sure Linus had fallen back asleep. Actual sleep this time.

"Amelie called." He glared down at Heloise's corpse like what would happen next was all its fault.

"I handled it." Sparing a final glance at my cousin, I amended, "I was handling it."

"This—" he pointed a shaking finger at her remains, "—will start a blood feud. The Marchands will come for you, and this time the gloves will be off."

"Funny," I murmured, riveted on the hand still curled as if to hold an artifact she no longer possessed, "I don't see any gloves."

Dame Marchand's interest in acquiring me had lit a torch within my heart. Maybe my parents had loved one another. Maybe they had *both* fought to keep me. Maybe the accident that claimed Mom's life wasn't so accidental. And if that were true, then how had my dad died?

"You could have been killed," he rumbled.

"Yeah, you're right." I was done tiptoeing around the truth. "And there wouldn't have been a damn thing you could do about it. Not even from across town."

Calling him out had Boaz flinching. Hard. "How did you find out I was in Savannah? Amelie?"

Now it was my turn to flinch. "Amelie knew you were still in town, and she didn't tell me." The confirmation stung. "That's why she's got you on speed dial."

"Don't blame her." He cast the house a lingering frown, searching the windows. No doubt for his sister's silhouette. "I made her promise."

"Why would you do that?" I voiced the conclusion I'd come to in Atlanta. "If the Grande Dame issued a gag order for you, you couldn't have told Amelie. Since you obviously did, that means you decided to withhold that information. You both chose to keep this from me."

"It's complicated."

"Are we together or not?" That's what hurt most. The wondering. "I thought we were trying. I thought that meant something."

"It did."

Past tense.

That sick clench in my gut twisted. "Are you breaking up with me?"

Judging by the look on his face, I wondered if he had already, but I missed the memo.

"This is so fucked-up." He stared at the ground. "The one time I want to stay with a girl, and..."

If this was the end, I wasn't going to make it easy. I was going to make him spell it out. "And?"

"I can't," he rasped.

"Can't or won't?" I kept my chin from hitting my chest by sheer force of will. "I thought you were all in."

For as long as it lasts.

"The deal changed."

"When? And why wasn't I told?" The way my palm itched, I didn't trust myself to get closer without slapping him. "Is that what the secret phone calls have been about? Is that why you haven't spoken to me unless I initiated contact?"

"Amelie put my family in a tight spot," he said quietly. "We have one chance to dig ourselves out of the hole with the Pritchard name intact."

An automatic step back bumped my hip against the van door. "You wouldn't."

He bowed his head. "I don't have a choice."

"Macon—" No, I wouldn't throw his little brother under the bus. After counting to ten, I tried again. "You don't care about reputation. You never have. You've spent your entire life cultivating an image, and newsflash—it's not one of the dutiful son."

"I hated being boxed in." His head jerked up, eyes blazing. "I hated being told what my life would be and who I would spend it with. How many kids I would sire and how much money I was required to add to the family coffers before lining up a successor." Muscle bulged in his jaw. "I wanted out, so I acted out. I tossed my good name in the mud and then I rolled around on it."

A slow burn started behind my eyes. "You told me I would be the one to make choices to preserve my line, my home, and my legacy."

"I also said you might not have a choice in the matter," he bit back.

At the time, the comment wedged beneath my skin like a splinter. "Did you mean it as advice for me, or as a reminder for yourself?"

"You're Dame Woolworth. That means you have the power. Whoever you marry will give up their last name and take yours. Whoever you wed will give up their family and become yours. Whoever I marry will take my name and my place. She will become the Pritchard heir. She will inherit my family, and there's not a damn thing I can do about it."

"You could say no."

"You still don't get it." He threw up his hands. "I've been groomed all my life, not to take control of the family, but to be a guiding influence for the wife I would one day acquire. She's a business decision, Grier. She's three big, fat checkmarks in the columns that matter most to my parents."

Tears veiled my eyes, and I couldn't see him through them, but I would be damned if I let them fall.

"She's an only child with a small family to support. She can afford to give up her name to take mine. She's the best hope we've got of coming out the other side of this scandal."

"What's her name?" I noticed I was rubbing the skin over my heart and dropped my hand. "You haven't spoken it once."

"Does it matter to you?" His bitter laughter almost choked him. "As long as she shows up to the Lyceum on time, it doesn't to me."

"This is why you were pushing me away." The radio silence was a precursor to this. "Were you going to tell me before I heard it from someone else? Before rings were exchanged?"

"Yes." His fists tightened at his sides. "I'm not that cruel."

"You got engaged behind my back. How is that not cruel?"

To think I had wanted a surprise in the romance department. Well, it didn't get more shocking than this.

"Our situation is complicated."

It hit me then, what he wasn't saying. "You've known about this for a while." It was the only thing that made sense, the only reason he wasn't tearing everything down around him. He'd had time to get used to the idea, to make peace with it. "But you worried how I would take the news because of Amelie. You strung me along so I wouldn't boot her to the curb when I found out."

"You're all she's got right now."

"What? Your darling wife won't look kindly on her sister-in-law?"

"Amelie is part of the deal."

Part of the deal. A *deal*. Not a marriage.

What a proper scion he was turning out to be. His mother must be so proud.

"She's been disowned," I rasped, shaking my head. "That can't be undone."

"I can't give her back her name, but I can give her a place, a home, access to her inheritance."

"Your mother—"

"Will no longer be Matron Pritchard." His jaw set. "If I step up, she steps down. That's my price."

My lips parted, but nothing passed them.

"The best thing for the family is to distance ourselves from the atrocities that occurred during her tenure as matron." How formal he sounded when he spoke, how practiced, as if reciting a speech. "The candidates they selected for me to choose from were desperate. Who else would marry into our line after this scandal? The former Matron Pritchard knew she had to act fast to mitigate the damage."

"Amelie will still be ostracized." Putting a roof over her head and money in her pockets wouldn't change that.

Quiet stretched long between us, the silence filled with things unsaid that could never be spoken between an engaged man and his...

Girlfriend? Friend? Neighbor? No, I was nothing to him now.

"I read the family histories for all the applicants," he began.

"Oh goodie." I clapped for him. "You and your new family should have tons to bond over then."

"The Whitaker matriarch died three months ago, and the title of Matron Whitaker fell to her eldest daughter. She's aware of our circumstances, and..." He wet his lips. "She lost her younger sister last year. Fibromyalgia and chronic fatigue syndrome kept her confined to the family home. She hadn't been seen in public since she was a child." His throat bobbed when he swallowed. "She was two years older than Amelie."

While I pitied them such loss with one breath, I resented them with the next. But what he implied... It was an elegant solution. One that never would have crossed my mind. "She's willing to let your sister masquerade as hers?"

"To provide for the family she has left, yes."

"This only works if Amelie doesn't stay in Savannah. People will recognize her. A new name won't fix that." The dybbuk scandal was big news thanks to my involvement, and the debacle too recent for the tittle-tattlers to forget. "You're sending her away?"

"We think it's for the best."

We. Already they were a *we.*

Already the pair was working together, solving their problems like...a team.

Blurred vision kept me from seeing his expression. "Get off my lawn."

"Grier," he pleaded, coming toward me. "You've got to believe this isn't what I wanted for us."

Us. There was no room for *us* in *we.*

"*Go.*" I shoved him. "Leave." He barely rocked back on his heels. "You're not welcome here."

"Grier," he whispered.

"No." I made a fist the way Taz had taught me, and I socked him in the jaw. Something in my hand popped, a knuckle cracking, but I was primed to go again when cool hands landed on my shoulders. I angled my head, catching sight of Linus behind me, and my bottom lip trembled. "He's engaged."

The cold fury banked in his ebony gaze as he stared at Boaz should have made me afraid for him. Instead it made me grateful to have Linus by my side. "You're a fool, and you will regret breaking her heart for the rest of your long life."

I'll make sure of it.

Unsure if that last part had been spoken out loud or implied, it still flung open the floodgates. Stupid tears spilled hot and fast over my cheeks. Linus was an auburn blur, his touch the only real thing in this world.

This time, I let Boaz watch. Damn if I was going to hide one ounce of the pain he had caused for his sake. Forget pride. Let him see. Let him live with this. Let him fall asleep tonight and dream about my splotchy face, my tears, my misery.

The shirt I called Old Grier tore, and I split down the middle with it.

A chorus of growls rose in response to my anguish, and the watchmen prowled over to stand with me. Lethe and Midas flanked me, the former nuzzling my hand, while Hood stalked Boaz until he backed away.

"Goodbye, Boaz." I glanced down at the watchmen. "Escort him off the property, please." I brushed my fingers down Lethe's nape. "Allow the Elite to claim my cousin's body, and then I want them gone."

With eager barks, they embraced their orders.

"You need to sit down before you fall down," I warned Linus, looping an arm around his waist to balance him, happy to fuss over him rather than linger over Boaz's announcement. "Should I call your mother?"

He offered me a weak smile. "Tomorrow."

Considering I had hidden the car accident from my family, I could hardly complain if he kept his in the dark too.

"I heard about Meiko," he murmured. "You were right. I should have taken her in hand long before this. It's my fault she felt entitled to make a move against you."

"This wasn't your fault." I worried my bottom lip between my teeth, wondering if it made him feel any better or if guilt would still cling to his bones as it did to mine. "She made the decision to compromise the Faraday. Not you."

And she would pay for it in blood.

While there was no love lost between Meiko and me, Heloise had led her astray. My cousin had as much as admitted to manipulating her, knowing the jealous nekomata might appear human, but her instincts were animalistic. So was her reasoning. That didn't excuse Meiko, but if I spoke on her behalf, it might keep the watchmen from killing her outright.

"Not my fault," he echoed. "I enjoy saying those words more than hearing them."

Huffing out a laugh, I murmured, "I bet."

"Hearing them, even when they're meant well, doesn't change anything, does it?"

"Nothing absolves the guilt, but it tells me I'm not alone." I gave him a gentle squeeze. "You're not alone, either."

With his arm slung around my shoulders, I managed to get him to the carriage house. He fumbled the door open, and we sidled in together. As weak as he was, I decided on a mattress over the couch and aimed us toward his bedroom. Once he sat, my knees buckled, and I sank onto the floor in a heap.

"I'm sorry," Linus said, and it encompassed my entire world and all of its fractures.

Fresh tears plinked on the hardwood, the puddle growing beneath me. "I don't want to see her."

"Amelie," he said, but it wasn't a question.

"She lied to me." A watery laugh escaped me then, because it shouldn't surprise me. Nothing she did ought to shock me anymore. "This hurts worse than the dybbuk." How pathetic was it that I would take a near-death experience over heartbreak? "She always said she would choose me. That if Boaz and I happened, and then we didn't happen, she said she would pick me over him."

A grunt reached my ears as Linus slid onto the planks beside me. He was dragging a blanket behind him, and he wrapped me up tight, insulating me against his cold. I slumped against his chest when he opened his arms, and I cried until I got hiccups, until my snot had washed away his healing runes, until I lost my voice and figured it was a good thing because I had run out of things to say that didn't boil down to *it hurts*.

The jagged mass twisting in my chest cut worse than Atramentous, worse than Volkov, almost worse than losing Maud. I kept looking down, thinking I ought to be bleeding to death, but the wounds he had inflicted were invisible, and I was only leaking through my eyes.

With exquisite gentleness, Linus gripped the wrist on my sore hand and turned it palm up. He must have fetched his pen from his pocket. He bit off the cap and held it between his teeth as he drew a healing sigil to fix what I had broken punching Boaz.

"Is there a rune that fixes a broken heart?" I murmured against his shoulder.

Cool lips pressed against my temple. "No."

"Figures the one time I would be willing to take an out, there's not one."

"He's going to regret you for the rest of his life."

The urge to wish that miserable future on him was too strong, so I kept my mouth shut.

"I ought to tell Woolly, but I don't want to do it over the phone, and I don't feel up to it tonight." Bitterness swirled through me, draining through the pit of my soul. "She really does love him. This is going to break her heart."

"Take my bed," he offered. "I can sleep on the couch."

"I've kicked you out of enough beds." It's not like where I started the night mattered much considering where I always ended them. "I'll take the couch." I unfurled the cover then helped him up and back in bed. "I won't be sleeping much as it is."

Linus shut his bruised eyes before his head hit the pillow, and I stood there for a long time, watching him sleep. Once I convinced myself he wasn't going to kick the bucket if I turned my back on him, I pulled the sheet up to his chin. A down comforter stretched across the foot of the bed, and I tucked it around him. Recalling his soft admission from weeks earlier, that he got cold, I added the plush gray duvet he had wrapped me in to his layers.

Backing from the room, I left the door cracked behind me so I could listen to him breathe.

Alone in the living room, I couldn't silence the noise in my head.

Boaz was engaged. *My* Boaz. Engaged.

No, not mine. Not really. Not if he allowed this to happen.

The sun rose while I sat there, hands folded in my lap, head hanging loose on my neck.

I didn't know what to do with myself, how a world without Boaz looked, and I didn't want to see.

When the phone rang, I didn't want to answer, but a sixth sense prodded me not to let this call pass.

"*Ma coccinelle,*" Odette sighed. "Today the sea churns with the salt of your tears."

Odette was the closest thing left I had to a mother, and hearing her voice unlocked a fresh wellspring of tears that flowed down my cheeks while I curled around my phone on the couch.

"I warned him he stood at a crossroads," she said sadly. "Had he chosen well, he would have had his heart's desire: freedom to live as his own man, power to enact change, love that transcends centuries. But he chose poorly, and he has lost that which matters most to him: himself."

"It hurts," I said thickly, voice catching. "It's never... Him choosing someone over me never hurt this much before."

I had plenty of experience in losing Boaz to other women. This latest ought to be yet another speed bump that jarred me to my senses. For a little while. Before I set my sights on him again. But not this time. The break felt...

"Marriage within the Society is forever." Odette sounded pained to remind me. "That ache you feel is a true ending, *bébé*. He can no longer cast his net wide then drag home to you when his arms tire. He has tangled with a whale, and she will drag him out to sea."

The mental picture of him hurtling toward the Atlantic like a water skier behind a speedboat almost made me laugh. But I was scared if I started that I wouldn't stop until the tears came again. They would masquerade as happy tears and hide behind my smile, but I would know the truth.

Singing me to sleep was off the table. Odette was no songbird. So, I asked for a different favor instead.

"Tell me a story," I murmured, eyes drifting shut, "about you and Maud and Mom."

Warmed by the ray of sunlight slanted over my shoulder, I listened to her retell the story of the time she convinced them to go sailing in the middle of a hurricane. Curled on the couch, her voice in one ear and Linus's breath in the other, I tumbled into fitful sleep.

SIXTEEN

Bacon woke me. Okay, the bacon didn't physically reach out and shake me until my eyes opened, but the smell did set my stomach growling. Sometime during the day, I had found an empty corner and huddled there with an afghan tangled around my legs. Judging by the stacked trunks blurred through my puffy eyelids, I was still in the living room.

"Coffee?" a towering god asked while extending a cup of ambrosia toward me.

"Yes," I rasped, voice ruined. "Thanks."

The god, who also happened to smell like bacon and resemble Linus, sat beside me.

"You're going to wrinkle your clothes."

"That's what irons are for," he countered. "How are you feeling?"

"Like my heart has forgotten its rhythm." After I gulped down a scalding mouthful, my eyes remembered how to open fully, and I raked my gaze over Linus. "How about you?"

"You saved my life," he said simply.

"Just returning the favor."

"Thanks all the same." A faint curl of his lips betrayed his amusement. "We make a good team."

"We do." I rested my shoulder against his, and after a moment, he leaned back. "All good partnerships ought to require both people to take turns being the damsel, like a team-building exercise." I tilted my head back and smiled. "I'll take you dress shopping next week. Though, I don't know where we'll find one of those pointy hat and veil combos."

"Hennin."

"Are you an encyclopedia spelled into a human skin? You can tell me. I'll keep your secret."

A flush stained the high curves of his cheeks pink, and the daisy under his left eye turned downright rosy.

"Amelie's called twelve times since I woke at dusk." Somehow, he made it into a question.

"I don't want to talk to her." I sipped my coffee, letting its warmth seep into me. "I don't want to see her, either."

"That's going to be difficult when you live together," he pointed out, not unkindly.

"I have a proposal." The reflexive closing of my throat warned tears were queued and ready to fly at a moment's notice, but I swallowed through the tight knot. "Poor choice of words."

After removing the fresh kitchen towel from his shoulder, he pressed it into my hands. "I'm listening."

"Move in with me."

Linus startled so hard, he banged his head against the wall. "What?"

"I can't do this." A strain entered my voice that hadn't been there earlier. "I can't look at her without seeing him, and I can't see him right now if I want to pull myself back from this." I peered up at Linus. "I'm a hot mess." I pushed out a sigh. "I need to be around someone who doesn't add to that."

"Woolly won't approve."

That wasn't a no. I could work with that.

"She didn't want to accommodate Amelie in the first place. I twisted her arm. After this? Woolly will evict her. Forcibly if necessary. Amelie will be lucky if her great-great-grandkids can step foot inside my house without getting expelled." I swirled the remains of my drink, careful not to slosh over the lip. "This is going to end one of two ways. Either I get a new roommate, or you do."

"Woolly can be reasoned with," he began. "You don't have to invite me in. I'm content staying here."

"She loved Boaz too," I told Linus. "They were friends. She trusted him." I set my cup down before the anger threatening the edge of my thoughts forced me to smash it on principle. "Boaz—" I choked on the name, "—is all the family Amelie's got left. He's going to want to visit her, and Woolly will not grant him entrance. Odds are high she'll toss Amelie out on her keister as soon as she learns what happened."

"These aren't the terms you agreed to," he said softly. "We'll have to talk to my mother."

"Can we not and say we did?" I left each of our encounters feeling like I had lost something.

"We have to do this the right way, or you'll be penalized, and Amelie will become a ward of the Society."

The temptation to wipe my hands clean of her glittered like a gem in my mind's eye, but I wasn't that cruel. I hadn't offered her sanctuary only to pull the rug from under her. Despite all she had done to me, for me, I loved her enough to spare her that fate.

"I don't want to go to the Lyceum."

"The only alternative is bringing Mother here."

"I'll pull on some pants."

"I'll pack the bacon."

I patted his arm. "Good man."

CITY HALL WAS as quiet as a tomb, for which I was thankful. While we took the elevator down to the hidden subfloor that housed the Lyceum, a transformation overcame Linus. His shoulders wound tighter, his chin jutted higher, and his expression flattened into a flawless mask of austerity. His ability to morph into this Linus, the version I considered Scion Lawson, fascinated me as much as it worried me.

Planting myself in front of him, I braced my hands on his chest and rolled up on my tiptoes. "Are you still in there?"

"I'm right here." He didn't break character, and the cut of his blue eyes—edging toward black—chilled me. "I'm still me."

"You don't look like you." A shiver tripped down my spine. "I don't like this side of you."

"Are you implying you like others?" The teasing question didn't belong on those lips.

"I like you," I allowed. "The *real* you."

"Thank you." His cool fingers traced the bend of one knuckle. "I'm glad one of us knows who he is anymore."

A perky *ding* signaled our arrival, and I followed him out into the hall tiled in blood-red marble.

The usual bustle was absent tonight, and I breathed a sigh of relief. We didn't even have to knock on the Grande Dame's door, though I wasn't sure if that was because Linus had called ahead while I got dressed or if the Grande Dame didn't stand on ceremony when she was alone.

Linus strolled right up to the threshold, the tips of his loafers toeing the invisible line. "Mother."

"Darling." Her head popped up, and joy suffused her features. "You're home."

"Atlanta is my home now," he told her in no uncertain terms.

"An old habit." All elegance, she rose and circled her desk until she could embrace him. "And you've brought Grier." She enveloped me in a hug that smelled and felt so much like Maud, fresh tears welled then dripped on her shoulder. "Is everything all right?"

"We should all sit," Linus said, steering the conversation as he shut the door behind him.

"Of course, dear." The Grande Dame reclaimed her chair, and I took the one across from her. "Now, what's all this about?"

"There's an issue with Amelie Madison." He perched on the edge of her desk. "We need to relocate her."

"I worried this might happen." She clucked her tongue. "Has there been more trouble? Is she attempting to remove her bindings? Has Grier or Woolworth House been harmed?"

"No," Linus was quick to assure her, for which I was grateful. "She's been a model employee."

A pucker gathered across her forehead. "Then I fail to see the issue."

"Boaz is engaged," I croaked, wiping my face dry only for it to dampen again.

The Grande Dame appeared more perplexed than ever. It was almost funny. Well, not really.

Cocking her head, she studied me. "Surely that's good—"

"Mother," Linus bit out the word to curb whatever she had been about to say.

Huffing out a sigh, she stilled. "Explain why this is a bad thing and how it affects the indenture."

"Woolworth House has developed an attachment to Boaz over the years." Linus traced the woodgrain beneath him with a fingertip. "She believed that, thanks to Grier's childhood infatuation with him, the two of them would marry."

Nothing short of him lunging across the desk and clamping his hand over her mouth could have stopped her guffaw from escaping. "Surely not."

"Woolly is unaware of the change in Boaz's circumstances," he continued, without acknowledging her outburst, "and it's our concern that she will react badly, perhaps violently, to this news."

As much as I wanted to protest on Woolly's behalf, she did have a mercenary streak. Linus could attest to that.

"Where do you propose we relocate her?" Her amusement waned into annoyance. "She is Grier's charge. The fact her brother will marry doesn't change that. Grier made a pact with the Society, and it cannot be broken."

"We understand," he demurred. "For her safety, all we ask is that she be confined to the carriage house rather than the main house."

"No." Her scowl could have cut glass. "She is a danger to all those around her. I respect Grier for sparing her in the name of friendship, such loyalty is commendable, but I will not allow her to live with my son."

"Grier has offered to allow me to move into Woolworth House, with her."

A stillness permeated the room. Shock, perhaps. Clearly, the Grande Dame hadn't anticipated this.

"Oh, well, that's a horse of a different color." Her expression smoothed into a flawless mask her son had learned to mimic well. "I have no issue with you taking up residence in your old room at Woolworth House."

No imagination was required to picture her clapping her hands under her desk. Her intention had always been to have Linus bunk with me, the better to spy on me. But after all Linus and I had been through, I was willing to extend the man a little faith. Maybe even a lot.

"We'll have to secure the carriage house, but we can make the transition by the end of the week," he told her, all business. "You're welcome to send a representative to oversee the transfer if you'd like."

"I trust you to spearhead this." She smiled softly at him. "Keep me updated on your progress, and I'll notify the council at our next meeting."

"Thank you, Mother."

"Thank you," I echoed.

The Grande Dame reached for my hand, and I had no choice but to let her hold it after the allowance she made for me. "I am sorry you're hurt, Grier, but surely you must see this is why Maud was so opposed to the pairing."

Maud had never been in favor of the match, true, but she had never said or done anything to make me think she minded our friendship as long as Boaz kept seeing me as kid-sister material. Had he taken an interest, sure, then she would have stepped in and put a stop to our flirtations. But he had never given her any cause for alarm on that point.

"Maud wanted more for you." She cut her eyes to Linus. "She wanted—"

"Mother," Linus said in a soft voice that spoke of exhaustion on a topic not worth revisiting.

The Grande Dame exhaled through pursed lips but caged whatever else she had to say behind her teeth.

That might have had more to do with the Elite who appeared in her doorway than him, but I'd take it.

"We'll leave you to your work," he said formally. "Thank you for your time."

"We'll discuss your trip at dinner on Sunday, darling," she said in dismissal before turning her attention to the new arrival.

Linus cupped my elbow, hauled me to my feet, and all but dragged me from the room.

Exercising that newfound trust between us, I didn't question him but followed his lead.

Not until the elevator doors swished closed behind us did I break. "What was that about?"

"You didn't recognize him?" Linus dropped my arm and got busy texting. "He was one of the Elite who responded to Amelie's call for help."

"He's going to report to her on the incident," I groaned. "She'll force us to go back and make a statement."

"She'll have to catch us first." Linus flashed a mischievous smile as we reached the lobby, and took me by the hand. He tugged me after him right up to the curb where a white van idled. Behind the wheel, Tony saluted with a can of energy drink. "Hurry before she sends him after us."

I wanted to laugh, goddess knows I did, but I didn't have enough light in me to manage. What smidgen of levity I possessed shriveled when reality struck home. "I have to break the news to Woolly."

"How do you want to handle it?" Linus exhaled once the door rolled shut behind us. "Do you want me there, or will that make things worse?"

"It's best if I do it alone. She might lash out, and I don't want you to make an easy target for her." I chewed on my bottom lip, mentally curating a to-do list. "We'll have to completely empty the carriage house before Amelie moves in. There are too many artifacts stored there, and the trunks in the living room have to go too."

"Can you wait and tell her when we're ready?"

"The wards are too strong." I shook my head. "Woolly senses my emotions when I'm in contact with her, and I'm a crap actress. I won't be able to fake it around Amelie. Not this time. Woolly will realize something happened, and she won't rest until I confess."

Nodding like he expected as much, Linus sat back. "We'll postpone your lessons for the time being. It's more important to get Amelie resettled."

"The Kinase pack needs debriefing too." But how to call them to me? *Here boy* would get me bitten, I was sure. "They might want to sleep under the stars, but I still have to feed them and teach them the rules. I can't have them accidentally eating the wrong people."

Though, to be fair, most of my visitors were of the edible variety.

In all my life, I can't remember ever dreading the moment when Woolly came into view, but the sight of her columns set my gut roiling.

I didn't want to break the news about Boaz to her. I wanted to keep on pretending like always. That this girl too would pass, that one day he would wake up and realize I was it for him. But engagements were serious business, and Odette was right. Divorce did not exist within the Society. Marriage was a contract that couldn't be voided.

Boaz had taken a crucial step toward an irrevocable bond, and nothing I said or did would change that.

It was time I let him go. For good.

After the van parked, I glanced over at Linus. "Wish me luck?"

"Good luck." The worry pinching his expression didn't sell it.

While Linus squared up with Tony, I dragged my feet across the lawn and trudged onto the porch.

Woolly lit up the second I touched her planks, fear and worry and dread blazing through our connection. Guilt that I hadn't come home the previous night weighed me down, but seeing Amelie after Boaz made his big announcement would have shattered me when I had already been too close to breaking.

One night later, I wasn't in much better shape, but I could speak without tears garbling my words. Maybe.

Aware of Amelie drifting through the house like a specter, I selected the front porch swing for the chat and sat, waiting until Woolly had gathered all her awareness to that point to begin.

"I've got some bad news, girl."

The boards groaned beneath my feet.

"I know how much you love Boaz. I love him too." Though now I would never get a chance to be *in* love with him. "But I need to not see him for a while."

The light above the door flared in question.

There was nothing for it but to put it all out there. "He's engaged."

The bulb shattered, pieces raining down onto the planks.

"His family needs him to marry well for them to save face after Amelie."

More tiny explosions, more glass tinkling as it hit and skittered.

Carving out my heart would hurt less than admitting, "He's doing the right thing for the Pritchards." The window beside me bowed, ready to crack, but I pressed my palm against the pane. "You can't hurt yourself over this. He's not worth it."

Face paler than usual, Oscar materialized at my eye level. "What's wrong with Woolly?"

The wards, that constant melody playing in my head when I was home these days, turned into a jumble of discordant notes, a primal screech of agony voiced the only way she knew how.

"One of her friends let her down," I told him. "She's upset, but she'll be okay."

"I'm her friend." He puffed out his chest. "I won't ever let her down."

"I know you won't, kiddo." I ruffled his hair. "We need a minute alone. Girl stuff. I'll be up to tuck you in in a little bit."

After casting the house one last worried glance, he walked through a wall and vanished.

"I'm sorry," I murmured, stroking the siding in the hopes it might calm her. "He told me last night. That's why I stayed in the carriage house. I couldn't..." I sucked in a breath. "I couldn't tell you. I couldn't face Amelie. Not when it hurt so much."

Given a target for her anger, the point of her consciousness arrowed toward Amelie. A surge of magic that made the hairs on my nape tingle struck her, encapsulated her, then expelled her out onto the porch with me. Woolly shoved and shoved until Amelie stumbled down the steps, her wide eyes seeking me out as she clung to the railing that Woolly turned into coiled snakes with rusty metal fangs, ready to strike out if she touched her again.

"I can't leave the house," Amelie pleaded. "The sentinels will come for me. I can't go back."

"Woolly, stop." I leaned my forehead against the cool metal chain suspending the swing. "Listen to me."

The pressure on Amelie didn't bow outward again, but neither did it release.

"I spoke to the Grande Dame tonight. She agreed to let Amelie move into the carriage house."

Amelie paled. "But Linus—"

"I want Linus to move in with us," I told the old house, ignoring Amelie. "We're responsible for them both, and right now he's what I need." Thinking of Neely and the likelihood Cruz would ever let me see him again, I admitted, "He's the only friend I've got right now."

"Grier..." Amelie bumped against the barrier when she tried to reach me. "I'm your friend."

"No, you're really not." I straightened and faced her. "You knew what he was planning. This whole time, he was confiding in you. You should have told me. You promised you would always pick me if things went south, and you lied. You chose him." A lightning bolt of comprehension struck me. "That's why you've been so weird around Odette. You were afraid she would glimpse the truth and out you both."

"He's all the family I've got left," she whispered, not bothering to deny it. "I can't lose him too."

"I get that. Things have changed since you made that promise. Everything has changed." I blinked until my vision cleared. "That's why I asked permission to relocate you when it would be so much easier to hand you over to them." I checked with Woolly before telling Amelie in no uncertain terms, "Boaz is no longer welcome in this house. The only way you'll see him while you're serving out your indenture is if you take the carriage house."

"I never meant to hurt you."

"I get that a lot," I said on a watery laugh.

"After Maud died—"

"You and me? We're not going there again. You can't base *your* life choices on what happened to *me*."

"You don't understand what it was like," she protested.

"You're right." I let my anger off its leash. "I can't imagine how it must have felt to stay at home, with my family—who are all safe—and keep living my life the way I chose." I tasted metal and realized I had bitten my cheek to hold back after all. "I don't doubt you thought about me, I don't doubt that you hurt for me, but you can't use my past as a crutch to lean on every time you make a bad judgment call."

"I wanted to protect you," she pleaded. "That's all I ever wanted."

Meiko's warning rang in my ears: *There's nothing wrong with lying until you start telling them to yourself.*

"You made a grab for power that almost killed me." It had cost several vampires their lives, and it was past time she owned her truth. "This? This hurts worse than that. This feels like someone punched through my ribs, fisted my heart, and squished it to a bloody pulp." I worked my jaw. "I'm not saying a heads-up would have made this hurt any less, but it would have given me someone to lean on, a shoulder to cry on. You should have been the one to hold me when I broke apart, not Linus."

"You can't trust him," she protested. "He's the Grande Dame's son."

"The thing I've learned about Linus is no one trusts him. Everyone doubts his motives. His actions are examined under a microscope, his every word dissected. No one believes there's any good in him. They all see him as the Grande Dame's son or the Lawson Scion or the Potentate of Atlanta." So many masks, I was sure I had forgotten a few of them. "Don't get me wrong. I'm guilty too. I have a hard time trusting anyone, believing in anything, but I like to think I've earned my paranoia."

Tears slid unchecked down her cheeks, glistening in the moon-light as she listened without protest.

"Do you know who has been there for me every single time I needed someone? Not my best friend. Not my almost-boyfriend. *Linus*." It hurt looking at her, so I stared over her head. "Is he in his mother's pocket? I don't know. Had you asked me the same question about Boaz last week, I would have said hell no. But I would have been wrong. Goddess knows, I'm tired of being wrong. I'm tired period. The people I've trusted most of my life have betrayed me. How can he possibly do any worse?"

"You're right." She wiped her cheeks dry. "We should have done better by you. *I* should have done better. You are—were—my best friend, and I wasn't there for you. I let you walk into this when I should have walked through it with you. I put my needs, and my brother's, above yours." She pressed her palm against the barrier. "I'll go upstairs and pack my things, if you let me, Woolly."

The old house didn't budge.

"Woolly, Linus and I need a couple of days to clear out the carriage house. She must stay with us until then. We have no choice."

The nearest window exploded in a fit of pique, the shards falling harmlessly to the porch when she could have shredded Amelie to ribbons with them. Lowering the barrier, she frog-marched Amelie into the foyer, but Amelie fought her there.

"I'm starting to understand," she whispered, "the burden of someone loving you too much."

"You're getting a second chance," I countered, fresh out of sympathy for the night. "Don't waste it."

With a concentrated shove of magic, Woolly forced Amelie into motion, guiding her up the stairs to her bedroom where she slammed the door behind her.

Needing a stronger connection to Woolly, I picked out a spot free of debris then slid my back down the wall to sit on the porch, stroking the boards with my fingertips, wishing there was some better way to lessen the sting.

"We're going to be okay," I promised her. "We've still got each other."

A cool wind sighed through the eaves, and the house moaned around me.

Shards of glass shimmered on the weathered planks like tears, and mine glided down my nose to mingle with hers.

Short of losing Maud, I had never hurt so much in my life.

Hours slipped through my fingers while Woolly and I grieved together. I stared across the lawn at the pinkening sky, waiting on the sun to rise so I could proclaim this miserable night over and done.

When the first rays of a new day caressed my face, the light touch was a benediction.

In embracing the new day, I accepted my new reality.

I had enemies. Ones I had earned and not inherited. Life had just gotten that much more complicated.

The Master, always so careful with me, had lost his patience. The

Marchands, who might have proven to be advantageous allies, had declared themselves my enemies. And I had as good as killed my own cousin.

A hot sting behind my eyes warned the tank wasn't on empty yet, and yep, fresh tears snaked down my cheeks to drip onto my shirt.

A throat cleared from some distance away.

Lashes gloopy and mashed together, I forced my eyes open.

Linus stood in the grass near the steps, hands shoved into his pockets. "Is there anything I can do? For either of you?"

Woolly's consciousness stirred itself to drift down the steps toward him, and he must have felt the viscosity in the air. He reached out a hand, his palm facing up in supplication, and she enveloped him to the wrist in magic before tugging him slowly to where I sat. As if that small effort had been too much when she had already grieved so hard, she winked out and left me alone with him.

"I think she just gave you her blessing." I patted the planks beside me. "Join me?"

Moving carefully, he lowered himself beside me, his gaze darting around like he expected Woolly to change her mind and expel him into the garden. "How did she take the news?"

"About as well as expected." I let my head fall back as sleep tugged on my limbs. "She popped every bulb in the house as far as I can tell, and that's only what I can see from out here."

He angled his head toward me. "How are you holding up?"

"I'm..." Leaning forward, I pinched a jagged sliver of glass between my fingers then held it glinting in the sunlight. "The part of me that believed in happily-ever-afters and true love triumphing against all odds is crushed to learn sometimes you fall in love with a prince who is actually a frog." I didn't fight Linus when he took the sharp point from my fingers before I cut myself. "Mostly I'm glad I can stop wondering."

"About?"

"How he kisses, how he tastes, all the stupid things I always wanted to know." It made me pathetic to admit it, but I hoped Linus wouldn't hold it against me. "I got to be his for a little while, and he got to be mine. It's what I always wanted, and I got to experience it. That makes me lucky, right? Not pathetic?"

Linus stretched his arm across my shoulders, and I curled against his side, resting my head on his chest.

Exhaustion tugged on me, leading me down a path I hated to follow but was helpless to resist.

"That makes you very lucky," he murmured. "Not all of us get to know how that feels."

Maybe Boaz was right. Maybe I was a masochist. Maybe pain was how I coped.

Or maybe I just wanted to sit here and ache with someone who understood how even the ends of your hair hurt when you pined for someone who either didn't—or couldn't—reciprocate. "I saw your office."

"Meiko?"

"Meiko."

"You've been my muse for a long time," he admitted, his heart thudding faster under my cheek.

The sketchbook Boaz had stolen from him when we were kids proved his words. "Why me?"

"You're not the only one allowed to carry a torch for the unobtainable ideal."

"That almost sounds romantic." I felt bad about wiping snot on his shirt now. "I had no clue." A yawn cracked my jaw that I muffled against him. "You never said a word."

"You had your heart set on Boaz." His cool fingers stroked down my arm. "You always have."

"Hearts are stupid." I fisted his shirt as my damp lashes kissed my cheeks and stayed there. "Life would have been easier if I had fallen for you."

As blessed darkness swirled away my consciousness, my breaths growing longer and slower, he brushed his cool lips against my temple and whispered, so soft I might have imagined it, "There's still time."

ABOUT THE AUTHOR

Hailey Edwards writes about questionable applications of otherwise perfectly good magic, the transformative power of love, the family you choose for yourself, and blowing stuff up. Not necessarily all at once. That could get messy. She lives in Alabama with her husband, their daughter, and a herd of dachshunds.

www.HaileyEdwards.net

ALSO BY HAILEY EDWARDS

The Foundling

Bayou Born #1

Bone Driven #2

The Beginner's Guide to Necromancy

How to Save an Undead Life #1

How to Claim an Undead Soul #2

How to Break an Undead Heart #3

Black Dog Series

Dog with a Bone #1

Dog Days of Summer #1.5

Heir of the Dog #2

Lie Down with Dogs #3

Old Dog, New Tricks #4

Black Dog Series Novellas

Stone-Cold Fox

Gemini Series

Printed in the USA
CPSIA information can be obtained
at www.ICGtesting.com
LVHW042230130624
783200LV00029B/229